LUXE TWO

ALSO BY ASHLEY ANTOINETTE

Luxe

LUXE TWO

A LaLa Land Addiction

ASHLEY ANTOINETTE

ST. MARTIN'S GRIFFIN
NEW YORK

This is a work of fiction. All of the characters, organizations, and events portrayed in this novel are either products of the author's imagination or are used fictitiously.

www.stmartins.com

The Library of Congress Cataloging-in-Publication Data is available upon request.

ISBN 978-1-250-06698-5 (trade paperback)
ISBN 978-1-4668-7489-3 (e-book)

Our books may be purchased in bulk for promotional, educational, or business use. Please contact your local bookseller or the Macmillan Corporate and Premium Sales Department at 1-800-221-7945, extension 5442, or by e-mail at MacmillanSpecialMarkets@macmillan.com.

First Edition: October 2016

D 20 19 18 17 16 15 14

I dedicate my tenth solo novel to my amazing son, Quaye Jovan Coleman. Quaye, the words to describe how much I love you have not been created yet. The human tongue isn't skilled enough to create such a language. Just know that you are my everything.

I

Bleu

Don't do this, Bleu told herself as she gripped the crack pipe in her hands. *Just call Iman. He'll come get you.* Sweat glistened on her forehead and her heart pounded furiously inside of her chest. Temptation called her. She could feel her gut twisting in anticipation of the incomparable feeling that awaited her. She hadn't even hit the pipe yet, but the anticipation of getting lifted had her dopamine levels on overload. It was like the moment just before an orgasm, when you could feel your clit swelling and you could feel the pleasure building and building. It was that achy feeling right before you exploded. It felt so good that it hurt. That's what Bleu felt as she sat there, high off the possibility of allowing herself to be sucked back into the abyss. She closed her eyes and her body shuddered as she remembered the way it felt. Her nipples hardened against the fabric of her thin shirt and she clenched her thighs together. She wanted to suck on a glass dick so badly. She was dying for it. Tears slid down her pretty face. The palms of her hands itched. She could feel the imaginary bugs crawling up her back already. She squirmed in her seat. *Just one hit,* she told herself. She wanted it so badly that spit pooled in the corners of her mouth. She was salivating for it. *Three months, seven days, seven hours*—she checked the Rolex on her wrist—*forty-seven minutes,* she concluded her thoughts. It was like she was starving and depriving herself of a meal, and it was becoming unbearable.

She was trying to hold on to those few months of being clean for dear life. Being clean was like time served in a penitentiary. She had earned every second of the past three months. It was the hardest battle she had ever fought. She remembered the cold sweats, the stabbing pangs in her belly, the blinding headaches, and the utter despair. Her body had been so confused as it tried to purge itself from the poison she had put into it. It had all seemed so unending as Iman had forced her to stop using. She had hated him. It had all seemed so cruel. Like he was bleeding her dry when in actuality he was breathing life back into her, freeing her of the substances that had taken control of her existence. He had helped her and oh, how she needed him now. She needed him to help her say no to this temptation, but he couldn't always be around. There was no possible way for him to shadow her every movement. It was times like these when she was afraid. She felt cornered. Bleu was trapped with just the company of herself and that was when the urge to smoke dope became the greatest. Iman couldn't help her in this moment. She had to find the strength to help herself. *I just can't,* she thought. Her thumb rolled down over the lighter and the sound it made as the flame came to life caused her heart to skip a beat. It was as if she had heard the voice of a long-lost love. The fire danced to the slight breeze in the room, and just as she was about to succumb to her desires Noah's name appeared on the screen of her phone.

Bleu dropped the lighter as if he had caught her red-handed and then hurriedly answered. If anyone could save her from herself, he could.

"Noah," she cried softly into the phone, not even bothering with the formality of *hello*.

"Where are you?" he asked. She could hear the worry in his voice. His tone was serious. Demanding. He didn't know exactly what was plaguing her, but he had known at first glance that something about her had changed.

"I'm at the Holiday Inn in Ventura, room 1128," she said, sniffing loudly as she wiped her nose with the back of her hand. With shaky legs she rushed to the dresser and placed the crack pipe inside. She then went into the bathroom and closed the door, locking it as if she was trying to take every measure to keep herself inside. She sat down on the toilet, put her feet up on the side of the bathtub, and placed her hands over her ears as she squeezed her eyes closed. Bleu trembled. She wanted to smoke so badly. She could feel the yearning in her bones. She just wanted Noah to get there already, before she could do anything stupid. "Please hurry," she whispered.

Twenty-five agonizing minutes rolled by before Noah finally

knocked. She bolted from the bathroom and pulled open the hotel door, distraught. Bleu rushed into his arms. He received her, inhaling her scent as he comforted her.

"Shhh," he whispered as he rubbed the back of her head, pulling her into him reassuringly. "It's okay, B. I'm here."

Her heavy sobs were uncontrollable as they stood there. She clung to him for dear life. "Talk to me," Noah said as he eased her into the room and closed the door. She buried her head in his chest as she balled her fists, resting them against his shoulders. Despair filled her. She knew that his presence was only a temporary gift. As soon as he left she would be susceptible to ruin again. There was no doubt in her mind that she was going to smoke the dope in her possession; the question was no longer if . . . but when. She wanted to tell him, but she couldn't. He was the one person who still looked at her through untainted eyes. He didn't know she was a recovering drug addict. To Noah, she was still perfection personified. She wanted to keep it that way.

Noah gripped the sides of her face and tilted her head back so that she was forced to look up at him. She closed her eyes, afraid that if she matched his gaze he would see through her. He was the person in the world who knew her best. Hiding her sins from him would be most difficult.

"I missed the shit out of you, Bleu," he admitted. "Did that nigga hurt you?"

She shook her head. Her throat was too constricted to form words. She was choking on a ball of emotion.

"Tell me something then, B. What's going on out here?" he asked. "Something is off with you. I can feel it."

All she could do was cry. She couldn't help but wonder what would have happened if Noah wouldn't have pushed her away. If she had stayed home in Flint while he served his time, she would have never come to L.A. She would have never gotten pulled in by the lights, the fast money, the clothes, the drugs. L.A. was a dirty city masked by glamour and lights. She was lost in a luxe world and she could feel herself losing control. "I missed you so much," she whispered. "You never wrote me. I needed to hear from you. I needed you and you shut me out."

"I couldn't do shit for you in there, Bleu. I'm here now," he said. He thought about the girl he had waiting at home for him. Naomi was everything he could have asked for in a woman. She was loyal and beautiful, but she wasn't Bleu. He didn't know if the feelings he had for Bleu would ruin their friendship. He was terrified of the possibility, but he couldn't deny the way his heart swelled when he was around her. He had forgotten the hold she had over him. To think he could ignore the way his heart weakened around her was foolish. Distance had caused him to tuck the thought of her into the back of his mind, but now that he was in her presence he was overwhelmed with feelings he had suppressed.

"Yeah, well . . ." She paused as she ran her hand through her hair, fidgeting as her eyes darted toward the dresser eagerly. "You're too late." Sadness laced her tone as he used his thumbs to wipe her tears while still holding her face in his hands.

"I don't know what's going on with you, but I'm sorry for not being here for you," Noah said sincerely. Wrinkles filled his brow as he frowned, observing her. "I don't like what I'm seeing when I look at you. You're not okay and I don't know why you don't want to tell me what's up? I will body somebody over you Bleu. You know that."

Bleu's heart raced because she knew he was speaking nothing but truth. He had killed for her before. She didn't doubt that he would do it again. Their bond was just that strong. She didn't want Noah involved in her mess. He had already sacrificed a piece of his life for her before.

"Come back home with me," he said. "I love you. Let me take care of you. I've got my own thing going now. It's major and I'm eating. We'll be straight."

He was saying words that sounded like music to her ears and she wanted to say yes. She wanted to run away with him, but she would ruin him. The toxic life she lived would destroy him. So instead of saying yes, she opened her mouth and said, "I can't."

He released her.

He licked his full lips and nodded his head. His ego was slightly bruised and she could see it. She felt like she needed to explain . . . to add more so that he didn't hate her. So that he would take back the feelings that he had just confessed. She wanted his love; she just didn't know how not to taint it. "It's not what you think . . . I love you too, but you just don't understand. . . ."

"It's cool, Bleu," he responded. He went into his pocket and pulled out a knot of money. He counted out twenty-five hundred-dollar bills to her.

Bleu immediately thought of how high she could get with

that much money. Her eyes lit up. Iman hadn't allowed a single dollar to touch her hands since she began her recovery because he knew what she would do with it It was too much temptation, so instead he bought her everything himself. Noah was handing her a loaded gun, because with that much money she would surely kill herself.

"I don't want your fucking money!" she yelled, fighting a battle inside that he knew nothing about. She came off harsher than she intended. Her reaction caught him off guard.

"Take care, Bleu," he said. Had he known what was at stake he would have forced her to come with him, but he was clueless as to what really ailed her. He walked out, leaving her alone.

Bleu wanted to race after him, but she wanted to smoke the dope she had waiting even more, so instead she let him walk out of her life. She rushed to the drawer and pulled out the pipe.

I can keep it under control this time. I won't do too much. Just a little bit, she thought as she licked her lips. *I can handle this.*

She wrapped her lips around the pipe and sparked the flame, but before she could apply it and melt the rock down—

Knock! Knock! Knock!

She didn't even hide the pipe this time. Noah was blowing her private party. She put the top latch on the door and opened it only slightly. "I told you, I'm not—"

She stopped midsentence when she saw Iman standing on the other side.

"Open this door before I knock it down," he said sternly. He had never spoken to her with such anger in his voice. *Does he know what I did to Cinco?* she thought, fear seizing her heart.

"Bleu," he said. She looked at him with teary eyes. He didn't need to say anything more. The authority in his voice let her know that he was coming inside the room one way or another. She unhooked the latch and he came inside. Bleu looked back at the bed ashamed.

"No, ma, no," he whispered as he swiped his hands over his face, overwhelmed. He grabbed her roughly by the arm and pulled her over to the pipe. "This is what you want?" he asked harshly, shaking her. "I give you everything, I love you, I protect you, and you go back to this? You want this shit that bad?" He was shouting and squeezing her upper arm harder than he meant to, but he was livid. He could tell that she hadn't smoked yet, but had he shown up even a minute later he knew that she would have.

"I wasn't going to—"

"You lying to me now?" he asked, not even trying to hear her lies. Iman didn't even know why he was so invested in Bleu. She was young, strung out, and more trouble than she was worth, but he loved her. He loved the shit out of her and it was breaking his heart to see that she was so weak.

She cried.

He grabbed the crack pipe and the lighter, setting up a blast for her. "Go ahead. Smoke it. You want it so bad. Smoke the shit," he said. "Let me know right now what it's going to be like, ma, because I'm not beat for this shit. You can have this shit or you can have me, but you can't have both. So what's it going to be?" he asked as he held out the pipe. "Smoke it!" he shouted.

Bleu wanted to inhale the smoke so badly that her lips tingled. Her eyes glazed over as if she were hypnotized. Iman could see the demon of addiction riding her, urging her. He could see the devil dancing in the reflection of the flame in her eyes and his stomach was in knots. This beautiful girl with so much potential was lost. She was gone. Addicted to the type of orgasm that he couldn't provide. He was all but crying as his heart clenched inside of his chest and his eyes misted. *Damn.* What had Bleu done to him to make him even care so much? Her detriment would be agonizing to him. He was about to give up hope when Bleu knocked the pipe out of his hands. She sobbed as relief flooded him.

"Come here," he whispered as she fell into his arms. She crumpled in his embrace, her knees buckling as he slowly lowered himself to the floor.

"It's okay, ma," he whispered as he kissed the top of her head while rocking her back and forth. "It's okay. I'm going to help you. I promise. Everything will be okay."

Iman didn't even know if he believed his own words. A part of him wanted to let this young, wild girl fly free. He had been in the game long enough to know that he couldn't trust a girl like Bleu. She would be loyal to her addiction before all else, but he loved her and he couldn't just let her self-destruct.

2

Naomi sat curbside in the midnight Range Rover eyeing the door in anticipation. She didn't know when or how it had happened, but she loved the hit out of Noah. Their relationship started out as a partnership . . . a hustle . . . a means to an end, but what started out as friendly had quickly transformed into something more. Like a flame their bond had ignited at a rapid pace and now he had her feeling things she had never experienced before. She hated how butterflies danced in her stomach whenever he was around and how her brain seemed to freeze whenever he asked her a question. He was the first man to hold her attention beyond the bedroom. She knew men were dogs. They strayed from one female to the next so easily that she had vowed never to trust them, but with Noah it was different. He had her head gone off the idea of what they could become together and, although she knew that he was still a man, she wanted him to be different from all the rest. When she saw him emerge from the airport she smiled. Hopping out of the car, she ran up to him in excitement and pounced on him, wrapping her legs around his waist as he greeted her warmly.

"You missed a nigga, huh?" he asked as he carried her effortlessly while nuzzling his face in the groove of her neck. He inhaled her scent as he gave her a quick kiss. The feel of his lips on her anywhere always set her on fire.

"You know I did," she replied. He placed her on her feet and gave her backside a light squeeze as he pulled her into him, kissing her as he pressed her against the truck.

"I don't even know what you do to me," she whispered. "I feel like a fucking schoolgirl around you."

"That's a bad thing?" he asked as he pulled back and looked down at her, staring at her.

"It could be. When niggas get ahold of my heart they tend to break it," she said as she crossed her arms and stared off to the side to avoid eye contact with him.

"Good thing I ain't that type of nigga then. I'm a man, Naomi, and I'm not into playing games. If I'm ever not into this anymore I'll let you know, but you don't ever have to worry about another lady stepping to you over what's yours. I'm not embarrassing you out here," he said.

"So you're saying you're mine?" she asked, lips pursed sexily as a faint smile graced her face. They had never defined what it was they were doing.

"I'm just saying you don't have to worry," Noah replied.

She didn't miss how he didn't want to put a label on things, but she dismissed it. "Hmm-hmm," she replied. "That's what they all say."

She slid out of his reach and walked around to the driver's side. They drove away without breaching the subject, each of them consumed by their own thoughts.

"So business was a'ight in L.A.?" she asked, changing the subject to erase the awkward vibe that had fallen between them.

Noah cleared his throat. "Yeah, it was good," he replied vaguely. Naomi was oblivious to the real reason he had abruptly hopped a flight to the West Coast.

"Just good?" she asked with a bent brow. It wasn't like him to keep her out of the loop where business was concerned. "That's all?"

"Nothing to talk about yet. Just a quick trip. I was in and out. If something comes of it, I'll put you up on game," he replied. He didn't know why he didn't tell Naomi about Bleu. A part of him knew that Naomi was just a consolation prize. Sure, he was feeling her. But she was meant to be queen to another man, one who would appreciate her more. Noah could never put Naomi first because Bleu would always trump her. Even halfway across the country, Noah felt loyal to Bleu. Whenever she needed him he would come, and he didn't want to worry Naomi by explaining the complexity of his bond with another woman.

Naomi pulled up to her apartment and cut the ignition before replying, "Okay." She could sniff out a lie like a bloodhound could prey and an uneasiness filled her gut. It wasn't worth pressing the issue, however. She was a firm believer that what was done in the dark always came to light, so instead of nagging she opened the door and hopped out of the car. He didn't miss the slamming of her door, however.

"Naomi!" he called after her as he climbed out. She turned, but before she could respond the red, white, and blue lights pulling up distracted her.

"Against the car!" an officer shouted as he immediately came off his hip with a 9mm handgun.

"What the fuck is all this?" Noah asked. His tone was calm as he raised his hands, palms out, revealing that he was unarmed.

"What are you doing?!" Naomi asked, concern and fear lacing her tone as she stalked over to the officer.

A second officer emerged from the car, stopping her. "Ma'am, have a seat on the curb and put your hands behind your head where I can see them," he said.

"I'm not doing shit! Why are you arresting him?" she screamed. "He didn't do shit!"

"You want me to arrest you, too?" the officer asked. "Huh? Sit down and put your hands behind your head."

Naomi pulled out her cell phone and began recording. "Fuck you. I haven't done anything. I don't have to do shit. I'm recording every second of this."

"Naomi, chill. It's all right. Just come bond me out," Noah said as he bit his inner cheek to stop his temper from flaring.

"Put the phone down!" the second officer ordered, this time much harsher as he snatched the device from her hand and manhandled her to the ground. "I gave you an opportunity to sit down and stay out of it. Now you're going downtown too!"

"Ow! You're hurting me!" Naomi shouted as he forced her onto the ground and put a hard knee in her back as he cuffed her.

Naomi's cheek was pressed against the concrete and her heart almost pumped out of her chest as she half-expected to be shot in the back. She watched as the police forced Noah's tall frame into the back of a police car. The officer who had taken him turned to the one apprehending her and said, "Cut her loose. We don't need her."

"Bitch has a chip on her shoulder," the second officer stated as if he was ready to fulfill a personal vendetta against her.

"Cu-u-ut her loose. Less paperwork."

Naomi rubbed her wrists as soon as the handcuffs were removed. The way the officer had handled her had Naomi seeing red.

"Run along before you get yourself locked up." They spoke to her as if she were filth beneath their shoes, only intensifying her temper. She had always been a hothead, and before she could listen to the voice of reason screaming for her to stop she picked up a large rock that decorated the apartment-building landscape and threw it at the back of the squad car.

The sound of glass shattering shocked Naomi as she put her hands over her mouth. She backpedaled as the officers quickly rushed her.

"Now I can collar you for assaulting a police officer."

The cop bent her wrist so far back she thought it would snap as she was thrown in the back of the squad car next to Noah. Tears stung her eyes, but she refused to let them fall.

"You fuck boys don't have anything better to do than to harass us. Hate you fucking pigs," she said.

"Chill out," Noah said calmly as he stared out the window. His tone of voice caused her to silence herself immediately. He was brooding, plotting, strategizing in his mind and she could see that her antics had only made things worse.

"I want a lawyer," Noah said as he found himself on the other side of an interrogation table, staring at who he thought was a plainclothes detective. The last time Noah had been inside this very room he had never walked out.

"You don't need a lawyer, Mr. Langston. This is just two people, talking. My beef isn't with you. I'm looking for Bleu Montclair. My name is Assistant District Attorney Tori Nixon—"

"I want a lawyer," Noah interrupted, uninterested in the introduction. He wasn't buying her act. He knew that if he was even sitting in front of her he was in trouble. There was no need to play the game of cat and mouse. He wanted a lawyer. He would be mum until he received one. He folded his hands over the table and squared his shoulders as he looked at the black woman sitting across from him.

"Noah, this can be easy or this can be quite difficult. You see, I know that you broke the stipulations of your probation by taking a trip to Los Angeles. I can have you arrested and have you thrown right back in prison. All I'm seeking is information to help bring Bleu back to Flint to testify in an investigation of the murder and armed robbery that she was involved in last year."

Noah was unmoved. His poker face was strong, but his heart was racing. Behind the cell of a prison wall was the last place he wanted to be. He had known that this was a possible consequence to chasing after Bleu, but when she had called him he felt inclined to check on her. There had been desperation in her voice. He had heard fear in her tone, so he hopped on the first flight smoking to L.A. to find her. Now the D.A. was trying to jam him up, but he couldn't give her what she was asking for. If Bleu stepped foot back into Flint, her life would be in danger. There was a bounty on her head, and as soon as word got out that she had returned every goon in the city would be chasing that payday.

"Lawyer," was all Noah said as he stared straight ahead, making eye contact with the D.A. to show that there would be no further discussion without his representation in the room.

District Attorney Nixon nodded. "Okay, Mr. Langston. Play hardball," she said as she stood and walked out of the room.

Noah swiped his hand over his face and let out a sigh of exasperation as he sat waiting impatiently. He didn't know why he took penitentiary risks for Bleu, but whenever it came down to him or her he always sacrificed himself. This time might just be the final nail in his coffin.

"Hello?" Naomi yelled as she sat at the metal table tapping her foot rapidly against the concrete floor. Her nerves were on 10. "I know you fucking hear me! You stupid fucking pig mu'fuckas!" she shouted. She hated this waiting game. She knew that the police were purposefully antagonizing her. She stood, determined, and stalked over to the mirror that she was sure had officers standing on the other side. Her balled fists beat against it as her rant only intensified: "Let me out of here!"

Naomi had been sitting there for hours. From the moment she had stepped foot into the police precinct they had separated her from Noah. Her mind ran wild as she thought of the possibilities. She wondered had she and Noah slipped up somewhere along the way? Had the cops found out about the heroin that Noah had flooded through the prison? Had someone talked? Had she and Noah neglected to cover their tracks? She spun on her heels in frustration as she picked up the chair she had been sitting on. "You want to watch me? Well, I want to watch you too," she said as she swung the chair against the glass mirror with all her might. The glass splintered, like a windshield in the wintertime, and she picked up the chair again, this time swinging harder. The mirror shattered, revealing the next room as two uniformed officers rushed into her room.

They quickly handcuffed her and grabbed the chair before forcing her into her seat. "You can't just hold me in here! Where is my lawyer!" she shouted.

"Well, well. You are on a roll with breaking things tonight, aren't you?"

Naomi rolled her eyes. "Who are you?" Naomi shot, her face turned up in distrust.

"I'm the District Attorney."

Naomi sucked her teeth. "You think you're important with

your fancy two-piece suit and them cheap-ass shoes. Girl, you're just another ass-kissing Uncle Tom. No matter how many of your own people you put away, you still won't be one of them. How many niggas you lock up today?"

D.A. Nixon smirked as she took a seat and pulled a manila folder out of her leather briefcase. She opened it and began flipping through the pages. "You're tough," she said. "Grew up in Baltimore, Maryland. Father in federal prison. You're related to the infamous Porter clan. Picked up for grand larceny, felonious assault. In fact, you have an active warrant for your arrest there. . . ."

Naomi's stomach went hollow as she listened to her past being thrown in her face. She had come to Michigan for a new start, but as she sat here she felt it in her soul that everything she had run away from was about to catch up to her.

"What do you want?" Naomi asked frankly. She knew that if the D.A. really wanted to turn her over to Baltimore P.D. she wouldn't even be wasting her time with threats. This wasn't about Naomi. The D.A. was interested in something else.

"Noah Langston is your boyfriend?" D.A. Nixon posed the question.

Naomi hesitated. *What is this about?* she thought.

"It's okay. You don't have to answer. I'll assume that he is," the D.A. said. "I'll also assume that as his girlfriend you aren't too pleased with the fact that Bleu Montclair is the reason he continues to have trouble with the law. He caught a five-year bid for killing her stepfather; now he is at risk of being sent back for violating his parole to go see her in California. . . ."

Naomi's disposition changed at that revelation. *He told me he went to Cali to handle business. Not to chase after some bitch,* she thought, slightly irritated.

The D.A. noticed her anger. "Oh. I see you are not familiar with Mr. Langston's relationship with Ms. Montclair," she said.

Naomi cut her eyes at the D.A. as a million things ran through her mind. She didn't know about the complexity of Noah's friendship with Bleu, but the fact that he hadn't told her about it bothered her deeply.

"You see, all I want is Bleu Montclair's location. She is a witness in an armed murder and robbery of a local business owner in the city. I think Mr. Langston knows where I can find her. He broke parole to go see her. For some reason, he would rather be shipped back to prison than let me know where Ms. Montclair is—"

"He went to Calabasas," Naomi said. She was pissed. The fact that Noah was willing to risk all that they were building to protect another woman had her vexed. Naomi was a territorial woman and she had already marked Noah. His loyalty to another made her sick to her stomach. In any other circumstance she would have given the D.A. her ass to kiss, but Naomi wasn't about to protect a girl she didn't even know. "I don't know exactly where ol' girl is, but he mentioned something about the Holiday Inn in Ventura when he was there."

The D.A. smirked and stood as she gathered the case file. As she headed for the door Naomi lifted her cuffed hand.

"Hey!" she shouted, expecting to be freed for her cooperation.

The D.A. looked at the officer standing in the corner of the room and said, "Let her cool off for a few hours and then cut her and Langston loose. And put an arrest warrant out for Bleu Montclair. She hasn't done anything, but I'll take her any way I can get her. If she so much as gets a traffic ticket in L.A. I want LAPD to detain her. I need her testimony to close this murder case against the two liquor store shooters. I want her back in Flint, Michigan, as soon as possible."

"Who is Bleu?" Naomi asked.

It was the first words that had been spoken since she and Noah had been released from holding nearly twenty-four hours ago. A thick tension filled the air between them. It was an uncharacteristic vibe for their relationship. Every interaction with them had been smooth, easy, and effortless. Now an awkwardness existed. Both were consumed with thoughts they didn't care to share, but the silence was deafening. Naomi awaited his response with bated breath. Her gut knotted because she had a feeling she wasn't going to like his answer. She saw the wheels turning in his head. He was choosing his words carefully. Perhaps overthinking his explanation, which only worried Naomi more. "It's a simple question," she added.

"With a complicated answer," he responded. He didn't look at her. Instead he stood in the window of Naomi's top-floor loft, overlooking the lights of the city.

Naomi knew better than to push. If she forced him to talk he wouldn't disclose the full truth to her, and she didn't tolerate dishonesty. The first time he ever lied to her would be the last. She would be in the wind before he even realized she was gone. Naomi wouldn't make herself susceptible to pain. She couldn't. Noah had a strong hold over her. Loving him could leave her broken, and she didn't like the vulnerability of it all.

"Just tell me if this girl is somebody I need to worry about," she whispered.

Noah turned toward her. The concern in her tone was surprising. He crossed the room and stood directly in front of her. Noah lifted her chin with his fingertip so that he could look into her tear-filled eyes.

"You don't have to worry," Noah assured her.

"You promise?" she asked as she placed her hands on the sides of his face and pulled him near.

"I promise," he answered.

Noah saw his words soothe her angst as the tension left her shoulders. Guilt filled him because even as he stood in front of Naomi Bleu occupied his mind. He couldn't shake the nagging feeling that she was in trouble. He couldn't place his finger on what exactly had changed about her, but Bleu was different. He told himself that his concern came from a friendly place, but deep down he knew. Being around her made him feel hollow inside and leaving L.A. without her had killed him. *Bleu out there with that Hollywood-ass nigga, riding her high horse. She's too good for you now,* he told himself. He had a woman right here in front of him who would do anything for him. Naomi was loyal. She was solid. Naomi wanted to be his, and that was more than he could say for Bleu. A part of him wanted to keep his heart on reserve. He felt disloyal for allowing Naomi to occupy such an intimate place in his life, but Bleu had made her choice. She was doing her thing, living in a life that he didn't quite fit into out in L.A. Time and distance had made them grow apart. They had walked down two different paths, and although his soul would always crave her, Noah couldn't wait around forever. Bleu was his past. Naomi had held him down during his bid and helped him break free. Naomi had proved herself time and time again. He owed her his loyalty. Naomi was exactly the type of queen he needed as he built his street kingdom. He knew this, but still his affections for Bleu resided deep within him. He pulled away from Naomi, conflicted. He wanted a young woman he couldn't have, but still their bond had been cemented in years of friendship. He couldn't help but love her. Bleu knew him better than anyone else in the world. Trying to let go of that bond was proving futile, but he had to try. He wasn't used to playing a sucker. He didn't like how much power Bleu had over his emotions. *Maybe it's a good thing she's so far away. I can't have her weighing on me this heavy and chase this money. She's a distraction,* Noah thought.

"What's wrong?" Naomi asked, sensing the inner turmoil that was conflicting him.

She snapped him out of his reverie. "I'm good," he replied distractedly.

Naomi closed the space between them and wrapped her arms around his neck, pulling him in for a kiss. "You're not good, but you will be by the time I'm done with you." Her kisses dulled his concerns as she dipped low, going south, then a little farther, planting her perfectly pouted lips against his skin to build the anticipation. Noah sighed and let his head fall back in pleasure as she helped him release all of his tension. As he fisted her hair he realized that she might not be exactly whom he wanted, but she knew exactly what he needed to take his mind off of the one woman he couldn't have.

3

Bleu could hear her heart beating in her ears as she stared out of the window of Iman's car. She was too embarrassed to look him in the eyes. What could she say? She felt like a child riding with a disappointed parent. The only difference was, Iman wasn't obligated to save her. He wasn't naturally designed to love her. His affections for Bleu had limits and she feared that she had tested them one too many times. A mixture of fear and wanting filled her. Had Cinco told Iman about her involvement in robbing him? Was Iman driving her back just to be punished? She had a feeling that there was a side of him that she had yet to witness. He was in deep with the Mexican Cartel. He ran an entire West Coast operation. Bleu wasn't naïve to the fact that there was a darkness inside of him. Good guys didn't make it to the position of power that Iman was in. His love for her had allowed her to witness a rare side of vulnerability, but as she stole a quick glance she no longer saw that in him. His frustration was written all over his face. The worry lines written on his forehead revealed the anger that he was trying hard to hide. His temple throbbed. He was like a kettle threatening to boil over. Bleu waited for him to chastise her. She would rather he yell and berate her, but he kept his composure, giving her nothing but silence as he drove her home. She didn't even feel like it was her place to speak. It was like she needed his permission to open her mouth and provide an explanation. He didn't give it, so she didn't make one peep. It was the first time she had ever felt intimidated.

When Iman pulled up to his Calabasas mansion Bleu didn't move.

"Iman . . ."

"Just go inside, Bleu," Iman said. "I need to go clear my mind, ma. Can I trust you to stay put until I get back?"

She could tell that he was trying his hardest to be patient with her. He was fed up and she couldn't blame him. He wasn't her daddy. He shouldn't have to put up with her stunts. Her bad-girl antics were tiresome and she could tell by his temperament toward her that he viewed her differently now. The first time he had snatched her off the streets she was a good girl who had lost her way. This time she wasn't so innocent. She was just some cracked-out fiend desperate for the chance to wrap her lips around a glass dick. *Why would he want to be with me now?* she thought.

"Bleu," he said, frustration lacing his every word. "Go in the house."

She nodded as tears accumulated in her eyes. Even now, under his judgmental gaze, Bleu still felt the urge to get high.

She hated herself for loving something more than she loved Iman. She was too weak to resist it and she was afraid of what she would do if left alone.

"I don't want to disappoint you," she whispered. "Can you just stay with me, please?" She swiped a tear that had escaped down her cheek.

Iman's face fell in devastation as he looked at her sadly. It was the first time he ever thought about the role he played in this disease. He just happened to love Bleu, a girl addicted to the very drug he flooded the streets with. It made him sick to his stomach because, although he knew how addictive crack cocaine was, seeing it affect someone so close to him was torture. He was trying to impose a strength on her that she just did not possess. He had to sniff back his emotions as he nodded.

"Yeah, ma, I got you," he said. The anger dissipated, giving way to sympathy and remorse. He was too fast-paced for this young girl. He was the bad to her good and before he thought that gave him balance, but now he saw that he had contributed to her corruption. He exited the car and walked around to open her door.

"Is anyone else here?" she asked, her voice shaking as she thought of the possibility of running into Cinco again.

"No, everyone's gone," Iman replied, frowning as he recognized the look of fear in her eyes. She averted her eyes from his intense stare.

"Why can't you look me in my eyes, ma?" he asked.

Bleu couldn't find the words to answer him. She was emotionally drained.

Bleu wanted to tell him what burdened her. She wanted to spill the secrets of her heart, her afflictions, and her worries, but she knew once she did things would never be the same between them. She knew that Iman loved her. The way he handled her told her that. His actions spoke louder than any words ever could, but to know that she had robbed Cinco and that Cinco had been inside of her . . . Even if Iman forgave her for the role she had played that night, he would never get over the fact that Cinco had been between her legs. That was supposed to be Iman's alone to explore. It was unspoken that he owned that pussy, and she had allowed someone he knew to occupy it. Bleu knew it decreased her value. No man wanted what everybody could get. *He probably won't even believe that Cinco raped me. It'll be my word against his. Cinco will never admit that. He's not going to say anything to Iman. If Cinco was going to say anything he would have done that already. I just have to keep my mouth shut. It's the only time I'll ever lie to him,* she thought. Her drug addiction robbed her of all credibility. Her mind went back to the elaborate stories her mother used to tell. They had all just sounded like excuses. *I don't want to be just another fiend telling crackhead tales,* she thought. *I can't tell him the truth.*

"I just want you to look at me the way you used to," she said honestly as she shifted her stance while hugging herself.

"Then you've got to be the girl you used to be," he said. His finger under her chin, his thumb rubbing her lips, his eyes penetrating hers so deeply that she felt like he could see through her. It was in moments like these that she realized how deeply she was invested in him. She loved everything about Iman. He melted her with one glance. The things he made her feel were intense. Loving him felt like looking directly into the sun. It was beautiful but bad for you all at the same time. Iman's love was scorching and blinding. It was blistering to a girl who had never truly felt loved, and she wanted to do everything she could to keep him. Bleu just wanted to hold on to this overwhelming feeling. The truth would only interfere with that.

He walked into the house and they stood awkwardly in the foyer. "Get some rest. I'll be down here if you need anything. I'm not going anywhere," he reassured her. He planted the simplest kiss on her forehead, but the emotion connected to it was the most complex she'd ever felt. He stood at the bottom of the stairs as she ascended. When she was behind the closed doors to the master suite she placed her back against the door and felt her legs giving out as tears fell from her eyes. She wished that she could fight this urge that she felt, but it was so strong. It was like a black hole sucking her in. Iman had said and done all of the right things to keep her clean. His love made her feel good, but she knew something that felt better. As much as she wanted to deny it, in the bottom of her gut, in her darkest place, she still wanted to get high. She cried her heart out because she knew it was only a matter of time before she gave in and, once she did, she would lose Iman for good.

Iman stood on the back terrace to his opulent home, staring out over his property. It was beautiful, expansive. He was the shining example of a man at the pinnacle of his success. Stone statues lined the rectangular oversized pool. Waterfalls trickled into the glowing Jacuzzi. Iman had every luxury at the tip of his fingers, but it meant nothing to him without someone to share it with. Once upon a time he had thought Tan would be his heart's joy; now it was Bleu and he didn't want there to be any other after her. Her age made it almost impossible for her and Iman to be soul mates. She was too young. She hadn't truly lived yet. Bleu didn't even really know herself yet. She was discovering who she was and what her impact on this world would be and Iman didn't want to stop that. He wouldn't mind being the audience to her life's show, but what he was witnessing was horrific. He could see Bleu disappearing right before his eyes. The intelligent, driven, focused young woman she once was had become a mere memory. He hardly recognized the desperate, thirsty version that the drugs had transformed her into. He could see her resolve wavering. Her struggle was evident. Sometimes her nerves were so bad that her body shook involuntarily. It ailed him greatly to see her deterioration, and as much as he wanted her, he knew that he was no good for her. His lifestyle didn't allow for her recovery. He made his riches off of the very drug that was destroying the woman he loved. Her quest to look good on his arm and to fit into a world where everything moved at warp speed had caused her to crash. It was all too much for her to handle.

I don't know how to fix this one, Iman thought. Iman was a man who calculated each move before he made it, so the fact that he didn't know what to do about Bleu troubled him. He felt helpless and he realized that this might be his karma. He had periled the next man's woman, mother, daughter, sister, with the crack cocaine that he put onto the streets. Seeing how much damage it caused up close to someone he cherished was agonizing.

Iman gripped the railing of the terrace as he lowered his head in despair. He had never felt a weight this heavy. Bleu's condition burdened him. The hollowness in his stomach reminded him that he was human. He had been so cold, so unmoved and detached from his emotions, for so long that the feeling was unfamiliar to him. He hadn't felt this vulnerable since Tan had lost the child she carried years ago. Iman wasn't an emotional man, but Bleu was his Achilles' heel. He was usually so calm and collected. This array of emotion was uncharacteristic of him and made Iman feel like he was out of control. He swiped his hand over his face and pinched the bridge of his nose as he blew out a breath of frustration. He wished he could love her to health, but he wasn't equipped to handle an addiction. He had tried and although for a while she was better, he knew it was only a matter of time before she backslid. Watching her demise would break him. He removed his phone out of his pocket and dialed the only person he could think of to ask for help.

"*Tía,* I need you," he said as soon as his aunt Marta answered the phone.

"Iman? It's three o' clock in the morning. What's wrong?" Marta asked, concern lacing her tone. Her voice was thick and husky due to her being interrupted from a good night's sleep.

"It's Bleu. She's in trouble," Iman said. "I just want her clean. I found her in a hotel room today. I busted up the spot moments before she relapsed. She had the pipe in her hands, *tía*." His voice cracked and he cleared his throat, trying to remain composed. He had loved before, but never in his life had he loved someone as deeply as he loved Bleu. She had penetrated him straight to the core. Her youth was like a breath of fresh air. Her tenacity revived a spirit in him that he had neglected at her age. She was honest, vulnerable. She was a young woman who would mature into a grown woman for him to cherish. He would grow her up. He would experience all of her firsts with her. He just had to get her through this rough patch in her life. He wouldn't have bothered to be burdened with anyone else in this dire situation. He would have dismissed any other chick but Bleu. His Bleu. She needed him. He couldn't help but feel like he was partly to blame for her addiction.

"We'll be there in the morning. Bright and early, Iman. Can you handle things until then?" Marta asked.

"I can. I can't see her like this and I don't trust anyone else to handle this for me," he said.

"No explanation needed," Marta said. "Good night."

Bleu didn't sleep all night. She lay on top of the covers. Despite the shower she had taken, she felt too dirty to climb underneath. She had a burdened soul, a guilty conscience, and it was eating at her. She stared out of the window all night, blinking only when her tears threatened to fall, until the darkness outside turned to light. She waited for Iman to come to bed. She knew that he was upset. Bleu feared what he might think of her. She could only imagine how disgusted he must be. She was waiting like an undisciplined child anticipating punishment but Iman never came. Her heart felt like it was being squeezed so tightly it hurt. *He can't even stand to be around me,* she thought. The sound of the bedroom door opening made her pulse race, but she didn't move.

"Get up, sweetheart. It's time to go."

When Bleu heard Marta's familiar voice she sat up in confusion. "What are you doing here? Where is Iman? Go? Go where?" The questions came one after another. She couldn't even get one out fully before she rambled into the next one.

"You can't stay here, Bleu," Marta said. "You need help, honey. Professional help."

"He wants me out?" Bleu asked, her eyes wide in shock as her brow creased in confusion.

"He just wants you to get better," Marta said. "Eddie is waiting in the car. Get dressed and we will be waiting for you, sweetheart. Take your time."

Tears pooled in her eyes. "I'm not leaving until I speak to him. He can face me. That's the least he can do!" she shouted, suddenly angry as she stormed by Marta. "Where is he?!" Bleu yelled as she rushed down the stairs.

She found him standing outside, waiting near Eddie's car.

"You're making me leave! You're abandoning me!" She pushed Iman and he grabbed her up instantly, pinning her hands at her sides and pulling her into him. "Please don't make me leave, Iman. I promise you I won't mess up. I won't. I just had a bad night. I promise. I don't want you to give up on me." She was sobbing hysterically.

"I'm not abandoning you, ma. I just need you better. I need you stable and healthy. I can't watch you twenty-four-seven.

You need to be somewhere safe, just for a little while," he said.

"Iman, no, please," she begged. "Don't throw me away."

Iman looked Bleu directly in her eyes and released her arms as his hands traveled to her face. He held her cheeks so gently that she let her head fall to the side as he caressed her skin with his thumb. She could feel him trying to wipe her tears away, but they were endless. "I'm so sorry," she whispered.

"You don't have to be sorry, ma. You're sick. You just need some rest. Do you trust me?"

She nodded.

"This isn't what I want either. I want you here with me, but this is what's best for you right now. We just have to take care of this for you right now. Kick this shit once and for all. I paid for you to go to one of the best rehabs in California. It's real exclusive. Private. Nobody will know you're there. They have yoga and all types of bougie shit," he said with a smirk. "It's a library full of books there. I chose this place because it fits you. It has all the things you like to keep you occupied while you're there."

"How long do I have to stay?" she asked somberly.

"As long as it takes," he said before kissing her forehead.

"You won't wait for me!" she cried, unable to stop her sobs from wrecking her.

"You know better than that. As long as it takes. I'm not going anywhere," he reassured her.

Bleu reached up and hugged him as tight as she could. He picked her up off her feet, closing his eyes as he took her all in. "The only way you'll lose me is if you lose yourself, Bleu. You need to get better, ma. I want that for you, but you have to want it too. If I had shown up a minute later yesterday you would have smoked that shit. It's not out of your system. If I could keep you here with me I would, Bleu, but I have to be able to trust you. Go in there and get your mind right, ma. When you get out I got you," he said.

Marta and Eddie stood back watching the young couple. Marta had never seen Iman so smitten. Not even by Tan. "I'm sorry, but if we don't get moving we'll get caught in traffic," she said, interrupting.

Iman nodded and released Bleu. He could see her reluctance as she moved toward the car. There were so many things he wanted to say to her, but he knew that hearing how much he cared for her would only make it harder for her to leave.

As they pulled away, Bleu turned and looked at Iman through the rear window. She felt like he was throwing her away. Rehab was just an excuse to get rid of her. As she turned her head forward, she wiped her tears and crossed her arms stubbornly. This was not what she wanted, but in the struggle to maintain control she couldn't see that. She couldn't handle this lifestyle, and if she didn't get out now it would kill her.

4

"We're here," Marta said. Bleu looked up at the sign on the building. *The Sanctuary,* she thought. She scoffed as she shook her head. Bleu knew that once she stepped inside it would be anything but a safe haven.

"I don't need to be here. I don't belong here. I've been clean for three months," she said.

"You're a grown woman, Bleu," Marta said as she turned around in her seat to look Bleu in the eyes. "You don't have to go in there, but we both know if you don't you're going to go back to the streets. You will try to stay clean because you love Iman. There's only one problem: you don't love yourself, and as long as you don't love yourself you can't stay off the drugs for long. So it's your choice. What do you want to do?"

Bleu's eyes watered, but she was so stubborn that she refused to let them fall. "I don't need you to walk me in. I'm a big girl," she said, angry as she gritted her teeth and pulled open the door before stepping out. She slammed the door so hard the car shook. Bleu knew that she had no right to be mad at Marta and Eddie. They were only trying to help her. From the first day she had come to L.A. they had supported her, but she needed someone, anyone, to blame. Eddie climbed from the car and grabbed her bag out of the trunk. "I've got it," she snapped as she snatched it from his hands.

"You can do this, Bleu. We believe in you. Somewhere deep inside you is the same smart girl I picked up from the airport not so long ago," Eddie said. His words affected her so deeply that a pit formed in her stomach.

"That girl doesn't exist anymore. A girl like that can't keep a man like Iman," she responded in almost a whisper. Bleu turned on her heels and stormed toward the entrance of the rehab.

The smell of lavender filled the air and arrangements of exotic flowers filled the white room. It was all so clean. It didn't match her expectations. She had thought it would be dirty and old, with the bare-minimum accommodations. This was like an upscale resort. It sat on a Malibu beach and only accepted the most elite of clients, movie stars, socialites, and somehow Iman had gotten her a spot among them. She had expected to be around the worst of the worst, the dirty, the desperate, the filth of society, but as she looked at herself in a mirror that hung on the wall she realized she didn't look like what she had been through. Over the past few months she had gotten her weight up and restored her health. If she never disclosed her addiction, one would never suspect she had been a full-blown addict. Anger filled her because she didn't think she deserved to be in a place like this. She didn't want to put her business out for others to judge. Cinco had thrown her off and made her crave an escape. She had slipped up momentarily and now Iman was punishing her. He didn't know that being in his presence was the only thing that soothed her. Tucking her away, no matter how lavishly he accommodated her, only made the urge to get high return. It filled her with anxiety to be alone because it was then that she was forced to look at what she had become. She was so lost and ashamed that she didn't recognize herself.

"Welcome to The Sanctuary. How can I help you?"

Bleu looked at the blond woman who smiled politely at her, but she didn't offer a smile in return.

"I'm here for treatment. My name is Bleu Montclair," she replied.

"Welcome, Bleu. Please have a seat and fill out this paperwork. I'll go fetch Gloria, our intake nurse, okay?" The woman held out a clipboard for Bleu and she hesitantly took it.

She flipped through the pages, scanning the questions.

How long have you been using drugs?
What type of drugs do you use?
What are your triggers?
Does substance abuse run in your family?

Bleu felt nauseous. This was too big of a commitment for her. She didn't want any of this. She didn't ask to be here. Iman had forced it on her, surprised her without warning, and put his love on the line so that she couldn't say no. She sat looking out the window while gripping the pen in her hand, but she didn't write one thing. She just sat, blankly staring at the waves of the ocean, thinking of how much her life had changed. Just one year ago she had come to L.A. with the entire world at her feet. Life had been hers to conquer. She should be starting her sophomore year at UCLA. This street life, this fast life, had run her into the ground. Bleu had come to California with dreams. She had planned her entire life out in her head only to let it slip through her fingers.

"Bleu?"

Bleu turned to find another woman standing in front of her. "I'm Jess. I've been expecting you," she said. She was beautiful, with dark olive skin and jet-black hair that fell down her shoulders. Her frame was model thin and she had a graceful smile that made Bleu feel as though they were old friends.

"I, um . . ." Bleu cleared her throat as she held up the paperwork. "I didn't get a chance to fill these out. I don't . . . I don't think I belong—"

"Of course you don't belong here. Nobody belongs here. Nobody sets out to use cocaine, or heroin, or meth, or alcohol, but somehow you're here. Somehow things got out of control. So why don't we just give it a try anyway. Okay?" Jess said.

Bleu nodded and followed Jess down a hall. Bleu passed a studio where a group of people were sitting on yoga mats, arms and legs folded, with their eyes closed and palms uplifted to the sky.

"That's the meditation room," Jess said as they bypassed it. "We have every luxury you can think of here. We offer exercise classes, cooking courses; we have a psychiatrist on staff who you will have one-on-one sessions with. There is a pool, a sauna. We offer massages and detoxification baths. All of our meals are prepared with organic foods and are gluten- and preservative-free. When you leave here your body will be purged of every poison. It's not just about getting the drugs out of your system. It's a complete cleansing."

Bleu listened as she tried to absorb it all. Jess gave her a tour of the entire property until finally she was shown to her room. She just wanted some privacy and a little bit of time to adjust to it all.

"There are no phones allowed on the property. Our clients value their privacy, so I'm going to need to confiscate any device you have. Laptops and iPads included."

"I only have a phone," she said as she reached into her bag and retrieved it. "How long is this program?"

"Seven weeks," Jess answered. "Don't worry. It will fly by and at the end you will thank yourself for sticking it out. Visiting day is every Tuesday. You have today to roam and get comfortable with this place. Tomorrow your treatment begins."

Bleu plopped on the bed as soon as Jess left the room. Seven weeks without Iman felt like a lifetime and she was sick thinking of all the random women who would try their hand at him while she was away. *He's going to replace me,* Bleu thought. A fire burned in her chest as despair filled her. She was so wrapped up in Iman that thoughts of him consumed her. She was younger than him, so her world revolved around him. She had never felt the things he made her feel and she didn't want to go a day without him. Bleu didn't know it, but a love this strong wasn't meant for a girl so young. She was dependent on it and whenever she didn't have him she would need something to fill the void he left behind. Something as intense as the bond they shared. Something that made her feel just as good. For her that "something" was crack cocaine, and as she buried her head under the pillow she realized the answer to one of the questions on the intake form.

What are your triggers?

She grabbed the pen from the nightstand beside her bed and picked up the application before writing her answer.

Iman. Her trigger was the man she loved, and if they expected her to let him go they had another thing coming. She would rather die loving him than live without him. Bleu didn't realize that in itself was an addiction, one that she needed to shake.

5

Noah stood in the middle of the cemetery, staring at the headstone in front of him. It was evident that not many people visited it anymore. While all of the graves of those laid to rest around it were trimmed and freshly flowered, this grave was unkempt. Apparently the street legend who had faked his death over a decade ago had been forgotten. Noah was still in disbelief that all these years he was the son of one of Flint's biggest kingpins.

"I remember the day they laid that stone. The graveyard was packed all the way down to the street. As soon as they bury you, they start to forget," Khadafi said as he walked up behind Noah.

"Nah. Flint didn't forget. I heard your name coming up before I ever knew you were my father. The entire city thinks you're dead. I haven't even wrapped my mind around the fact that you're standing next to me in the flesh. You'll have to tell me the story about why your name is on this rock one day," Noah said.

"One day," Khadafi confirmed. They stood side by side and stared out into the distance as they spoke. Despite the fact that they shared the same blood, they were still strangers and an awkwardness existed between them. They didn't know each other, not in the way that they should.

"If I had known about you, I would have been around," Khadafi said, clearing his throat as he shifted his stance uncomfortably.

"No need to address that. Mom dukes did just fine. She had her reasons for keeping me from you. It's not my business why. I'm not crying no rivers. I'm good. Let's move forward and talk about this money," Noah said.

"How much can you handle?" Khadafi asked, switching gears.

"I need fifty this time," Noah answered matter-of-factly.

"That's a lot of heroin. You've been flying under the radar, moving low, but you're gaining a reputation in the city. You're building your own empire and you need a team around you. You're too hands-on. You need a right hand and Naomi ain't it," Khadafi replied. "I want to introduce you to someone."

"Nah, I don't rock with new niggas," Noah protested.

"He's new to *you*. I've known him since he was a cub. Practically raised him—"

"Must have been nice," Noah replied sarcastically.

Khadafi paused. "You're my son, but you're a man and no man has ever disrespected me. You show me respect and I'll do the same. Same goes for the clowns you deal with in the streets. Don't let a nigga take a tone with you. You're not a boy. You're a man. You make sure people treat you like a man. You accept less and the next thing you know they start thinking you're equals. Once they start thinking that they begin plotting on your spot. Now you ready to listen or you got more to say? Because you can't absorb knowledge when you're talking. Niggas that talk too much miss the lesson."

Noah stopped himself from replying because he knew if he spoke he would tell Khadafi something he didn't want to hear. Khadafi was kicking game that would have fascinated a young boy, but Noah was far removed from those influential years. He was a grown man, one who was unsheltered, one who had done a bid already. It was too late to school him. Khadafi had missed those years, but out of respect Noah didn't remind him of that. Khadafi could see that Noah was uninterested in the direction of the conversation, so he detoured. "Bookie has a son. Messiah. I want you to bring him in. He's solid and he's thorough. He isn't afraid to get his hands dirty. I'll set up the meeting."

Noah nodded and then turned to head back to his Range Rover. He stopped midstride and faced Khadafi, staring him in the eyes. "I respect you. Every little knucklehead running these streets grows up respecting you. We've all heard the same stories. What you need to worry about is the love. I don't got that. I don't know nothing about having love for another man. You learn that by loving your pops growing up. I didn't have a father to admire, no pops showing me how to change a tire or how to throw up a jump shot. So the respect is there. The love, that's the main lesson I missed."

"So we both have a lot to work on as we develop this bond," Khadafi said.

"Agreed," Noah said before walking away. He wondered if he would ever view Khadafi as more than a connect. *The nigga don't even know the day I was born,* he thought. Noah shook his head as he reminded himself, *He ain't been a part of any other birthday. I made it this many years without him. I don't need him. Fuck him.*

Noah climbed inside of his truck with a myriad of awkward emotions filling him. He was a man with no emotional compass to guide him through the ups and downs of life. It was because of Khadafi's absence that Noah felt like the knots in his gut made him weak. He couldn't admit that his father not knowing his birthday had hurt him or even attest to the fact that having Khadafi in his life excited him. He was unbalanced with pride and ego because it was what he used to navigate his way through childhood. He had taught himself to be a man, and having Khadafi show up after all this time was difficult for Noah to process. Nothing but time could forge their relationship in stone.

Noah put his truck in gear, and when he focused on the road ahead he noticed a black envelope stuck under his wipers. He frowned as he retrieved it. When he opened it a piece of paper with an address written on it fell out. *Fuck is this?* he thought as his eyes shot back toward the gravestone, but Khadafi was nowhere in sight. Noah figured that the address was the location where the bricks of heroin would be left. They had never done business this way before and he wasn't really comfortable with the change of plans, but he would have to roll with it. The streets were drying up and he was eager to re-up so that business could go on as usual. He wasn't the type to miss a dollar, so instead of going home to Naomi as planned, he started his engine and entered the address into his GPS.

It didn't take him long to make it across town. He found himself in Grand Blanc, one of Flint's prestigious neighborhoods. Prestige of course was relative when speaking in terms of Flint. Anything outside of the city limits was considered an upgrade. Grand Blanc was where the doctors and lawyers lived. It was only a stone's throw away from the most violent city in America, but for some reason when you drove into its neighborhoods they felt far removed from it all. It was a hot place to do business. *Why would he bring me to the burbs to do this type of business? I stick out like a sore thumb out here,* Noah thought. He pulled up to a massive home and frowned. Nothing moved around the house. There were no cars in the driveway, no people in sight. It was just him. He picked the key out of his cupholder and exited the truck. He fidgeted uncomfortably and looked around cautiously before making his way to the front door. Noah was hesitant to use the key. He had no idea what was waiting for him on the other side. There was too much mystery in the air, and tension filled him as he opened the door.

"Yo!" he called out. He didn't know whom he was talking to, but he just wanted to let his presence be known. The empty house only echoed back to him, and when he was sure he was alone he stepped inside. "Damn," he whispered, marveling at the exquisite home. He had never been inside a place so grand. This was the type of neighborhood he used to come trick-or-treating in as a kid because he knew they would be giving out the big candy. It was where the rich folks lived, where they actually ran water that people could drink, and where the police actually responded. He immediately felt out of place. A hood nigga with hood swagger wasn't even supposed to be this far out of the city limits. He wondered why Khadafi had sent him here. As he made his way through the house he noticed a bottle of Dom Perignon sitting on the mantel above the travertine fireplace. There was a red bow tied around it and a card leaned against it. He opened it.

Every king needs a castle. I had many good years in this house. Take good care of it. Happy Birthday, Son.

Noah smirked. "You mu'fucka," he said with a chuckle as he realized Khadafi had known all along. Noah looked around, marveling at the details of the enormous house. Nothing had been spared. This had been Khadafi's home once upon a time. The hood had spoken for years about how the government had seized it years ago. Khadafi had purchased it back just to give to his only son. Perhaps having his father in his life wouldn't be that big of a challenge after all. He placed the bottle of champagne back on the mantel and then walked out. He had a birthday celebration to get to. Before he drove away he looked up at the mini-mansion. It symbolized so much. His father had been the greatest hustler the city had ever seen. Noah only hoped he could follow the same path.

Get money and stay out the way, he thought. Noah didn't need the street fame. If he was too flashy the same streets that loved him would turn on him. He wanted to make silent paper. Get in, grind to the top, and get out before the hungry niggas beneath him came for his head.

"You know this ain't my flow," Noah said as he pulled up to the club.

"What do you mean? This is your city, baby. These are your people. The whole city came out to celebrate your birthday with you. Just loosen up and try to have a good time. What's the point of making money if you don't enjoy it?" Naomi replied with a pretty pout as she leaned over the armrest and kissed his lips. "It'll be fine. Just give it thirty minutes. If you not feeling it after that we out, a'ight?"

"Yeah, a'ight," Noah replied as he stepped out of the truck and handed his keys to the valet.

Naomi held out her hand for him as he walked around the front of the truck. Noah cleaned up nice. He looked like new money as he entered the club, but he was easily outshined by his lady. The short, skintight Valentino dress she wore turned the heads of every man and woman in the room.

"You make me have to knock a nigga head off in here tonight," Noah whispered in her ear.

Naomi gave him a coy smile as they were led to their booth in VIP. The music in the club was deafening and Noah was out of his element. He didn't vibe like this. He was too low-key for the spotlight, but when Naomi grabbed a bottle of champagne and sprayed it on the crowd below he knew they weren't leaving anytime soon. It was just the two of them, like Bonnie and Clyde, turning up in their own little world. All eyes were on them. Word had spread throughout the city that Noah had risen to the top. He was the man to see if you were trying to make a little paper. While other hustlers was putting bullshit product on the street, Noah had grade-A dope, straight off the boat. He had the plug, so he had the power, but as he sat in VIP he realized Khadafi was right; Noah needed to build a team. He was feeling too naked. He only had two eyes circulating the club. He was heavily outnumbered by the hundreds who were trying to take a peek at him. He couldn't watch everybody at once. There were too many hands tucked and too many niggas full of envy for him to monitor dolo. It only added to his discomfort. Naomi noticed and walked up to him, winding her body to the beat circulating through the club. "Relax, babe," she said. She handed him a glass of champagne and lifted her own.

Noah downed the drink and then said, "I need something stronger. The waitress is too slow. You want something from the bar?"

Naomi shook her head and Noah descended the steps as he squeezed his way through the thick crowd. He was halfway through the crowd when he locked eyes with someone familiar. Noah couldn't place the face, but the look of malice coming toward him made the hair stand up on the back of his neck. Noah reached for his hip, but he lost the draw when he looked up and saw a .45 pointed in his direction. He couldn't react quickly enough. He froze, anticipating the gunshot that would end his young life.

Bang!

A melee erupted and Noah turned just in time to see a man behind him drop instantly. Noah turned in bewilderment as he realized he had almost had his head blown off. He turned back to see the gunman fleeing with the rest of the crowd. Noah looked toward VIP and didn't see Naomi anywhere.

"Naomi!" he shouted as he aggressively pushed through the frenzy.

He made his way outside, his hand planted firmly on his hip and his head on a swivel as he searched for Naomi.

A black Mercedes-AMG truck with tinted windows pulled up on him and Naomi jumped out of the passenger side. "Oh my God!" she screamed as she hugged him.

Noah noticed the shooter behind the steering wheel. Noah lifted his shirt slightly, exposing the burner he carried.

"No issues, homeboy," the driver said before speeding off.

Noah grabbed his truck from the valet and hurriedly pulled away from the club.

"You know that nigga?" Noah asked.

"*You* don't? He said he was your people," Naomi replied, confused. "That's the only reason I even got in his truck. I saw what he did for you. If it weren't for him, you would have been the one circled in chalk on the dance floor. The guy he shot had a gun pointed at the back of your head. I thought you knew him."

Noah didn't respond as he tried to filter through his memory to pinpoint how he knew the shooter. He was drawing blanks, but he knew that his days of walking around unprotected were over. His one-man army was no longer enough.

He was grateful for Khadafi's gift. It was time to switch up his routine.

"Where are we going?" Naomi asked as she looked out of the back windshield. "Aren't we going the wrong way?"

"Sit back, I've got a surprise for you," Noah said.

"Whose house is this?" Naomi asked as Noah pulled up to the new home.

"It's mine," Noah replied.

"Quit bullshitting," Naomi said jokingly as she hit him playfully.

"No bullshit," Noah said humbly as he pulled out the key. He handed it to her and she looked at him, mouth wide open as her chin hit her chest in disbelief.

"Go ahead," Noah said as he nodded toward the house.

Naomi rushed out of the truck excitedly and ran into the house. As Noah followed he was stopped by the flashing of headlights. He turned to find the same black truck from the club. Noah pulled his pistol without hesitating and held up his arms.

The driver of the truck drove toward Noah and rolled down his window. Noah saw the man from the club, only this time much clearer. "You can put your burner up, fam. I come in peace," the guy said. "Khadafi sent me. I'm Messiah."

"Bookie's son," Noah said.

Messiah reached his hand out the window and they shook before clasping fists in respect.

"Good looking out on that work you put in back there," Noah acknowledged.

"We don't even got to speak about that," Messiah replied. "You too large to be moving dolo, though, bruh. I see you got Shorty in there waiting on you, but let's rap when you get a minute. I got a team. We ready to work when you ready. Everybody solid too."

"Yeah?" Noah asked.

"All day battle-tested, my nigga," Messiah answered with a subtle arrogance that let Noah know it was fact.

"Hit my line tomorrow so we can chop up the details," Noah said. "I'll bless you for that play you put down tonight."

They shook hands once more. "Real niggas don't do it for that, but I'm looking forward to it, bruh."

Noah watched Messiah pull away before joining Naomi inside. His mind ran rampant with thoughts of how close he had come to death. He hadn't even seen it coming. Messiah had proved himself loyal without even trying to and Noah would put him on because of it. Noah had the connect and Messiah had the muscle. It should have been the perfect street marriage. Noah had always believed in doing his dirt alone to avoid the inevitable betrayal among friends that came with the game. He only hoped that going into business with Messiah wouldn't be a decision that he would later regret.

6

Iman sat eating alone at the head of the rectangular table as silence filled his estate. There had been a time when he appreciated the emptiness of his home. It was his solace, his retreat, his escape from the chaotic underworld he navigated in and out of every day. Today, however, he felt alone. He had become accustomed to Bleu's laughter infiltrating his space. Her presence made the vastness seem small, giving him an intimacy that he had never known. Bleu made his house feel like a real home and her absence was driving him insane. It had only been a few days and already he wanted to drive to Malibu and bring her back. He hadn't realized it, but he needed Bleu. Yes, he had everything that money could afford him, but she had shown him something that couldn't be purchased. She had given him something priceless . . . her heart. There was something about loving a woman that renewed him. Iman had been cold before Bleu. The ups and downs of a young marriage had taken its toll on his outlook on love. He had separated himself from his emotions to avoid dealing with the aftermath of his failed marriage to Tan. He hadn't wanted to feel the loss of it all. He couldn't allow himself to be distracted by the painful hole in his chest, but when Bleu came along and began fill the void in his life he softened. He began to live again. Her vibrant love had forced him to open up to her. Before her he had been a shell of a man, ironclad in business and ironclad in life, but with her he was able to separate the two. She made him "feel" again, but with that came despair now that she was away. Iman wanted to be selfish and bring her home, but he knew that she was exactly where she needed to be. Away from him. It was best for her. She couldn't handle his lifestyle. Being with him would lead to her demise. After seeing someone he cared for afflicted by the very drug he peddled, he began to wonder if the money was worth it anymore. He thought about all the other "Bleus" he had served over the years. From his come-up on the street corners, hustling blocks, to moving kilos, to now running the largest movement in all of California, he was a part of the problem. He was man enough to admit it, but he was too far in to just step out. He had worked too hard to just give it all up. The game didn't work that way. There was no for-sure exit plan. Iman had come to terms with the fact that he would die as a result of his participation in this deadly game . . . before he met Bleu. Now everything was just so uncertain. A part of him wished she were older, wiser, more mature. She hadn't even begun to truly live yet, and while he was ready to settle down, was she? *What if I give all this up for her and this isn't what she wants?* he thought. It was that possibility that kept his feet firmly rooted in the game. While he was plotting a lifetime with Bleu, he didn't know if she was interested in forever. He trusted her, but he knew that as she grew she would change just as Tan had done. He didn't know if time would allow him and Bleu to grow together or if they would inevitably grow apart.

The ringing of the doorbell interrupted his thoughts. Iman was grateful for the distraction. When he pulled open the door, much to his surprise, Tan stood on the other side.

"You knocking now? Last time you were here you came busting in on some rah-rah-type shit," Iman said.

He expected her to respond with her quick wit, but when she removed her sunglasses he saw nothing but raw emotion in her eyes. Her flushed face was puffy and swollen from crying, her normally perfect hair was disheveled, and her forehead was wrinkled in worry.

"What's wrong, Tan?" he asked.

"Everything," Tan whispered.

Iman frowned. "Tan, you're shaking. What's wrong? You've got to talk, T. I can't read your mind," he said.

"It's Papa," she replied. "I think there is something wrong with him, Iman—" She couldn't even finish speaking before she broke down. A part of him wanted to doubt her intentions. He had asked her for a divorce. *Now she here with these tears,* Iman thought skeptically. He felt she was trying to work him. A relationship as long as the one they shared came with strings. They would always be attached and she knew that seeing her so disturbed would bother him. Iman had taken his last name back, but there was a piece of his heart that she would always have, simply because she had been down for him since day one.

"Calm down, T. What are you talking about? I just saw Sandoza a few days ago. He seemed fine."

"He's not fine," Tan snapped. "There is something different about him, Iman. He's absentminded. There is worry in his eyes, Iman. I've never seen Papa afraid of anything. He's distracted and evasive when I ask him what's wrong. There is something wrong, Iman. I don't know what is going on; Papa is in trouble."

"You're jumping the gun, Tan. Sandoza is fine," Iman replied, losing patience.

"Please check on him for me, Iman. Please. He will talk to you. He will tell you what's going on," Tan said. "Please, *papi*."

Iman exhaled in exasperation because he knew that Tan wouldn't have come to him unless she was genuinely concerned.

"Okay," he said. "I'll go down there and check on him."

"Promise me, Iman," she insisted.

"Have I ever lied to you?" he asked.

"Yeah. You once said we would be together forever," Tan replied. Sadness dripped from her words, crushing him. Iman had never wanted to hurt her, especially this version of her standing in front of him. Life had hardened her over the years. Tan hadn't shown him this side of herself since the day she lost the baby he had planted in her womb. He had missed this part of her. He knew that her unraveling was a product of the divorce papers he had sent her, and knowing that he had caused her so much pain was like a blow to the chest.

Sympathy filled him as he replied, "I don't know what you want from me, Tan. Do you think I want to hurt you like this?"

"You didn't even try. You just met this girl and you slid her right into your life, in the place I used to be!" Tan cried.

Tan's devastation was real. Her pain was palpable and so great that Iman felt it. She wore it all over her. She was drowning in grief from love lost, and despite all the bad they had been through, he was the only one who could comfort her. Love was crazy in that way. He was to blame for her hurt but was the only one who could heal her. It was irony at its finest. Iman knew that it had taken so much out of her to even come to his house after what had gone down between them. She hated him for moving on, but she loved him for everything that he had been to her. He could feel her soul yearning for him. The long history they shared didn't allow him to disregard her need for him. Iman knew that Tan was capable of weaving a sticky web and he felt himself being caught in it. He opened the door wider and stepped to the side, inviting her inside without saying a word. She walked in and he grabbed her arm, pulling her close. Iman knew that the lines were blurring. He shouldn't have been holding her; she shouldn't even be in the home he planned to build with Bleu. Or was it the other way around? *Did I destroy this with Tan by having Bleu in the home I bought for her?* Iman didn't know, but he couldn't deny that it felt good to hold his wife. It felt good for her to let him hold her. Tan melted into him, sobbing into his chest as he caressed the back of her neck. So many emotions pulsed through him that it was hard for him to focus. Bleu crossed his mind, but when Tan placed her lips on his all guilt was erased. Iman wasn't in the business of breaking hearts, but the way his body was reacting to Tan made it impossible for him to stop. Before he knew it he had her pinned against the wall and her thighs were wrapped around him as he slid into her.

"Damn," he whispered, kicking himself as he fell into a rhythm. This was wrong. He knew it, but the way his name fell off her tongue in the throes of their lovemaking made it too hard to stop. They were animalistic, carnal, as she dug her nails into his back in an attempt to keep up with the pace. It had been so long since he had touched her, since she had let him, but it was like riding a bike. He chased her to the finish line, letting her win before getting his second prize. Her chest heaved up and down. She was exhilarated. "Iman," she gasped. "What does this mean?"

"I don't know, Tan," Iman replied as he rested his forehead against hers.

"Figure it out, Iman," Tan whispered. "And don't forget who was here for you when nobody else was. I want you back, and based off what just happened, a part of you wants that too." Tan adjusted her dress and cleared her throat. "Go check on Sandoza. You owe me that much."

She left just as quickly as she had come, leaving Iman with a whole new set of problems. He had betrayed Bleu, but re-connecting with Tan hadn't felt wrong. He loved them both and the thought of hurting either of them tore him right down the middle. He would eventually have a choice to make, but he knew that no matter what he decided, someone he loved would grow to hate him in the end.

Iman was always uneasy when he stepped foot on Mexican soil. In this country he had no muscle, no pull, no advantage. It wasn't his kingdom to reign. Mexico was run by the most ruthless drug cartels in the world. Sandoza was the head of one of them, so his word was law. As Iman walked out of the airport and stepped into the waiting black town car an uneasiness filled him. Iman wasn't big on making the trip back and forth. He didn't want Customs to flag him for visiting too frequently. Tijuana was known for its drug activity and Iman preferred to avoid suspicion. He only came when it was absolutely necessary, but his promise to Tan was something he wanted to keep. He didn't know if she was overly emotional or her concern was valid, but he felt inclined to see for himself.

He hadn't given Sandoza warning of his arrival. He only hoped that Sandoza welcomed him with open arms. Their interactions had been less frequent lately. Iman had expected Sandoza to all-out war with him over divorcing Tan, but instead he had been met with indifference. Sandoza had said he was okay with it, but the shift in the interaction between them revealed that there was conflict. Sandoza's silence meant he was brooding and plotting. Iman was prepared for anything. As his driver took him out of the city's limits he thought of the work he had put in for Sandoza over the years. Building his own L.A. empire didn't come without a price.

He had sold his soul to Sandoza over the years to prove his worth. Iman didn't like to think of the wives he had turned to widows on his climb to the top or the children he had turned to crack once he got there. His thoughts wandered to Bleu. *She thinks I'm a good man, but I'm one of the bad guys,* he thought. *She can't handle me. I'm knee-deep in the game and I can't foresee the end anytime soon. She isn't built for this life. Tan can handle this, but it'll destroy Bleu. If I choose her, I'll kill her slowly.* The thought of letting her go sent a stabbing pain through his gut. He loved her so much that it ailed him . . . it physically haunted him to even think of being without her. She haunted his thoughts, distracting him so greatly that he didn't realize that he had arrived at Sandoza's estate. He was used to the grandness of it all. He had been a guest many times before.

He rolled down the back window. "Estoy aqui para ver Sandoza," he said, his baritone commanding authority.

"Sí, señor, bienvenidos," the guard greeted him. They knew him well and allowed him access without second-guessing.

"Gracias," Iman answered before rolling up the window as his driver entered the gates. Security was never sparse at Sandoza's estate. Armed men protected the perimeter at all times. Sandoza took no shortcuts when it came to his safety. It was how he had persevered in the underworld for so long.

The car came to a stop at the top of the circular driveway and Iman emerged. He removed the jacket to his Tom Ford suit and rolled up his sleeves in an attempt to adjust to the smoldering Mexican heat.

Sandoza came out to greet him before he could even approach the door. It didn't surprise Iman. Sandoza had eyes all over his property. If his men didn't radio him to let him know he had a visitor, then the high-tech security cameras would let him know.

"This is unexpected," Sandoza said as he held out his hand. Iman shook it and then hugged Sandoza, giving him a tight squeeze before letting him go.

"I had some business across the border. I figured I'd stop in and have a drink," Iman said.

"Good. It's long overdue," Sandoza said as he welcomed Iman into his home. Iman stepped inside. He looked around, impressed. Iman was well off, but Sandoza was wealthy. He had a few million dollars in art hanging on his walls alone.

Sandoza retrieved a bottle of scotch and two glasses from the bar before heading into his study.

Iman sat across from Sandoza and waited patiently as he poured both drinks. Iman studied Sandoza, wondering what it was that had Tan so alarmed.

"So are you going to tell me what really brings you here or are you going to bullshit me all day?" Sandoza asked while holding out the glass.

Iman chuckled as he accepted the drink. "You've always been able to call my bluff," Iman said.

"I raised you. We may not share blood, but you're still my son," Sandoza said.

"I just wanted to make sure everything between us is square," Iman said as he took a swig of his drink, allowing the burn to roll down his throat slowly. He didn't want to expose Tan's worry by telling the truth and he couldn't lie to Sandoza, so instead Iman spoke of one of his personal concerns.

"I've never minced words with you before and I'm not going to begin now. There comes a time in a man's life when he knows the end is near. I don't have a lot of days left, Iman. I can feel it, and before anything happens to me I want to be clear on what I want. You're like a son to me. I've known you since you were a teenage kid chasing after my daughter's skirt. I trust you and I have seen how you run your business in L.A. I want you to fill my seat with the Five Families if something happens to me," Sandoza said. "All of this, my entire operation, is yours if you want it."

Iman didn't know how to respond to this. They were clearly having two different conversations. Iman thought Sandoza would take issue with him over Tan, but here he was offering him an entire empire. "What about Cinco?" Iman asked.

"I expect him to be upset. He is like a spoiled child with his temper tantrums and his entitlement. By blood everything should go to him, and I wish I could give it to him, but he isn't ready. Every player doesn't make a good coach," Sandoza said. "I want him involved of course, but I can't hand over my life's work to him. He isn't diplomatic. He would have us warring with the other families before the dirt covers my casket. He can't do this job. It has to be *you*," Sandoza stressed. He was so passionate that the veins in his forehead bulged as he spoke.

"Why are we having this conversation now? Why the urgency, Sandoza? Ain't no funerals happening anytime soon. We have time to iron out the details," Iman said.

Sandoza reached over the table and gripped Iman's wrist. "The time for the details is now," he said seriously. It was then that Iman noticed it: the fear that Tan had told him about. He saw a foreboding in Sandoza's stare. Sandoza was indirectly telling Iman something heavy. There was deeper meaning behind this generous offer. A lump formed in his throat. Something was up. He didn't know why and he respected Sandoza too much to dig deeper, but he heard him loud and clear. If, or, inevitably, when, something happened to Sandoza, Iman was next in line. *Is he telling me he's about to die?* Iman asked. *Is he sick? Is he beefing with one of the other familes? Is there paper on his head?*

"I'm ready whenever you need me. Just say the word," Iman said, nodding.

"An introduction to the other heads of the Five Families is necessary. They won't like you sitting among them. The seat is supposed to go to the first blood-born son. You will meet much resistance, but my word will bond your position. Once you're in, you're in for life. This part of the game isn't optional. Once you accept, the only way out is when the last breath leaves your body. You'll have more power than you've ever dreamed, more money than you can spend in two lifetimes. Right now you're selling drugs, but when you get to my level it goes beyond that. You'll own a piece of the world. Mexico is mine, and when I'm gone it will be yours."

The offer was enticing. It was what young hustlers aspired to and what you heard about in rap songs. Iman thought he was at the top of the game. He had developed a network of some of the most notorious criminal organizations in the country. He had no idea there was another level and he never imagined being inducted into it.

"Why me?" Iman asked. "I know Cinco isn't ready, but what about Miguel? He's been your right hand for over thirty years."

"Sometimes it's best to not let your right hand know what the left is doing. Miguel has been a good confidant, but he did something twenty years ago to disrespect me that he has yet to be punished for."

"What's that?" Iman asked with a raised eyebrow.

"He fucked my wife," Sandoza responded.

Iman smirked and Sandoza shrugged. "No need to lose a good shooter over pussy. I never said one thing. When I bypass him for you, he'll know why. Besides, I taught you everything you know," Sandoza replied. "So even when I'm gone I will still influence the decisions you make in my seat." Sandoza paused and Iman could see that he was choosing his next words wisely.

"What is it?" Iman asked.

"This comes with a condition," Sandoza said. "You have to stay with my daughter. I am offering you generational power, but I have to know that the generations I am providing for are my own. Tan is your wife, and as long as she remains your wife you will maintain your seat among the Five Families."

There it was, the other shoe that Iman was waiting for. It had dropped and with it came a heavy blow to his chest.

"She's my daughter. I've discovered some things recently that have me getting my affairs in order. I may not always be around to take care of her. This is my way of making sure that you do. You loved her once; this shouldn't be too much of a sacrifice, considering what you are gaining in exchange," Sandoza said. "Do we have a deal?" Sandoza was forcing Iman's hand, letting him choose his own fate in the game. He was stuck between love and money, and as the burden rested on his shoulder he was visibly undecided.

Bleu crashed into his thoughts like a hurricane hitting land, drowning him in visions of her. The things he felt for Bleu made him feel like a new man. Life had been black-and-white before her, but the moment he met her she had colored in the darkness, adding vibrant shades to his drab existence. Bleu made a masterpiece of his life like Picasso. Iman's love for her was new, but it ran deep and he didn't want to cut it off. *She's so young*, he thought wearily. He thought of her, strung out and addicted. He knew that staying with her would be a challenge, one that he would be willing to commit to for life. *But is she?* Again, his thoughts ran wild. He was older. He had lived. He had loved. He had experienced different facets of life that were unexplored by her. He wanted a couple of forevers with her, but was it fair for him to rob her of her youth? She hadn't seen anything, hadn't been anywhere. She still had all of her ho years ahead of her. Now was a time for her to be wild, to be free, to date, to find out what she liked and what she didn't prefer. *Maybe she only wants me because I'm all she knows.* Suddenly the option of turning Sandoza down seemed ludicrous. Bleu was just beginning her life. Iman was one of many lessons she would learn along the way on her path to self-discovery. She didn't know herself yet and that was evident. If he declined Sandoza's offer for Bleu, life would eventually take her away from Iman. She would grow and time would change her, the same way it had done to Tan. He couldn't take the risk. Betting on Bleu to hold him down would be foolish. He knew it; he just didn't want to admit it. He couldn't take a chance on Bleu. Not when there was so much at stake. It pained him to speak his next words.

"We have a deal," Iman agreed.

"I don't need to remind you that discretion is important. My daughter doesn't need to know about business between men," Sandoza reminded Iman.

Iman nodded. "I'm just a man trying to make his marriage work," Iman agreed.

"I'll have a talk with Marcincio," Sandoza said.

"He won't be happy," Iman said.

"No, but it is not his decision to make," Sandoza replied.

Iman stood and Sandoza did as well. He looked at his mentor, his father-in-law, sympathetically. He seemed to have aged overnight. Iman didn't know exactly what ailed Sandoza. He knew Sandoza wasn't preparing for his own demise for nothing. Iman wasn't eager to bury his mentor, but should the unspeakable occur . . . he would be ready to take the throne.

7

Iman stared out of the window of his private plane as it descended over the City of Angels. These were his streets, his territory. He had muscled his way to the top of L.A.'s cocaine trade, and as he sat overlooking it he felt godlike. Sandoza had placed so much power in his hands that most men never attained. He should have been ecstatic. He should have been plotting moves to expand toward the East Coast and even areas of the South, but he couldn't think clearly. He had sold a piece of his soul to secure his place on the throne. He would be Sandoza's successor, but it had come at a hefty price.

Iman was stoic as the plane landed and he headed for his waiting bulletproof SUV. He slid inside as the driver closed the door. Iman didn't like the "ain't shit" feeling that came with discarding Bleu. To just throw her away felt wrong, but Sandoza's terms were clear. Iman gave his driver the address of his L.A. condo. He was rushing home to the wrong woman and he knew it, but still he pressed forward. It took him an hour to even talk himself out of the car once he arrived. He found himself at Tan's doorstep. He had the key. He could have easily entered the condo, but instead he rang the bell. When she opened it her beauty stunned him. She was prepared for bed. Her plain face glowed and her hair was pulled up into a messy topknot.

"Those shirts always did look better on you," he said with a short smile as he noticed she still slept in his button-down oxford shirt and tall socks.

"What are you doing here?" she asked with a smile. "How was Tijuana? Did you see Papa?"

"I saw him. He's okay," Iman lied.

"Really?" Tan asked, frowning in confusion. "Are you sure?"

"I'm sure," Iman confirmed.

"Thank God," she whispered as she played with the diamond cross necklace around her neck. She sighed in relief. "You want to come in?" she asked. She could see despair in Iman's eyes. She had known him long enough to notice his distress, no matter how hard he tried to hide it.

"I want to come home, Tan."

There. He had said it. He couldn't change his mind. She recoiled in shock as he walked into the condo without allowing her to respond. He knew there was no need to wait for permission. She wanted him here.

"I don't understand. What does this mean? A few days ago you had divorce papers sent to me and now—"

"Now I want my wife back," Iman finished for her. The

words in his mouth tasted like vinegar. All he could think of was Bleu.

"And the bitch you had in my house? What about that situation?" Tan asked.

"It's done," Iman replied. "That's finished."

Tan looked at him skeptically.

"I know you've built walls over the years. That was part of the problem between us. You shut me out. You lost our first kid and then another and another—"

"Iman, don't," Tan whispered.

Iman took a seat and placed his elbows on his knees, then tented his fingers against his forehead. He took a deep breath. He loved Bleu, but that didn't mean he didn't love Tan. He realized that there had been so many factors that had contributed to the destruction of his marriage. This was a hard conversation. One they had never had the courage to have, and so many things needed to be said.

"I was there too, Tan. Right there with you, right there feeling it. I never blamed you. I only wanted to help you through it, but somehow shit got all messed up. The love got lost. You needed someone to take it out on and that was me. It tore us apart, and I fell out of love with you. You changed and I changed. I gave up." He lifted his head and looked at her. "I want to come home and see if we can get back what we lost. You deserve that."

Tan was speechless. Every word Iman spoke chipped away at her hard exterior. "You can't just come in here talking like this after you paraded another bitch in front of me. You chose somebody else. You put me out of a home we built together and kept her there with you. What was it about that girl? You've had hoes before, but this was different. She wasn't like the others. You moved her in. Do you love her?" Tan asked, unable to accept the fact that there had been someone significant in Iman's life.

"She is the opposite of you. When she wanted to cry she cried. She was vulnerable. Soft. Those are the things that made her unlike the others. Unlike you."

"She sounds weak," Tan spat, crossing her arms and turning her nose up in disgust.

"She is," Iman admitted. "She's recovering from a crack addiction. So when I tell you that it's done between me and her . . . I mean that. You don't have to worry about that."

"Well, good," Tan said as she crossed her arms, and she looked nervously at her feet. She wanted to kiss him, but she refrained. He could tell she was holding back.

"Be weak," he said as he stood and crossed the room, stepping into her intimate space. He was so close that she was uncomfortable. She placed a flat hand to his chest to keep a bit of distance between them.

"Iman," she resisted.

He removed her hand. "Be weak," he demanded. "Submit to me, ma." It didn't even feel right, calling her what he affectionately called Bleu. He needed Tan to lower her defenses, to be more like Bleu. He needed Tan to make him feel even an inkling of what Bleu made him feel.

"You'll hurt me," she whispered.

"I didn't hurt you the first time," Iman said. "Life hurt us. Heal with me. Show me what you're feeling, Tan. No more walls, no more blocking me out. Let me love you."

Tan lowered her head and a tear escaped. Iman swept the tear away with his thumb and then rubbed his fingers together as if he wanted to see if it was real. He pinned her against the wall, lifted her chin, and then placed his lips against hers. She melted, right into him. Tan pulled away first and looked up at him, seduction glazing her eyes as she began to unbutton her shirt. She bit her lip as she began to walk toward the bedroom. With every step she took she left a piece of clothing as Iman admired the view. "I've got something soft for you," she said. She beckoned him with her fingers as she headed into the bedroom. Iman loosened his tie and followed her, hoping that their lovemaking would further help him shake the hold Bleu had on him.

8

Bleu stood at the window overlooking the ocean as hints of orange and yellow began to lighten the morning sky. It seemed the entire world was moving on, time was passing, but she was stuck in the same place. She couldn't put one foot in front of the other. Emotionally and mentally she was lost somewhere between sanity and insanity. The world around her was coming to life, introducing a new day, but Bleu felt nothing but darkness. It had been a week and Bleu had been holed up in her room, curtains drawn, her tears her only company. If it hadn't been for the trays of food Jess had placed outside her door, Bleu would have starved. She just didn't have the motivation to do anything but sulk. She was lonely without Iman. It wasn't the fact that she was away from him. They had been apart before, but this wasn't regular distance. She felt abandoned; like a baby dropped off on a firehouse doorstep; she had no one. It hurt. Unlike anything had ever hurt before.

Jess had been patient with her. No one had forced her to participate. She just wanted to be left alone. She was angry that Iman hadn't visited and when she called she received no answer. He was cutting her off. *I knew it,* she thought. There was a cloud hanging over her head causing a gloom so dark that it felt like life was raining on her. Anxiety filled her. She was suffocating.

Knock. Knock.

"It's open," she said.

Jess came through the door. "Good morning, Bleu."

Bleu gave her a tight-lipped smile in response but didn't speak as she turned back toward the window.

"I know you're hungry. No more room service, Bleu. If you would like to eat, you will have to come to the cafeteria," Jess said.

Bleu heard the door close and then huffed in frustration. If she could stay in this room forever she would, but she was starving. She slipped on sweatpants and a hoodie before wandering out of her room. Bleu grabbed a cup of coffee and then wandered out to the beach. She inhaled deeply. The scent of ocean filled the air and she closed her eyes as the mist soothed her. Bleu was so low. She was never supposed to be this girl . . . the kind who threw her goals away as if they never mattered. She was stupid and materialistic. *I've made so many bad choices. I could have stayed in Flint for this,* she thought in disappointment. She really just wanted to go home, but she feared that if she walked out of rehab eventually she would go back to smoking. It was always present in the back of her mind. It was a high that felt so good that nothing else compared. Smoking crack was better than sex, better than love, than adventure, than money. She had never understood why her mother couldn't stop until she took her first blast. It wasn't until then did it all make sense. *I need to talk to him. I just want to hear his voice,* she thought. Bleu couldn't stay here guessing whether or not Iman still wanted her. She needed him to tell her that he would still be there when she got out. That he still loved her and that he would stand by her. That was the only thing that would get her through the next six weeks. She turned and found Jess heading her way.

"Hey, I need my phone to make a call," Bleu said.

"Okay," Jess said in a soothing tone. "How about I make you a deal? If you come to morning group, afterward I'll take you in my office and give you your cell so that you can make your phone call."

Bleu rolled her eyes, not really feeling the bargaining game Jess was playing.

"It's the only way you're getting your phone, Bleu," Jess said. "Come on. Just give it a shot. If you don't want to do it in a group setting, I can arrange for you to meet with a counselor one-on-one."

Bleu nodded. "The private session sounds okay," she agreed, but as she followed Jess inside she was already regretting it. Bleu wasn't naïve about the skeletons she had tucked in her closet. She tried hard to hide them. Coming up, she was always the daughter to crackhead Sienna. The entire hood knew that Bleu's parents were on drugs and she had been embarrassed by that for as long as she could remember. She remembered her mother inviting men to their apartment when

Bleu's father was gone. It was the smell of them that haunted her the most. Sienna had done anything to get high. Bleu had been exposed to so much. She had blocked out the rough hands that had fondled her little body. When her mother had become worn-out and the local D'boys no longer found her attractive, she sold Bleu's innocence. It was a part of her life that she had blocked out. No one knew about it. Not Noah, not Iman. All of these things had led up to this moment. She was hurting inside. She had tried running from her past. It was half the reason why she had wanted to go to college so far away from home. She loved that she had a fresh start. It had been her chance to start over. No one knew who she was or the nothingness that she came from. She was just a girl on her grind from a little city from the Midwest until she made people think otherwise. She had messed up . . . royally and fallen into the same trap that her parents had been lost to. *Maybe it was supposed to end up this way. I was running from fate,* she thought. She didn't need a therapist to tell her that she was fucked up. She had known that for a long time but had tried to cover it by overcompensating in other areas. First she dived into her studies as a distraction from the madness. Then there was the lifestyle, the weave, the clothes, the makeup. Living luxe in the big city was like playing dress up every day. She had changed so much about herself that she didn't recognize the little girl who had allowed random men to violate her. Moving drugs in and out of Mexico made her feel in control for the first time in her entire life. Then there was Iman. Loving him was so intense that it made her forget about everything and everyone before him. He made her feel so worthy, so priceless, but she couldn't help but wonder if she provoked the same emotion out of him.

Bleu entered one of the offices and was greeted by a friendly-enough face. Bleu didn't pay attention to the name or even hear the words that were coming out of the man's mouth. She wasn't open to this. It was bullshit. They couldn't force her to divulge her innermost thoughts. Some secrets should just go to the grave. So as the therapist inquired about her, Bleu just told him what he wanted to hear. She smiled amicably and did more listening than speaking until it was over. She didn't realize she was blowing off something that could actually help her. This session was just a means to an end. She had to give a little to get something and she desperately needed that phone call. Jess was waiting outside of the door for her, leaning against the wall with Bleu's cell phone in her hand.

"Here you go," Jess said, handing Bleu the phone. "You've got fifteen minutes. Perhaps next time you'll take the session more seriously." She walked away, shaking her head, as she gave Bleu privacy to make her call.

Bleu dialed Iman's number as a ball of nerves formed within her. Her breath caught in her throat as the phone rang in her ear.

"Hello?"

The female voice that answered the phone put an instant frown on Bleu's face. "Who is this?" Bleu asked.

"This must be my husband's side chick. Listen, little girl,

I'm back in his life now. Your services are no longer needed. Don't call this number again. I'm not the type to blame the other woman. You were only around because Iman allowed you to be around, but all of that is over now. You don't want a problem with me, so let this be your last time calling."

Hearing Tan's voice ruined Bleu. "Bitch, put Iman on the phone!" Bleu said. She didn't even realize she was shouting until people around her took notice.

"Look, you junkie bitch. Your fifteen minutes are up. Take the hint and beat it."

Click.

Bleu's heart dropped. *He told her about my rehab. He's back with her. He sent me here so that he could get back with his wife. That's why he hasn't visited. He lied to me,* Bleu thought. The phone fell from her hands and she reached out to balance herself against the wall. The room spun and her chest felt so heavy that it was hard for her to breathe. "Oh my God," she whispered. "Oh my God, oh my God." This feeling was too strong to mourn silently. She had to let it out. She had to scream. Bleu doubled over gripping her stomach in agony. It was the second time Iman had made a fool of her. The first time when she had discovered he was married and now this. He was killing her slowly, torturing her with his potential to love her. He gave her just enough to get her hooked, then snatched it away repeatedly. It was cruel. *I have to get out of here. I have to see him,* she thought.

"Bleu?" Jess rushed over to her, but Bleu pushed her away. Bleu didn't want Jess's fake love, her pretend caring, the false concern. Bleu saw the I.D. card that hung from a lanyard around Jess's neck. She snatched it off and bolted for the door.

"Bleu!" Jess shouted. "Security!"

Bleu didn't even look back. She just wanted out. She needed to get to Iman . . . to hear it from him. She wanted him to look her in the eyes and tell her that he didn't want her.

Bleu didn't stop running until she was sure no one was chasing her. When she finally did, the contents of her stomach erupted. She was lovesick. Her legs were so shaky from the revelation Tan had thrown at her that she sank to the ground. Suddenly she felt weak, light-headed, and so full of angst that she wanted to give up. She planted her head in her hands as she allowed herself to have a good cry. She was tired of holding it in. For an entire week she had pretended that the knots in her stomach didn't exist. She had tried to dull the ache building in her chest. Her heart felt too heavy to beat and it made the rise and fall of her chest feel unbearable. She just wanted to die. Surely death would be easier than living without love.

Bleu looked around in despair. She was sitting on the side of the Pacific Coast Highway, without her wallet or a cell phone. She was stuck. There was nothing around for miles except the place she had just run from. *I'm not going back there,* she thought. She composed herself as she stood and began to walk on the side of the winding elevated highway, hoping someone would take sympathy on her and save her from the rising Malibu temperatures. Bleu walked for an hour before a car pulled over for her. Relief flooded her until she turned to see Jess's face through the window. Bleu blew out a breath of frustration and raked her hand through her sweaty hair.

"I'm not coming back to rehab," she protested. "It's not the place for me. I just need to get back to Iman. I don't belong there! The Zen and the yoga and the talking and the . . . ugh! I'm over it."

"We can't make you stay at The Sanctuary, Bleu," Jess said. "I've packed your things. They are in the trunk. Now are you going to walk to the bus stop? Or are you going to get in so that I can drop you off?"

Bleu reluctantly got inside the car.

"My name tag please," Jess added with displeasure.

Bleu gave it to her and then sat back as they rode the rest of the way in complete silence. When they arrived, Bleu couldn't get out of the car fast enough. Jess looked at her sympathetically and said, "You're the worst kind of addict, Bleu. You're in denial that you even need the help. You don't just stop smoking crack, Bleu. It's an everyday struggle that you fight like hell to maintain for the rest of your life. You're going to slip up because you don't want to admit what you are. You can't face yourself, and until you do you won't ever recover. Good luck."

Bleu didn't respond. She simply grabbed her luggage and walked away. *She doesn't even know me,* Bleu thought with an attitude as she went to buy her ticket. There was only one person's approval that she needed; everyone else's opinion held no weight with her. There was no way she was going to sit in self-imposed seclusion for six more weeks while Tan weaseled her way back into Iman's bed.

• • •

Bleu's cab pulled up to Iman's house and devastation slapped her in the face when she saw Tan placing the last of her possessions out for the trash.

"It'll be fifty-six dollars," the cabbie said.

"Oh." Bleu fumbled through her bag. She didn't have any money. Iman never trusted her with large amounts of cash and she had spent the last she had on the bus ticket to get back to L.A. "I need to go inside to get your money," she said, embarrassed. "Just give me one minute." She looked up at the house as Tan got into her car. Bleu's stomach turned. She hated her. Tan was exactly the type who looked like she deserved to be with Iman. She symbolized all of Bleu's insecurities. Bleu wasn't pretty enough, fancy enough, sharp enough, thin enough. She was nothing compared to Tan. She was childish compared to Tan. As Tan pulled out of the driveway in her Aston Martin Bleu cowered in the backseat of the cab. She waited until she was sure Tan was gone before climbing out of the cab. "I'll be right back with your money."

"Don't make me call the police," the cabbie threatened.

"I got it," Bleu said impatiently as she slammed the door. As soon as she turned toward the house her feet felt like they were planted in the cement. She knew Iman was home because his car was parked horizontally in the driveway. She had seen with her own eyes that Tan was back but wanted to hear him say it. She wanted to ask him how he could let her set her things out for the trash. Was she trash? Was she that easily forgotten? She walked up and rang the bell, trying her hardest not to cry.

Do not let this nigga make you cry. Don't give him the satisfaction. Fuck him, she thought. The tough visage was shattered the moment Iman opened the door.

He saw her hurt. Visibly. It emanated from her like a radiator spreading heat. The look in her eyes was pure grief and the fact that he had caused it filled Iman with guilt. He hadn't expected to see her for another six weeks. He had thought he had more time to explain to her why he had to let her go. Absence had dulled the potency of his affections for her. He had underestimated how hard this moment would be. Her tears were love personified and he was wasting it. He was letting it spill down her cheeks as if it weren't one of the hardest things in the world to find. They stood there just staring at each other. They were silent, but so much was said in their gaze. He knew her questions: *Why? How could you?* Now the answers didn't seem to make sense.

"I'm sorry, ma," he said, suddenly ashamed of himself. He reached out to touch her, but she recoiled as if he had burned her.

She backpedaled while shaking her head and he advanced on her.

"I can't do this," she whispered, and then turned and hustled back down the driveway.

"Bleu!" he shouted. She didn't stop until she saw the cabbie getting out of his cab.

"Where is my money?" he shouted.

Iman frowned and pulled out a knot of money, throwing it at the cabbie. Bleu reached for the door, but Iman closed it.

"Just give me a minute," he said. He turned to the cab-driver. "She's good, my man. Beat it."

The cab drove away.

"How dare you!" Bleu shouted. "You sent me away so you could get back with your wife. My stuff is on the curb. You threw me away!" Bleu was hysterical. She braced her hands on her knees and cried, then stood, then bent over again in agony. She was going crazy. Iman made her crazy. He brought back the itch to smoke dope. He awakened her addiction. *He's my trigger,* she thought. *I have to get away from him.* Bleu began to walk away.

"Bleu. Don't make me chase you, ma." His voice was stern, commanding, and she stopped walking instantly. She refused to face him. She covered her face with her hands and sobbed so hard that her shoulders shook.

Iman felt like shit. How could he hurt this beautiful girl? Even the melody of her cries was the sweetest thing he had ever heard. Bleu was imperfectly perfect, like a priceless piece of china that had been cracked. He had developed a great appreciation for her character. Yes, he loved his wife, but she had never quite evoked this level of affection from him. Bleu had the key. She was like a fingerprint; there was only one of her.

Iman walked over to her and scooped her up in his arms. She didn't know how it was possible, but she hated and loved him at the same time. Iman put her in the passenger seat of his truck and fastened her seat belt. "I'll be right back, ma. I swear to God I'm going to make this right." She didn't believe him. He was the world's greatest liar, but she needed an explanation. He locked up and came back out, pulling away from the house that he now shared with his wife.

Bleu couldn't even look at him. He didn't know where to start with her, so they rode in silence.

"Why aren't you in rehab?" Iman asked, genuinely concerned.

"I'm not going back there. I don't know where I'm going, but it's not there," Bleu replied somberly as she watched the scenery pass by outside her window. He took her to his condo. Tan had already moved out of it and he was supposed to put it on the market, but he couldn't see Bleu out on the streets.

She followed him up to the penthouse condo and when they were behind closed doors she finally faced him. Her tears were still there. They fell effortlessly.

"You're back with Tan?" she asked the obvious.

He wanted to give her an excuse, even to tell her about the deal he had struck with Sandoza, but it didn't matter. At the end of the day he had chosen Tan over Bleu. He had to be a man and admit it to her. "I owe it to her to give it a real try."

"You owe it to her," Bleu repeated in disbelief. She scoffed as she shook her head. "And what about me? What about all the times you said, 'I love you'? What about the way you touched me? The things you promised me?" She was shouting. "A week ago I was sleeping next to you and now my clothes are in the street! Did I mean anything to you? Or was I just some stupid college girl that you took advantage of?"

"I meant it all, Bleu," Iman replied as he wiped his hand over his goatee. He felt stress consuming his body. He wanted to keep her, but he couldn't let Tan go. Tan was good for business and good for him in ways that Bleu couldn't be. He didn't have to worry about Tan. He didn't have to watch her every move out of fear. Tan was strong, but even with all of Bleu's flaws she was food to his soul. Her energy kept him full of happiness and that was hard for him to send out into the world for the next man to enjoy. She was his. He had claimed that pussy.

"If you meant it how can you do this? Is it the drugs? Is it because you found me in that hotel with a crack pipe in my hands?" she asked.

"That's not it, ma," he replied. He didn't need to make her feel any worse than he already had. "It's not a good time to end my marriage, Bleu. I didn't mean to deceive you. I planned to tell you once you finished your program. I'm sorry about your things. Tan was out of line. She was supposed to put your stuff in the garage, not the trash. I'll replace it all; you know that."

Bleu wiped her face. This was unreal. "I don't know anything. I don't know you. You never loved me. This isn't what it's supposed to feel like," she whispered. She headed for the door, but Iman grabbed her arm, pulling her back into him and caressing her face as he looked her dead in her eyes.

"Don't ever let that come out your mouth again," he said, his eyes betraying him and letting emotion cloud his vision. He sniffed it away.

"You make me feel like I'm nothing!" she shot back as she snatched away. Iman was right on her heels as she opened the door. He placed a palm on it, slamming it and then pinned her against it.

"I want to leave," she said, resting her forehead on the door in despair. She could feel his breath on her neck as he leaned into her.

"Please stay," he whispered.

"Stay where?!" she shouted, turning toward him and looking at him incredulously. "You gave my spot to your wife!"

"Stay here, ma. I'll furnish it; I'll pay all the bills. I just can't let you walk out of my life. Not like this," Iman said. "I can't leave Tan, but I can't leave you alone either, ma. I know what I'm asking is a lot, but I'm crazy about you, Bleu. I love you in ways that I have never loved anyone else. You do something to me. Stay." Iman wasn't a pleading man, but he was willing to sacrifice his pride if it would keep her near him.

"I don't want to be the woman you come see after you're done at home. I don't want to be the one you call using hushed whispers, or the girl who gets her gifts the day after Christmas. I want to be a priority!" she cried.

"Fuck is you talking about? Day after Christmas shit," he scoffed. "You're not a side chick. I would never play you like that," Iman said.

"What do you mean? You let her put my shit on the street! You have chosen to stay with your wife!" she shouted. "That's exactly how you would play me."

Iman was trying to hold his tongue, but he could feel Bleu slipping right through his fingers. She was going to leave him and he couldn't blame her.

"Sandoza is letting me take over his entire empire if I stay married to Tan," he said through gritted teeth.

Bleu exhaled. It was like a weight had lifted from her shoulders. It didn't make his decision right, but she understood how he had come to it. Tan was good for business.

"Do you love her?" Bleu asked.

"I won't lie to you and say no. I love her, but she's not you," Iman replied.

He kissed her and she did nothing. She stood stoically still, refusing to kiss him back, but he was relentless. He moved to her neck, stirring up feelings in her that she tried to fight off. She winced in resistance as he went lower, on his knees as he lifted her shirt to plant kisses on her belly. He pulled down her sweatpants and panties and she moaned. When he placed her legs on his shoulders she knew where he was headed next. He planted kisses on her southern lips and she reacted. She couldn't help it. Her back arched and her mouth fell open as Iman pulled back her labia to uncover her pearl. He attacked it slowly, passionately, applying pressure, then taking it away, as she writhed beneath him. "Stay," he whispered between kisses. "Say you'll stay, ma."

"Hm-m, I'll stay," she moaned as he brought her to orgasm.

She tasted so sweet on his tongue that even after she came he kept going, exciting her all over again. She fed him her honey three times before she couldn't take any more. He released her legs and she grabbed his hand and led him to the kitchen island. He laid her down, the cold tile against her back causing her nipples to harden. He took notice. His attention to the details of her body amazed her. He took one nipple in his mouth as he rolled the other one between his fingers. She could feel his need for her. It pressed against his jeans and she ripped at his clothes, uncovering the masterpiece that was his body. Iman was a beautiful man. Bleu reached down and massaged his strength, guiding him between her thighs. She gasped when he entered her. He always fit her just right. He went to work, grinding her deep as he gripped under her behind, pulling her into him each time she tried to run away.

"I love you so much," he groaned in her ear, but instead of the words warming her, they sent a frigid shiver down her spine. Bleu could differentiate truth from lies and nothing he told her anymore resonated genuinely with her. Not anymore. He had told a lie so damaging that it made her question everything that came out of his mouth afterward. She wanted to believe him, but she couldn't. No matter how good he made her feel, he had chosen someone else. He left her spent. Every part of her body was sensitive to the touch. She was naked as a newborn baby, but it wasn't her body that she wished she could cover. It was her soul. She wished she could rewind time and erase him from her life. If she had never allowed him access to her, he would have never been able to disappoint her. Her expectation of him had exceeded the reality of him. She sat up and Iman stood between her legs as she leaned her head into his chest.

"Look at me, ma," he said.

She did and he was disheartened by the change he saw in her eyes. "I love you," Iman stated. She was grateful for the sound of his ringing cell phone. She didn't know how to respond to his declarations of the heart. She hated him, but she loved him enough to want to stay here, knowing she wasn't a priority. It didn't make sense. She didn't even begin to know how to explain these things to him. So as he picked his phone out of the pocket of his pants she was grateful for the interruption. He looked at the screen and then silenced it.

"It's her, isn't it?" Bleu asked, crushed.

"You can stay here," Iman said, ignoring her question.

"But you have to go," Bleu finished for him. "Right?"

"I'll be back for you. Just stay here. I'll set you up. You can furnish it, decorate however you want."

"What about money?" Bleu asked, and he froze. He couldn't hit her off with a pocketful of cash. It would be too hard for her. It would be temptation at its finest and Iman feared that she would fall back into the trenches of her addiction. She noticed his hesitation. "I'm not going to get high. I have to eat. I need clothes."

He sighed, unsure of how to play this. Iman wasn't naïve. He couldn't trust Bleu. Just a week ago he had barely made it in time to stop her from smoking a straight shooter. He knew what would happen if he put cold, hard cash in her hand. She would try hard to stay clean, but eventually she would give in to the devil's smoke. Iman finished dressing and then pulled an American Express card out of his wallet. "Whatever you need, just charge it on my account. I'll call and have you added to it."

Bleu drew her lips into a flat smile, but she took the card, knowing she would need it. "Fine," she said.

Iman twisted the key off his ring and placed it in her palm.

He balled up her fist and kissed it. "I'll check in with you later, a'ight?"

Bleu nodded as she watched him walk out of the door. She shook her head as she realized what she had just agreed to. She had become Iman's mistress and the sad part was that she would rather accept that than lose him altogether.

9

Noah rode through the city, his city, sitting safely behind the tint of his luxury truck as he headed to meet Messiah. He didn't know much about him. Only that he got money on the city's south side. The fact that Khadafi had vouched for him gave Noah reassurance, but trust was earned. It would take more than the words of a third party for Noah to feel at ease. Time and consistent loyalty would prove whether or not Khadafi was right about Messiah. Too many niggas claimed friendships too quickly nowadays. Yeah, Messiah had let his cannon bark in the club on Noah's behalf, but Noah wasn't naïve. Messiah would have to prove loyalty to gain Noah's trust before knocking off his mark as well. Real men moved in silence and Noah didn't want to be caught lacking by calling Messiah a friend too quickly. He pulled into the car wash that Messiah owned and rolled down his window. It was a known hangout spot for made men around the city. When the wife was on your neck at home, you came to the wash. When you wanted to politic with other players in the city, you came to the wash. When you wanted to find out information, you came to the wash. Even if you wanted to dabble in a new flavor of pussy, you came to the wash. It was low-key and the hangout spot when the sun was sitting pretty, burning up the sky. With the pretty girls in their tiny shorts and bikini tops it was a black man's Hooters. All the O.G.'s in the city hung out there.

A pretty girl with short hair and even shorter shorts opened his door for him. "Hi, handsome. What can I get for you?"

Before he could respond Messiah came walking out of the office. "His money is no good here. Hook him up. Detail the inside and out," Messiah instructed as he slapped hands with Noah.

"Is that all you need hooked up?" the girl asked flirtatiously as she bit her perfectly painted bottom lip. She wore red, the devil's color, and the look in her eyes let Noah know she was game for anything.

He scoffed. Thirsty women weren't his type, so he declined. "I'm good." He pulled a knotful of hundred-dollar bills out of his pocket and handed one to her. "Go buy yourself some class, shorty."

The girl sucked her teeth and snatched the money from his hands before taking his car to be cleaned.

"You selling pussy now, my g?" Noah asked with a chuckle as he followed Messiah into the office.

Messiah laughed. "These hoes in here selling themselves,

man. I just hire the pretty faces with the fat asses. What they do on the side is their business," he said honestly.

"I've got some news for you, though, fam. The nigga I laid flat in the club last night was from the south side. You know a nigga named Keon?" Messiah asked.

The name registered with Noah. He would never forget the name of the first man he had killed. Bleu's face popped into his mind. He had done it all for her and would do it again in a heartbeat. "Yeah, I blew the nigga head off," Noah said frankly as he stared Messiah in the eyes without apology. Noah wanted Messiah to know that he would put his murder game down whenever necessary.

Messiah smirked. "We about to be legends in these streets, my g," Messiah said. "Follow me."

He unlocked a steel door that led to the basement and Noah followed him down the stairs. A single lightbulb barely lit up the underground space, but Noah saw the outline of a body hanging from the ceiling.

"My man that I left slumped in the club was Keon's cousin. Apparently his people got a beef with you. I don't know how they know it was you behind the trigger, but it's a problem. Homeboy here is Keon's little brother," Messiah said. "I thought you would want to have a talk with him."

"Who saw him come down?" Noah asked.

"Not a soul. He been down here since last night," Messiah said smugly. "The basement is soundproof."

Noah pulled the tape from the boy's mouth. "What's your name, little nigga?"

"DeMario," the boy replied.

"How old are you?" Noah questioned.

"Fourteen."

Noah could tell the kid was trying to be tough, but his voice betrayed him. It shook at the thought of death. Messiah had already gone to work on the kid. He was bloodied and beaten. Noah could smell the scent of piss in the air from where the kid had emptied himself. Fourteen years on the streets of Flint were different from the life a normal kid lived. Noah knew that this type of warfare came with the game. It was the mentality that crippled his city. A life for a life. Age didn't beget sympathy in the hood because there was no finger too young to pull a trigger.

He turned to Messiah. "Close the car wash. Clear this bitch out," Noah said.

Messiah nodded and then headed up the steps.

"Please, man, don't kill me," the kid said. There was fear in his eyes. Noah knew that it was necessary for the streets to fear him, but the look of dread in this boy's eyes made Noah feel like a monster.

"You know who I am?" Noah asked.

The kid nodded his head. "You killed my brother."

"Who told you that?" Noah asked.

"Keon's baby mom," the kid said. "Keon told her he was meeting up with you. Next thing you know he ends up dead and his stash was gone—Man, I don't got no beef with you. Please, man, I swear I won't say shit, man."

"Who tried to clip me in the club last night?" Noah asked. His voice was stoic.

"I don't know. I'm not in the streets, man. I just hoop. I play ball at Southwestern. I don't be on the block like that. That's my brother, man. I don't have nothing to do with that!" the boy shouted. He was crying now, like the kid he was; he was terrified.

"Your brother who?" Noah asked.

The kid's lip trembled as he stifled his cries. "It's my brother, man," he said, pleading because he realized he was being asked to sell his own flesh and blood out.

"Your brother sent somebody to blow my head off last night. I'ma off that nigga on switch. You can die quickly or I got all day. Choice is yours, kid. Now I'ma ask you again. Who is your brother?" Noah asked.

With tears streaming down his face the kid broke down. He was blubbering, but it was clear that he wouldn't tell on his family. Noah respected it, but he didn't show it. If the kid wanted to let his pride lead him to the grave then who was Noah to stop him? Noah looked at the torturous instruments that Messiah had already laid out for him. He picked up the hunters knife and walked over to the boy and placed it against his pinky finger. "His name or your finger, which one it gone be, lil' nigga?" Noah asked.

The kid played tough until Noah began to apply pressure to one of his digits. The first sign of blood made him yell out, "Demarcus, man! His name is Demarcus!"

Noah placed the tape back over the kid's mouth. He didn't want to hear the screams to come. The kid broke down. He was crying like a newborn baby as he realized the Grim

Reaper was standing in front of him. Bile filled the back of Noah's throat and his stomach felt hollow because he knew that he was about to do one more thing that moved him further away from God. Murder wasn't something he could take back. He knew that with each life he took his soul darkened more and more. It was the price to pay for street fame. On the rise to the top, the bodies of his enemies would be left in his wake.

Messiah came down the stairs with plastic tarp and duct tape in hand.

"We don't need that," Noah said.

"Fuck you mean?" Messiah asked.

"Sometimes you got to fight hate with love," Noah said.

"Love? You gone show love to this nigga family? These the same mu'fuckas that tried to murk you. You've got to make the city fear you, my G."

"Nah, I got to make the city love. A scared nigga will kill you, but a nigga who got love for you will kill over you," Noah said, hoping he wasn't making the mistake that would cost him his life.

"You sure about this?" Messiah asked as he pulled up to the small one-story house on the south side of Flint.

"We playing by new rules. No women, no kids, no innocents. I'm with the gangster shit, but it's time to end the nonsense. This little nigga ain't in the game. You snatched him off the hoop court. If he not a part of this life he shouldn't die behind this life," Noah said sincerely.

"That's some real shit," Messiah said as he palmed the gun

that sat in plain view on his lap. "It's your move. I got the back. I got the goons behind us in case his people want a problem."

Noah climbed out of the car and pulled his chrome 9mm from his waist before popping the trunk. He looked behind him and saw the two cars that parked behind him. All it took was a head nod for bullets to fly. With Messiah as his right hand, he acquired an army by default. He was a street king with an army of killers.

He pulled the kid from the trunk and walked him toward the porch. The kid tripped up the steps he was so nervous.

"Relax, homie," Noah said. He knocked on the door hard, and a short fair-skinned woman with silver hair answered.

"Oh my Lord," the woman said with a gasp as she covered her mouth.

"I have something that belongs to you," Noah said as he pushed the kid toward her.

She opened the screen door and hurriedly ushered him inside. "I mean no disrespect by coming here, ma'am, but I've got a message for your grandson Demarcus. You tell him that I don't want no smoke."

The woman's eyes watered as she nodded her head in understanding before she slammed the door closed in haste.

Noah turned around and headed back to the truck as Messiah followed. They got inside and pulled off with a caravan of shooters trailing behind them.

"Fuck was that, bruh? You know we got to find this nigga now," Messiah said.

"It's already taken care of," Noah replied knowingly. "I got somebody on it as we speak."

"I'm lost, fam; I can't even lie. It would have been easier to put two in that little nigga head you just let go. Send a message to anybody else out here thinking shit sweet," Messiah said.

"That message would have cost me my freedom. I've been on the inside. I ain't trying to go back. You kill a fourteen-year-old hoop star the police gone be on us. He go missing for too long and Granny back there calls the cops. The kid is innocent. He don't got nothing to do with this. I dropped him off and declared peace so when his brother turns up missing no fingers will be pointed my way. The next relative I send home will be in a coroner's bag, but we got to do it right," Noah said. "Snatching homie in broad day light isn't how I play. No slipups, no mistakes, no witnesses. It's being taken care of as we speak."

"Penny for your thoughts?" Naomi asked as she slid onto the barstool next to a man who sat, head lowered over the glass of cognac he swirled in his hands.

"No thoughts. I'm just chilling," the guy said as he lifted the glass to his weed-darkened lips, finishing the liquid. He motioned for the bartender and said, "Another one." He turned to Naomi. "And whatever she's drinking."

Never fails. Niggas smell pussy and get stupid, she thought. Her smile didn't match her sinister thoughts as she replied, "Lemon drop martini please. . . . Thank you." She had so much sugar in her tone that she thought she would get a toothache.

"Anytime, gorgeous. I'm Demarcus," he said as he held out his hand to her.

"Lisa," Naomi replied as she accepted it and shook it. "Thanks for the drink." Naomi stood and grabbed her drink and her handbag as if she were preparing to leave.

"You just gone take the drink I bought you and dip?" Demarcus asked.

Naomi turned, her forehead wrinkled in contest as she replied, "First of all, it's only a ten-dollar drink. I don't owe you anything. Second of all, I knew I was going to leave this bar with you before I even sat down. So we can play this game or you can follow me and take me back to a room. Fair warning: I only fuck with five stars." She winked and he smiled, completely enamored by her cancor.

He chuckled as he peeled off a hundred-dollar bill and placed it on the bar before sliding off his stool. She led him to the door as he placed his arm around her waist, palming her behind as they made their exit.

Naomi removed his hand. "Slow down, boy," she said.

Her chest grew heavy once they were outside of the comfort of the crowded bar. She surveyed Demarcus, knowing that he had at least a hundred pounds on her. She knew that Noah needed her to come through. He needed Demarcus's head served up on a platter in a not so obvious way. She loved Noah and this was a chance to prove to him just how much. Noah had been crowned king and she wanted to solidify her place as his queen. She didn't want to just sit pretty and spend his money, she wanted to help him earn it and protect everything he had earned, but she had never killed before and the thought of it made butterflies form in her stomach. *He has a hundred pounds on me. If it goes wrong, I could easily be the one going home with my toe tagged*, she thought. They climbed into his old-school Chevelle, and while she was more intrigued by foreign whips, she had to admit that the restored car was attractive. He opened her door and she slid inside as she smiled uncomfortably. She wasn't feeling being trapped inside the small space. She needed to hurry and get him to the hotel so that she could get this over with.

"Cat got your tongue, love? You was all talk in the bar. Now it's time to get it popping and you like a church mouse over there," Demarcus said.

"Just a little nervous. I don't usually do this," Naomi responded with hidden innuendo. Her manipulative nature came easily, but she had never murdered anyone. She wondered if she had what it took to get her hands dirty, because she was too far in to turn back now. The sick feeling that consumed her was hard to control. She just wanted to throw up. Her nerves were fucking with her and she took a deep breath to try to control her energy. She didn't want to appear too jittery and throw red flags.

"So you're a good girl?" Demarcus asked, intrigued as he licked his lips and peered at her briefly out of the corners of his eyes before focusing on the road ahead.

"I know how to be bad, though. Don't misunderstand," she flirted.

"I'm speaking your language fluently, my baby," Demarcus replied. Naomi laughed at his play on words. "The casino hotel str8?"

Naomi knew that downtown Detroit would be too congested. Her face would be caught on cameras everywhere if they went to that location. She would have to lower her standards and choose a hole in the wall in order to remain low-key. "It doesn't have to be fancy; I'm not tripping."

"I ain't gon' take you to no bum shit, my baby," he said. "Got to up the ante when you fucking with a queen, you feel me?"

She was grateful when he turned up the radio. It stopped them from having to interact. She didn't want to get to know details of the life she was about to end.

When they pulled up to the popular casino and hotel in the heart of the city, she tensed. She tried to keep her head bowed slightly to avoid the camera picking up her full face. On top of the city seemed to be alive; everyone was on the scene. *He would bring me to the most popping spot in the fucking D. With all of these people out here, somebody is going to be able to I.D. me once they find his body,* she thought.

He placed his hand on the small of her back as he guided her to the front desk. She played the back as he acquired the room key.

"You a'ight?" Demarcus asked as he walked up on her. "We ain't got to do this if you're uncomfortable. We can keep it casual or we go to the room and turn up. Whatever happens tonight, you're in control."

Naomi wished he could have been more of an asshole. It would have been much easier for her to deceive him.

"I'm fine. I just need to get in the room and get a drink," she said.

"You sure?" he asked.

Stop being so nice! she shouted in her mind. He was really trying to kick it with her and she was trying to run game. His sudden charm was causing her conscience to come into play and Naomi didn't like it.

When he hit the penthouse button Naomi felt guilt weigh on her shoulders. He was trying hard to impress her. He had no clue that she was a snake in his grass and her bite was deadly.

When she stepped into the room, she was in awe at the view that greeted them. The darkness of night was illuminated by the Canadian bridge that sat over the Detroit River. It was beautiful from this height and she was drawn to the window to admire it. "Wow," she whispered.

"Here is that drink, my baby," he said as he handed her a small bottle of vodka.

"This is poison," she replied with a chuckle. "I like my drinks pretty, like me. I'll whip something up. You just relax."

She sashayed over to the bar as his cell phone rang. He looked down at the screen.

"Please don't tell me I'm out here bopping around town with another woman's man. Is that Wifey calling?" Naomi asked with a smirk.

"Never that. I'm not that kind of nigga," Demarcus replied. "But I do have to chop it up with my nigga real quick. I'ma step out for a second."

She gave a polite smile, and as soon as he walked out Naomi popped open her purse. She pulled the Rohypnol out of her purse. She popped the pill into the cognac and Coke drink she had prepared and quickly snapped her handbag closed just as he walked back into the room.

"Everything okay?" she asked as she carried his drink over to him.

"Yeah, just a little business," he said. His body language was tense and his brow furrowed.

"Look, I don't know what the call was about, but we can end the night early if you have to shake. Your mood seems off," she said. She grabbed her handbag, bluffing as she prepared to leave.

"Nah, it's cool. My apologies," he said as he grabbed her bag and slid it off her shoulder, setting it on the counter as he held both of her hands. "I'm all about what's in front of me right now."

"What's wrong?" she asked.

"Bitch niggas trying me right now, that's all. They can't touch me, so they fucking with the people closest to me. My baby brother in high school. I hustle so he ain't got to fuck with the streets like that. He still getting wrapped up in the middle of my shit, though. I got a two-year-old baby boy at home, my granny, and my bro. I was hustling with my people until my other bro got killed a few years back. Now it's all on me. I don't get this money, my family don't eat," Demarcus said.

Naomi didn't know what to say. "Well, hopefully I can distract you for the night," she said.

"You can most definitely distract me," he replied as he sipped his drink.

Naomi watched his Adam's apple lower as he downed the drink. A pit filled her stomach. She hadn't expected herself to empathize with the other side. He really seemed like a decent guy. Suddenly it felt awkward to be in the business of men. Perhaps she should have let Noah handle this beef in the streets. Trying to end it in this way no longer felt right. She wasn't heartless, and although she was a hustler, she wasn't a killer. That had never been her M.O. By trying to prove her loyalty she suddenly felt like she was crossing her own lines of morality. She never minded getting over on a nigga. She felt like if somebody got "got" he or she deserved to get "got," but she didn't know if she was down to go this far.

"Let me freshen up," she said as she grabbed her bag and walked into the bathroom. She didn't breathe easy until she was behind the safety of the locked door. She hurriedly opened her purse and pulled out her cell phone.

I'm up the block waiting for you. When it's done, slide out.

Naomi read the text from Noah, feeling pressure on her back. He was depending on her and she didn't want to let him down. Naomi looked at herself in the mirror, conflicted. It had even been her idea to do this. He hadn't forced her hand. Naomi had wanted to prove her love to Noah and this was her grand gesture. Talking about it and actually doing it were two different things entirely, however. This was a life she was playing with and her humanity was at stake. Now that the time had come for her to bust her gun she didn't know if she could see it through. Naomi wasn't built for this. The honey blond wig she wore changed her appearance slightly but not enough for her comfort level. *What if someone I.D.'s me? What if I leave a fingerprint behind? What if I'm sloppy?* A million questions rang out in her head as she removed her clothes, revealing the dangerous curves of her body. Her gut was telling her to proceed with caution. Her intuition was warning her to stop, but she stayed the course and walked out; her only accessory was the La Perla lace that adorned her.

"Playtime," she said.

She could see the groggy look in his eyes. The effects of the rophy had kicked in and her tension eased slightly. She had a mental one-up on him.

"Damn, my baby," he commented as he approached her. She could see the change in his saunter. His motor skills were off too. *Even better*, she thought.

He couldn't stop himself from groping her cantaloupe-sized breasts. They were full, perky, and he lowered his lips to her taut nipples as he kissed them gently.

"We don't have to rush," she said as she pushed him onto the bed. "I like to take things nice and slow. It's all in the foreplay." She spread his legs and grabbed the bedsheet. "Let me tie you up and take advantage of you."

"Shit, you can do whatever you want looking like that," he replied with a lust-filled tone.

Naomi started with his hands, tying them to the bedposts before she also tied his feet. His manhood stood straight up by the time she was done. The anticipation alone had him ready to blow.

"Come set that pussy on my face," he said.

"You on one, huh?" she asked as she smirked, knowing that the drugs in his system had him extraloose. Once he was secured she stood on the bed over his face and squatted down until she was positioned directly over his mouth. "You smell that?"

"Hell yeah, smell good like a mu'fucka. Now let me taste it," he said.

She dipped a little lower and let him kiss her clit. She gasped slightly as he slid his tongue between her lips.

"Mm-m," he moaned.

She stood.

"What you doing? Let me get that," he said.

"Nah," she answered. "I just thought you deserved a little taste of the pussy that you about to die over."

"Quit bullshitting," he said, chuckling slightly, still not realizing how dire his situation was.

Naomi looked him dead in the eyes and the look he saw reflecting back let him know she was serious.

"Can't just pick any ol' bitch up in a bar," she schooled him. Naomi wore her poker face well. He had no idea that she was just as terrified as he was. She talked a good game despite the fact that her heart felt like it would leap out of her chest. She couldn't let him know that she was wavering. He bucked, trying to tear free from the sheets, but the drugs had his arms feeling like noodles. He was weak and drowsy.

Naomi retrieved a .22 out of her purse. She attached the silencer, her gut wrenching each time she screwed it tighter.

"I got a son," he said as he saw her take aim. "I'm all he got."

Naomi knew as soon as he said it that she wouldn't be able to pull the trigger. She had a son once. He had died of SIDS before she ever got a true chance to prove she could be a good mother. Now even the sight of a baby boy took her back to devastation. She had buried that fact about herself a long time ago. No one, not even Noah, knew about that part of her life.

"Come on, Lisa. Don't leave my son out here bold. What you want? Cash? I got bread. That's nothing. You ain't got to take my life over no paper—"

"Shut up!" Naomi shouted as she swayed back and forth with the gun pointed directly at him. "It's not about the money," she whispered. Her finger curled on the trigger. Somehow, she knew that if she pulled it she would be forever changed. The action would endear her to Noah forever, but now she wondered how she would feel about herself. "This isn't my game. This is the one thing I can't do.

"Take your son and get out of town. Leave Flint. If you don't, the next person that comes for your head won't even blink," she said with tears in her eyes.

She rushed to the bathroom and slipped on her clothes before rushing out.

Naomi knew that this was a mistake, but killing him would have been an even bigger one. She practically ran down the block until she spotted Noah's Range Rover. She slipped into his truck and as soon as she closed the doors she wept. Her cries were loud and she bent over, placing her head in her lap as she promised herself that she would never put herself in that position again.

"The first body is always the hardest. I owe you my life, baby girl. I love you," Noah said.

Naomi knew that after hearing those words she could never tell him that she didn't go through with it. He would take the words back and she had wanted to hear them from him for so long. "I love you too," she replied as he wiped the wetness from her face. Naomi hoped and prayed that Demarcus heeded her warning and disappeared so that Noah never found out.

10

Bleu stood at the window to the apartment that Iman had gifted her, overlooking the entire city. L.A lit up at night. She stood there, the picture of perfection, but internally she was struggling to keep it all together. She was beautiful in her Miu Miu wrap dress. It accentuated her curves and dipped in a low-cut V in the back. She felt like money in her twelve-hundred-dollar Valentino pumps and flaunting her jumbo Chanel bag. Even the cost of the nail polish on her fingernails was more than some people's light bills. Bleu was kept. Perhaps even more now that Iman had demoted her to mistress. It had been two weeks and she hadn't seen him since he had given her the key. He had made good on his promise and allowed her to splurge, hiring a driver so that he would know her whereabouts at all times. With him unavailable to her she spent her time perusing Saks Fifth catalogs and going on shopping sprees in Beverly Hills.

She picked up her cell phone and called Iman. She had gotten used to his voice mail. It seemed that whenever she tried to reach out he buttoned her. The only time they spoke was when he contacted her. She felt worthless, and no matter how many things she purchased to make her feel better, none of it made her feel better. She was growing bored and to an addict that was a dangerous thing. Idle time made her antsy. Bleu had thought about going to cop something to smoke so many times, but she didn't want to disappoint Iman. She never knew when he would pop up on her and she desperately wanted to show him that she could be who he wanted her to be. *He doesn't need Tan,* she thought. Bleu felt like she had to one-up Tan. She was competing with a woman who had already won. *Tan is his wife. It doesn't matter how many red bottoms I buy, how many times I make him cum, or how many times he says he loves me. She will always win. As long as she has his last name and he has that ring on his finger, she will win. He will never belong to me,* she thought sadly. Her stomach churned. It had been twisted in knots since the day Iman had found her in the hotel. She just wanted to get high. She was trying to keep up this act for him, this visage of a beautiful high-class woman. No amount of expensive things could help build her self-esteem. She was trash dressed up like treasure, but still she was rotting on the inside.

"You've got me going crazy," she whispered. Bleu was angry, but with nothing but four walls around her she had no one to lash out at. She sat down and picked up her phone, practically stabbing the phone with her stiletto nails as she sent him a text.

I swear to God if you don't call me I'm going to flip the fuck out. Where are you?

Iman glanced at his phone briefly and sighed deeply as he dismissed the message. He missed Bleu, but lately business had made it hard for him to get away. Sandoza had requested Iman's presence more frequently over the past few weeks. It was necessary for Iman's face to become familiar to Sandoza's men to make for a smooth transition once the time came. Iman knew that Bleu would be in her feelings, making assumptions about where his time was being spent. He didn't have time to cater to her every whim at the moment. It was her neediness, her lack of independence, that frustrated him. She needed him around her 24-7 and the type of lifestyle he led didn't allow for that. Her insecurities came out in immature ways and she put pressure on his back that he didn't need. Any time he was around Sandoza he needed to be on point. With her blowing up his phone all times of the night, she was a distraction. He worried about her constantly and it was exhausting. He wanted her to have something going for herself . . . to have her own life, separately from him. She needed something to occupy her time. School. *Shit, anything.* He would settle for a hobby. She had gotten sucked in by the luxe life and it had completely changed who she was. Gone was the independent, ambitious college girl he had fallen in love with. She was a shell of her former self. He loved her still, but her fire had been put out the day she had been introduced to crack.

"You good?" Cinco asked.

Iman nodded, refocusing his attention on the task at hand.

"I know you ain't call me all the way to Calabasas to blaze Cohibas and bullshit. What up?" Cinco asked, getting straight to the point.

"Cinco, sit your ass down and chill with your family for a little while. We hardly see you. We've been back together for two weeks and you just now making your way over here. You probably didn't even know," Tan chastised as she came out carrying a bottle of aged whiskey. She set down the bottle and kissed Iman on the lips. "I swear you were raised by wolves."

Cinco stuck up his middle finger at Tan's back as she headed back toward the house.

"I saw that!" she yelled without looking back.

Iman sat back observing Cinco. It was obvious why Sandoza had bypassed his only son to give Iman his seat. A mixture of immaturity, ego, and a temper made for a bad combination when running an empire.

"We've been in this for a long time. We've had a good run," Iman said.

"Had? You talking like we done? There's a lot of money to get out here," Cinco said.

"Absolutely," Iman said. "It's time to take this to the next level. Sandoza and I have been speaking about what's next. . . ." Iman paused. He wanted to choose his words carefully. With anyone else he wouldn't have held his tongue, but he had known Cinco since they were teenagers. He knew that Cinco desperately wanted to prove himself to Sandoza. Iman didn't want Cinco to take offense that Sandoza had chosen him, but he knew it was inevitable.

"*You've* been speaking with him?" Cinco asked.

Iman nodded. "I have. He wants me to take over. Not right away but eventually. I'll need a number two, Cinco. I don't trust none of these niggas out here . . . not with my life," Iman said.

Cinco leaned in and grabbed the decanter of whiskey. He poured himself a glass. "I guess you've always been the son he never had," Cinco said with a chuckle.

"Nah. A man don't send his son to battle," Iman said. "He don't want this life for you. Something go wrong niggas come for the head. They'll come for me, not you. You are Sandoza's only son. He can't jeopardize the legacy of his last name. If you die, his name dies with it," Iman said. He was telling the truth from his own perspective, giving Cinco an easier version to digest. If Cinco knew the real reason Sandoza had bypassed him, Iman knew he would harbor resentment. It was fact that Iman needed Cinco. He needed a shooter. He needed someone to help run his organization. He needed a buffer between himself and the streets so that he could call the plays without getting his hands dirty. "I need you in this with me. We're familia."

"That goes without saying," Cinco said. "You don't even got to keep talking. I'm good with it."

"Good," Iman said as he indulged in his drink. "Shit ain't official. I've got to get in good with the Five Families. No introductions have been made, but I just want to put you up on game. I need you in the loop," Iman said.

"Appreciate it, bruh," Cinco replied.

Iman's phone went off again and this time he silenced it.

Cinco looked at him with a raised brow. "Better turn that bitch off before Tan come back out here," Cinco said with a laugh. "You know she nuttier than a mu'fucka."

Iman couldn't help but chuckle at that.

"That's the pretty little bitch you was fucking with? You still on that?" Cinco asked.

Iman frowned. "Watch your mouth, fam," he said.

"Oh shit, no disrespect. I ain't know it was like that," Cinco commented.

"You good, but it's like that," Iman confirmed. "She's work, though. I'm back with Tan—"

"Because Sandoza said if you divorce her, you're out," Cinco said. He knew his father too well not to know that it was a part of the deal.

"Nah, I care for your sister. She's been here since day one but my lil' mama. She's . . . I fuck with her, but she gets wild. She gets caught up with the drugs and shit. I got Tan over here and I'm not trying to fuck that up, but I got her in the condo in L.A. and I'm trying to keep her on ice too," Iman said.

"I don't want them problems. That's why I don't wife no bitch." Cinco chuckled.

"I'm about to take this trip with Tan. She planned this anniversary vacation, but it's going to keep me away for two weeks. Shit's fucking with me," Iman said.

"I can check in on your girl for you, fam. No issues. I'll stop in every few days to make sure she straight," Cinco offered.

Had Iman known the malicious intent in Cinco's offer he never would have divulged so much information about Bleu. He had no idea of the sadistic things going through Cinco's mind. Iman thought he was sitting among family, and perhaps he was, but family is sometimes the most likely to snake you.

Cinco would never wear his heart on his sleeve, but the news Iman delivered hadn't been received well.

This mu' fucka telling me he want to put me up on game. Like his last name is Sandoza. My own fucking father looked over me for a nigga that's fucking over his daughter. So much for family, Cinco thought. It took everything in him to keep his cool.

"Yeah, maybe, man. I'll let you know if I need you to swing by," Iman said, brushing off the notion. He made a mental note to see about Bleu before she grew restless and did something to jeopardize herself.

Bleu held her phone in her hand, gripping it tightly as she went back and forth in her mind.

Just call him, she thought.

Her fingers dialed the numbers and she put the phone to her ear only to hang up as soon as it started ringing. *This is stupid. Just call him. Why are you tripping?* she chastised herself as she hit the number again and waited as it rang in her ear. She didn't know why she was so nervous, but butterflies filled her stomach.

"Bleu?"

Click.

She hung up as soon as she heard his voice. She closed her eyes and shook her head. "Oh! I'm an idiot!" she shouted in embarrassment. *Five, four, three, two . . .*, she counted down in her head, and on cue her phone rang. She took a deep breath and answered.

"Hi, Noah," she greeted him. "I'm sorry. I think I butt dialed you by mistake."

"Oh yeah? Twice, huh?" he said, teasing her.

Bleu rolled her eyes. "I miss you," she admitted. "I'm sorry about the way I treated you when you came here."

Bleu had never been too proud to say what was on her mind when it came to Noah. He was her very best friend.

"All is forgiven, B," Noah said.

"I'm kind of fucking up out here," Bleu said vaguely. There was no way she would tell him about her addiction. She knew that it would taint his perception of her. If there was anyone who put her on a pedestal it was Noah, and knowing that she shared the same love for the same glass dick as Sienna would disgrace her. No memory of her would ever be the same.

"You seem different," Noah said. "I don't know if that is a good thing or a bad thing, but you're not the same."

Tears came to her eyes and her voice quivered as she replied, "I know."

"How's school?" Noah asked. "I know you filling that big-ass head with hella knowledge." He laughed and she did too.

"Nigga, I know you're not on me, though? You never outgrew that hook in the back of your shit," she replied.

"You cold, B," Noah said, enjoying the childish banter. This was what they did. They laughed, they clowned, they enjoyed each other without the pressure of trying to impress each other. She didn't have to be a glamour girl, have her face made or her hair done. Noah could be dead broke with no clout at all. They were bonded at the most basic level. Their love was so genuine that they only showed their true selves to each other.

The rest of the world was greeted by their representatives . . . the masks that they put on when it was time to leave the comforts of home. Her voice grew serious as her laughter faded.

"I'm not even in school," she admitted.

"Fuck you doing? You fucking up. You know that, right?" Noah said, dead serious. "Why do I feel like that lame-ass nigga you fucking with is the reason why you're not in school?"

Bleu shook her head. "No, it's not on him. I promise. It's me. I kind of lost my way. I'm . . ." She thought about just telling him. He was the one person she could trust not to judge her, but she just couldn't. "I'm just lost, Noah."

"Come home," he said. "Come back home and I'll make sure you're all right. I'll make everything better. Whatever it is you're not saying . . . I can fix it." Noah knew that Bleu wasn't divulging everything to him. It was just a feeling he got. Her vibe was off.

"I can't," Bleu said.

"Then you got to work on getting back to you, B. I'm not playing with you. Don't make me come all the way back to Cali to fuck you up. Go back to school. Remember who you were before you let that la-la land shit change you. You're not from there. You're not Hollywood. Don't let that fake shit throw you off, B. Look at all the shit you survived. I was there when you pulled your mom out of dope houses and when they shot up your pops in the middle of the street. I saw what you made it through. You really gon' let the silicone and socialites be the shit to stop you?"

"I'm so far behind, though. You don't know how hard it's been for me," Bleu protested.

"Sounds like you the only one stopping you," Noah said honestly. "Think about it. For me, a'ight?" he asked.

"I will," she replied.

Bleu heard the sound of a woman in the background and dreaded what he would say next.

"I've got to go, B. You need me, you call me. You sure there isn't anything else you want to talk about?" he asked.

"I'm sure," she said, her heart growing weary that the conversation was about to end.

"Is that nigga treating you right?" he asked.

Bleu didn't know whether she should say yes or no. Things weren't ideal, but Iman wasn't necessarily treating her wrong. She was doing herself wrong by accepting less than what Iman had originally promised her. Or had he? Did she assume? She was so confused.

"I'm okay," she answered.

"That ain't what I asked you but I'ma let it slide," Noah said. "Take care of yourself, B. Love you."

"I love you too. Bye."

He had given her something to think about. *Maybe it ain't too late to go back to UCLA. They don't know about the drug use. I'm behind, but I can catch up. I've done it before. I can do it again,* she thought. Bleu knew she needed some type of direction, something to focus on to stop her from focusing on the urge that was growing by the day. She had already developed a thirst for addiction. She had tapped into the generational curse that coursed through her blood. Addiction was in her DNA, but maybe, just maybe, if she found something constructive to become addicted to it would negate her need to get high.

Ding-dong!

The sound of the bell ringing was the only thing that stopped her tears from falling. She sprang to the door, hopeful that Iman had come to check on her after reading her distressed text.

"Surprise, bitch," Cinco said.

Bleu was like a deer in headlights. Her heart fell into her stomach and she slammed the door only to have Cinco place a foot in the door, stopping her before muscling his way inside.

Bleu backpedaled. "I'll scream," she threatened as her chest heaved up and down. It felt like it would cave in on her and she was slightly dizzy as anxiety seized her. Bleu's eyes scanned the room for something, anything, that she could use to protect herself.

"Relax, Xena, warrior princess. Ain't nobody gon' do shit to you." Cinco chuckled, finding amusement in her fear of him.

"Why are you here?" she asked.

"Your boy told me to check on you. He's with my sister. His wife, in case you forgot," Cinco chortled. He was in rare form. He was angry at the fact that Iman was taking over for Sandoza. *The nigga want to be me. He want to be Sandoza's son. Maybe I should see what's it's like to be him tonight . . . sample some of this pussy he financing,* Cinco thought. His mind was maniacal. He couldn't show how much he hated Iman, not yet at least. When the time was right he would show his hand and make sure that Iman never sat on Sandoza's throne. Cinco was like a kid with a "mine" complex. If Cinco couldn't have it, nobody would.

"Why wouldn't he come himself? It's been two weeks. He wouldn't send you," Bleu defended as she rushed to the couch to call Iman. Cinco didn't stop her. He was sure that Iman wouldn't answer.

"What's wrong, shorty? He ain't answer? He's on a trip with Tan," Cinco informed Bleu.

Bleu gripped her stomach and her knees gave out at the revelation. For some reason she had made herself believe that Iman wasn't romantically involved with Tan. *Is he fucking Tan the way he fucks me? Is he putting his mouth on her body? Is he nuzzling her neck and wrapping his arms around her? The same way he is with me?*

Her thoughts drove her crazy as she sat down on the couch, shaking her head back and forth. "It's supposed to be about business," she whispered.

Cinco laughed aloud. "That's what he told you?" Cinco was taunting her, throwing salt in an open wound.

She knew there was no reason to get mad; she had done this to herself. Here she was pretending that she was happy with the way things were. The penthouse apartment with the luxury fixings wasn't enough to keep Bleu content. Not when she occupied it alone while the man who bought it for her went to sleep next to someone else every night. *I'm allowing him to make a fool of me,* she thought.

"Shit got you sick, huh?" Cinco said. "He's not going to leave Tan. They've been together for years. It's the same routine. They love each other, they hate each other, just to do it all over again."

"Stop," Bleu whispered.

"Yeah, okay," Cinco said. He headed toward the door without saying another word, leaving her alone with the seeds of doubt he had planted in her head.

Bleu's anxiety was at an all-time high. She stormed over to her phone and froze when she noticed the white Baggie that was sitting on the counter. She froze, more fear filled than when Cinco had invaded her space.

He left this here, she thought, panicking as she instantly thought about using it. Her mouth watered as she stood there staring down her demons. It wasn't her drug of choice, but it would do the job. She had been yearning for this for weeks, the opportunity to get high. There was nobody here to stop her. She was back with Iman, but he wasn't present. He wasn't there to stop her.

Bleu picked up the Baggie and opened it. Her eyes were widened in awe as she licked the tip of her pinky finger and stuck it in the bag. She brought her pinky to her mouth and traced the white powder on her gums. They numbed instantly and Bleu closed her eyes, squeezing out a tear. It was cocaine. Not quite as addictive as crack. *I can control this,* she thought as she emptied the powder onto the countertop. She hurriedly grabbed her handbag and pulled a dollar bill out, rolling it up. She hovered over the dollar bill when Noah's voice echoed in her mind: *Remember who you were before you let that la-la land shit change you.*

She stood abruptly and swept the cocaine off the counter, sending it flying all over the floor. Bleu sighed in relief, feeling victorious for the first time. It may have been a small feat, but to her it meant the world. She had said no. "I have to get myself in rehab," she whispered, realizing for the first time that she needed help. "I can get clean for good and get back in school. I can't stay here with Iman. I just need to get back to me."

Knock. knock.

She froze and walked cautiously to the door, this time placing the security chain on it before opening it.

"You get my gift, shorty?" Cinco asked. "I thought you might need a little bit more," he enticed her as he held up the bag, waving it back and forth.

She quickly closed the door and rested her head against it as she prayed, "God, please. Please, God. I'm not strong enough to say no twice." Bleu's stomach growled, but she wasn't starving for food. Her hunger was for something else. She opened the door and Cinco stood there, leaning against the frame with a devilish smirk on his face.

"Good girl," he said as he pushed by her. "Now let's have some fun."

As soon as Bleu let him in she knew it was a mistake, but he had something she desperately wanted. She wished she was who Noah thought she was, but that girl no longer existed. She was kidding herself to think she could ever go back. Certain things, once done, defined you. She would forever be the pretty girl who smoked dope. The crackhead who used to have a good head on her shoulders. No one would ever respect her. Men like Cinco would always think they could come at her bogus because she would do anything to get high. *So what's the point?* she thought. She had wanted the euphoric feeling for weeks now, but Iman had her on a tight leash. The driver he hired would never take her to cop even if she could have gotten her hands on some cash. Getting high with Cinco was her only option. *It's just cocaine. It's not as bad. I can handle myself,* she tried to convince herself.

"You're too uptight, shorty. Come here," Cinco said, setting up a line.

"I just need to use the bathroom," Bleu said.

Cinco pulled a fresh Baggie out of his pant pocket. He tossed it to her. "Get yourself right while you in there," he said. "Maybe the good-girl act will be gone when you come out. Loosen yo' ass up."

Bleu couldn't make it to her bathroom fast enough. She closed and locked the door behind her, partly for privacy, mostly because she needed refuge from Cinco. Bleu avoided the mirror. She couldn't look at herself. She didn't want to face the judgment in her own stare. If only Cinco had gone about his business that night . . . she would still be clean, but as she set up two fat lines of cocaine she knew that ship had sailed. Gone were her aspirations for anything except the high, and she was settling with the coke. What she really craved came in rock form, but she would take what she could get. Bleu didn't think to bring a dollar bill into the bathroom, so instead she dived in nose first. She plugged one nostril with her finger and vacuumed up the white in one sniff. The burn was a painful pleasure, and she paused as she waited for the infamous drip. That moment when the cocaine reached the back of her throat was the absolute best, and she closed her eyes as she sniffed and then squeezed her nose tightly. Her nose and throat went numb. The rush hit her and she laughed as she realized how much she had missed it. Why had she ever deprived herself of feeling so great? She opened the door to find Cinco standing on the other side.

"See, I'm not the Big Bad Wolf, shorty," he said.

"No, you're still the Big Bad Wolf. I'm just not Little Red Riding Hood anymore," she countered.

"I like bad girl Bleu so much better," Cinco complimented her.

"Move, boy," Bleu said as she pushed past him and walked back into her living room. All of a sudden there was more pep in her step. She had a sudden moxie that she hadn't previously possessed.

"You know what. I'm done waiting on Iman to come walking through the door. Next time he comes by, I might not be here. I might disappear on him. Let him see what it feels like," she said, feeling herself as the effects of the cocaine urged her on. She had a false sense of self. Perhaps that was the real reason she liked to be high. It gave her confidence. She said and did things that she wouldn't have the balls to otherwise.

Bleu walked out onto the balcony. She was fifty stories high, literally and figuratively. She felt like she was flying. "Sometimes I just want to jump," she said as she stood on the rails. She looked up to the sky wishing that it could all be so simple, but the truth was her ills hadn't plagued her enough for her to end it all. Bleu was overwhelmed enough to say it but too afraid to do it. She had no follow-through, so instead she was forced to live through the hurt and feel every pain that life threw her way.

She stepped down and went back inside to see Cinco leaned over the counter to snort a line.

"You on this with me or what?" he asked.

It was too late to feel bad now. There was no turning back. She had already messed up. *I might as well enjoy it,* she thought. She joined him and bent over. She felt him move her hair out of the way as she bent over. He was too touchy-feely for Bleu. She stiffened as she felt him begin to massage her neck. She snorted the line and stood up, easing out of his reach.

"That shit's official, right?" Cinco asked rhetorically.

"Hm-m," she agreed with a nod as she licked her dry lips slowly. Her entire mouth was dry, like sandpaper. She could barely swallow, but the side effects were worth the magnificent bliss she was feeling. "The best."

"You know I can get you right. Whenever you feel like you want a little taste, I got you," Cinco said. She recognized the look in his eye. The lust. The malice. The animosity. It brewed within him, he could barely hide it from her, and she quickly remembered whom she was dealing with. They weren't friends. She had tried to kill him. He had raped her. How she had found herself alone in a room with him was beyond her. Her desire to get high had overridden common sense and now she just wanted him gone.

"It's getting late," she said as she tried to walk past him. He grabbed her hand, gripped her wrists so tightly that she winced.

"Cinco," she said nervously.

He looked down at the grip he had on her and eased up. "I'm just saying," he said as he walked toward her. He advanced and she backed up until she had nowhere to go. "I can hook you up when you need that get right." He brought his face into the crook of her neck and inhaled her scent while he flipped her hair. She squirmed at his touch. Everything about Cinco made her skin crawl. Flashbacks of him forcing her to her knees in the sands of Mexico hit her and she turned her head. He had taken her body before, forcefully, brutally. She didn't want that. She couldn't take that again, but to fight him off would be suicide. He would kill her. "I ain't got to take it this time. You got something I want and I got something you want. I know cocaine ain't your thing. You like to suck a glass dick, don't you?" he asked as he licked the side of her face. "I can get it for you, shorty, but you gon' pay me with that pussy. I remember how good that shit was."

Bleu wanted to say no, but what Cinco was offering her was worth more than keeping her morals intact. "You got it with you?" she asked.

Cinco pulled back and reached in his pocket, retrieving a twinkie. Her eyes lit up. Crack was a different monster. Just the sight of it caused her nipples to harden in anticipation.

Bleu knew she would need that high in order to give him what he wanted. She had been so close to saving herself. Instead she was about to sell her soul. In that moment so much hatred filled her. She hated Iman for leaving her vulnerable and alone; she hated her parents for afflicting her with the disease of addiction. It was a generational vice to her family and she was falling victim to it. She hated herself for not being the type to use her background and motivation instead of an excuse, but most of all she hated God for making her life so hard. Why couldn't she be like the other students she had met on campus with their trust funds and entitled attitudes? She had come from the bottom and because of the choices she had made it didn't seem like she would ever escape the allure of the streets. Moving across the country hadn't helped her escape her fate. Bleu snatched the rocks from Cinco's hand and rushed into the kitchen. She pulled out every drawer in the condo, looking for something, anything, resembling a pipe.

Cinco pulled out a bag of weed and a cigarillo. "Sit down. Relax," Cinco said as he rolled up. "Give me the shit."

He laced the weed with the rocks and Bleu shook her head. "I don't mix it," she said. She was antsy. Her foot tapped nervously against the floor as she crossed her arms and watched him work.

"You don't really got a choice now, do you?" Cinco shot back. It was the first time he realized how bad she had it. He had thought her drug use was recreational. All the times he had seen her high, she had been the life of the party. Dancing on tables in clubs until 5:00 a.m. or partying with friends. It had all been social. Everybody in L.A. got lifted. It was a way of life in Hollywood, but the girl he saw in front of him was so desperate to get high. Too desperate. She was a crackhead, and if Cinco had a conscience he would have thought twice about what he was encouraging. He had zero fucks to give, however, and handed her the laced blunt.

"Enjoy," he said sarcastically.

"You not on this with me?" she asked, trying to pretend as if she didn't want every single morsel to herself.

"Nah, that's not my preference. You have fun now and I'll have fun later," he said, grabbing himself obnoxiously and reminding her that there was a hefty price to pay for getting high off his supply.

Bleu fired up and within minutes she was in outer space. It felt so damn good. So much pleasure . . . intense . . . sinful . . . unadulterated. *Oh shit,* she thought. She had forgotten what it did to her. Her clitoris swelled and she felt herself orgasm without any stimulation. If this was the sin that would send her to hell, it was worth it.

Cinco's manhood hardened at the sight of Bleu. She had forgotten he was even in the room. Cinco was going to keep her high until he was ready to use her to get back at Iman. In her right mind she would never go against Iman, but with Cinco in her ear, slowly filling her with animosity, it would only be a matter of time before she agreed to the plot Cinco was manufacturing.

11

"Bleu!" Iman's voice carried through the condo as he entered. It was the middle of the day, but nothing moved inside. "You here, ma?" he asked. He walked back to the master bedroom to find the room cloaked in darkness. The blacked-out shades were drawn closed, letting no light inside. The smell of weed permeated the room.

A mixture of worry and fury pulsed through him as he marched over to the drapes and pulled them open. Bleu was sprawled out on the bed, naked, her face peaceful as her chest rose and fell softly with the rhythm of her breathing. His eyes fell on to the ashtray that sat on the nightstand. As soon as he saw the roach inside he gritted his teeth in anger.

"Get up!" Iman growled as he snatched the covers off of her.

"Hmm," Bleu moaned groggily.

"Get up!" Iman repeated as he grabbed her feet and began to pull her out of the bed.

"Let me go! What is wrong with you?" Bleu screamed in alarm as she hit the floor with a thud. Iman had come by unexpectedly and her heart beat furiously as she looked around in anticipation to see what evidence she had left lying around. Seeing the disappointment in his eyes made her heart fall into her stomach. She was sick because now that he had come back around she could see that his intentions were never to harm her. She couldn't be trusted by herself for two weeks. *What have I done?* she thought.

Iman was usually a man of composure, but he was so livid that he picked up the ashtray as he shouted, "What's this? Huh, ma? You in here getting high?" He threw it aross the room, shattering it against the wall. Bleu jumped and stood to her feet in defense.

"No! It's just weed!" she lied. She knew she looked a mess. She had gone on a three-day binge, alternating between smoking and letting Cinco have his way with her. She couldn't even remember if she had washed Cinco's stench off her body before she had passed out in her bed. She stood to her feet and ran her fingers through her hair. Insecurity filled her as she saw the doubt in Iman's eyes. She had never seen him so angry. He had never spoken to her without love lacing his tone, but today the bass in his voice was terrifying. Bleu knew that Iman wouldn't strike her. She didn't fear him in that way. She feared being ostracized by him and having his love stripped away without warning. Despite her destructive behavior, she truly did not want to lose him.

"I don't give a fuck if it was a cigarette! You don't smoke shit in my crib. You know your situation. Weed ain't just weed with you, ma!!" He was shouting, something he never did. "How are you getting this shit? Huh? I don't leave you with no paper. Who sold this to you? You gon' make me dead one of these little niggas for bringing shit to my crib."

Bleu was glad she had thought to hide her last few rocks beneath the mattress. If Iman knew just how badly she had fucked up he would really flip his lid.

"No one!" she shouted. "I bought it from some white kid at the mall!" Bleu was making it up as she went along, adding false details to make him believe her.

"Wake the fuck up, Bleu," Iman said passionately as he grabbed her shoulders, trying to shake some sense into her. "You're an addict. I've been sugarcoating this shit and trying to help you through it, but I'ma give it to you real, ma. You're a fucking crackhead. You're no better than bitches on the street that swallow dick in order to get high. You can't smoke weed. You can't smoke shit. I can't even trust you around a medicine cabinet. The shit is serious. Do you know what you're doing to me, ma?" Iman released her and stormed out, headed for the door.

Bleu ran after him. "Iman, wait! Please!" She grabbed his hand as he reached for the door, squeezing her body between him and the exit. He pushed her out of the way, but she stood her ground, refusing to let him leave.

"Move out of the way," he said in a lower tone.

"No," she said sternly.

"Move," he said again, losing patience.

"No! Iman, no!" she shouted, this time pushing his chest. "I was stupid. I was bored and I did some dumb shit. I was going crazy here. I hadn't heard from you. You didn't come by. You weren't answering my calls. For the first time since I met you, I felt like I wasn't important to you. I acted out. I didn't even like it. It was just something to do and I'm sorry. I promise you, Iman, I'm not going back to how I used to be. You have to believe me!"

Iman stared at her. His mind told him one thing while his heart said another. The two were in direct conflict when it came to Bleu. This young, wild, reckless girl had her hooks in him so deeply that he was acting out of character. All the signs were there to tell him that she had fallen off track. She couldn't be saved. He had never been a sucker for love type of nigga, but Bleu had snuck her way into his heart.

"I'll never do it again," she promised.

Iman grabbed her by the upper arm and pulled her to the couch.

"Sit down." He said the words so sternly that she had to comply.

He sat across from her and tented his fingers under his chin. His forehead creased in contemplation as he let silence take over the room.

She dared not speak. She barely wanted to breathe. Anger radiated from him.

"You got to decide what type of woman you're going to be, ma," he said. "Cuz if this is who you are, I can't fuck with you. If you gon' keep making the same mistakes, over and over, we might as well call this curtains. If you can't shake this shit solo you can go back to rehab. I'll finance it, but I can't make you. I can't be here every minute of every day—"

"But you weren't here at all," she interrupted. "You keep trying to ship me off to rehab. Do you know how much support it takes to make it through rehab? I have no friends, no family. Just you, and you just dumped me there like I was supposed to just magically come out cured. No more crackhead Bleu!" she argued.

"I know and I apologize for that. I'll be better for you," Iman said as he sighed in exasperation. "But you got to be stronger than this, ma. I can't be with a weak woman."

"What don't you get? You're not with me anyway!" Bleu shouted. "You're with her! You're with your wife! So if I smoke weed, or meth, or crack, it doesn't matter! There's no reward for good behavior, Iman. Don't you get that you completely abandoned me?" she yelled.

He is my trigger, she thought as the stress from it all just made her want to say fuck the world and get high.

"What do you want me to do?" Iman asked.

Bleu was spent. Mentally and physically, spiritually and emotionally . . . loving Iman drained her in every way. Sitting here arguing with him, lying to him. It all just took too much effort. It was futile.

"Right now I just want you to go. Or can I even put you out? Seeing as how you own everything in here," she said sarcastically.

He didn't respond and she stopped her tirade. "I do love you, Bleu," he said.

"I know," Bleu replied. "But you just can't choose me. So what are were doing?"

"I don't know," Iman said.

Bleu stood and walked to the door. She opened it, letting him know it was time to leave.

"You really putting me out my own shit, huh?" he asked as he walked up on her. There was no such thing as personal space when it came to their interaction. He was so close she could smell the scent of his aftershave. She could feel the tickle from his growing beard. When he exhaled she absorbed his breath, wishing it could give her life . . . strength. . . . Oh, how she wished she could be half the woman he thought she could be.

"I can leave if you don't want to," she suggested

"I'll let you cool off," Iman said. He kissed her. Deeply. The type of kiss that made her soul stir and caused tickles to creep up her spine.

"Come back when you're ready to make me number one. I can't do this, us," she said, pointing between them, "not like this. So you have to choose. Tan or me." A sadness swept over her. She knew what the outcome would be. Pitting herself against Tan, a woman he had been with for years, would end badly.

Iman left and she closed the door before she embarrassed herself by begging him to stay. Bleu headed straight to her bedroom and retrieved the rocks from under her mattress. She couldn't sit here feeling the things she was feeling. The despair, the heartbreak, the loneliness. *Fuck that.* Not when she could just make it all go away with one little . . .

12

Bleu didn't feel anything . . . not anymore. This had happened to her so many times that she was no longer disgusted with herself. She had given Iman a choice to make and apparently he had not chosen her. It was a bitter pill to swallow, and to mask the sorrow that threatened to drown her she relied on drugs to see her through it all. It was either that or blow her head off. She figured self-destruction was better than suicide. Cinco gripped her hips so hard that his fingernails left impressions in her skin as he humped furiously from behind. There was nothing gentle about him. He fucked her. This wasn't even mutually gratifying. She was just a hole for him to get his rocks off and he inflicted more pain than pleasure as he pounded relentlessly. His sweat dripped on the small of her back and the smell of him, ugh. The scent of his flesh was the worst. He wasn't a dirty man, but everything about him made her sick to her stomach. The cologne he wore caused her stomach to turn. The stickiness of his perspiring skin was torture. The patch he wore over his eye creeped her out. His mentality was disgusting. His arrogance was a turnoff. His cruelty was sickening. Vomit tickled the back of her throat, but she held it in as his grunts filled the air. She wanted him to finish fast. Her fists gripped the sheets from the pain. With every thrust he was stabbing her insides. She was so turned off that she couldn't even get wet. Guilt filled her, but she was at his mercy. He had the power because he had the dope, and he hung it on a string above her head like she was a mule chasing a carrot. Cinco knew that she was more manageable when she was high, and whenever he came knocking with that rock in his hands she complied with his demands. It didn't matter that they were in the bed that Iman had purchased for her. All that mattered was that Cinco left her reward on the nightstand before he left. If this was the price to pay for her high she would do it every time. If this was what it took to forget that she was utterly heartbroken over Iman then so be it.

Cinco had been spoon-feeding her crack cocaine since the day Iman had left. Bleu hadn't heard from him since. *He hasn't even called to check up on me. Ugh! Stop thinking about him. Fuck him,* she thought. Bleu reached for the pipe that sat on the nightstand. Bleu needed a hit immediately. There was no way she could stomach Cinco's strokes without a bit of incentive. She fired up like an expert without ever missing a beat. The rock sizzled and Bleu inhaled the smoke, closing her eyes as she began to feel it. "Oh my God," she moaned as she came to orgasm.

"Damn, shorty. That shit got wet," Cinco said as he slapped her ass, stinging her as he wrapped his fists around her hair.

The dick would be decent if he weren't such a pig, Bleu thought. She was tired of feeling him inside of her. He had been chasing a nut for over half an hour and he still hadn't cum yet. Bleu sank her chest all the way to the bed, which caused her behind to stick up higher and her flower to open wider. She threw it back at him, matching him stroke for stroke.

"Damn. Hell yeah. Throw that shit," Cinco cheered her on.

Bleu rolled her eyes and looked over her shoulder. "Hurry up," she said impatiently.

She could feel Cinco's pace quickening. "Pull out," she said. She tried to get up, but he pushed her down, gripping her neck tightly. Flashbacks of the first time he had raped her erupted in her mind. That night on the beach when he had drugged her was the night that she had become his pawn, whether she knew it or not. "Pull out!" she cried. Simply because she had asked, he refused to. She felt him empty himself into her and she cringed.

"What are you doing?!" Bleu shouted as she crawled frantically off the bed. She scrambled to the bathroom and jumped directly into the shower. She turned the water on so hot that it burned as it hit her skin. She scrubbed her body and then rested her hands on the walls as she dipped her head. She wished that it was as easy to cleanse the inside of her as it was to wash away the outside. Bleu was rotten. She was so lost that she didn't even think she deserved a good life anymore.

Bleu hopped out of the shower and didn't bother to cover her body before walking back into the bedroom. Cinco had seen every part of her anyway. There was no point in being coy now.

Cinco smirked at the work of art in front of him. She was gone forever. Her bad-girl swag was much more interesting anyway.

"I better duck out before your boy slide through," Cinco said.

"He ain't coming. He's too busy with your bitch of a sister. I gave him a choice. His wife or me. You see how that turned out," Bleu said.

"Only reason that nigga still married to Tan is because of Sandoza," Cinco said. "That don't stop a nigga from keeping some pussy on the side."

"Why are you talking?" Bleu asked. "We don't talk." Bleu went into her drawer and pulled out a casual denim jumper.

"I'm just saying. Seem like Tan is in the way. Get her out of the picture and you'll have Iman to yourself," Cinco said.

"It's that easy, huh?" Bleu said as she rolled her eyes. "And how do you suggest I get her out of the picture?"

"Murk her." Bleu froze as she studied him. He said it so casual, as if he were talking about the weather.

"She's your sister," Bleu said, shocked.

"My sister's a bitch," Cinco replied with a dismissive wave of the hand. "Something happens to Tan on Iman's watch and Sandoza will never forgive him. He'll be out of business for good and I can get what's rightfully mine. Tan will be gone. You can go running back to your man. It's a win-win for everybody, shorty."

Bleu was speechless. She didn't know what to say. Was he joking? Was this some kind of test? She had never seen treachery of this kind. It was during moments like these that she remembered whom she was dealing with. Cinco wasn't wrapped too tight. *If he would do his own sister like that, imagine what he would do to me,* she thought.

"If I got to do all that, I don't want Iman," Bleu said.

"Whether you want that nigga or not, you're gonna do it," Cinco said. The threatening tone of his voice let her know he meant every word.

"Are you threatening me?" Bleu asked, her voice trembling slightly.

"Call it what you want," Cinco stated. "But I don't think you want me to tell Iman you been exchanging pussy for dope. I can tell him exactly how sweet that pussy taste and about that pretty little mole you got."

Bleu's stomach went hollow. Iman knew her body well. The birthmark between her legs was right on her outer labia. He would know exactly what mole Cinco was describing and there was only one way for him to know it was there.

"This is crazy. Is this some kind of game to you?" she asked.

"No games," Cinco said. "I'm dead ass."

Bleu was livid with Iman, but in no way did she want him to find out about her dealings with Cinco. She would do almost anything to keep this secret from Iman. She had hit rock bottom. Sure, she was living lavishly in a sky-rise apartment and she had more labels in her closet than you would see on a runway, but her peril rested beyond the surface. If Iman had been around he would have seen through her. He would have noticed the shift in her, but since their fight he had been MIA. She didn't know if he was leaving her alone or if he just needed time to figure things out, but either way it hurt. She just wanted to be with the man she loved, but could she kill for him? Was he worth that much?

"Look, you ain't even got to do the dirty work, but you can help me out. I know Iman keeps his safe in the house. I know you know where it is. I need to empty that shit while we in there to make it look like Tan was murdered in a robbery gone bad. We'll go in and you can hit the safe while I take care of Tan. I don't even need the bread. You can have that shit. I just need it to look legit. You can't lose, shorty. You get to keep your nigga and you leave out the spot with enough paper to change your life. Ain't you tired of not having your own dough? This nigga babysitting you like you not old enough to handle no cash? After this you won't have to ask him for anything," Cinco said.

"I just don't know if I can," Bleu said. "Please don't make me be a part of this."

Cinco nodded and picked up his phone. He put it on speaker as he dialed a number and listened as the phone rang.

"What's good, familia?"

The sound of Iman's voice sent Bleu into a panic as she reached for the phone.

"Hey, bruh. I got something I want to rap with you about.

You remember that little bitch you used to fuck with?" Cinco asked.

"Please don't," she whispered Cinco pushed her off.

"Nah, who you talking about?" Iman asked. "You know I don't fuck around out here with these birds."

"What's her name?" Cinco said as he snapped his fingers. "College girl?"

Bleu's eyes widened as she whispered, "I'll do it."

"You know the bitch that used to move weight for me. China," Cinco said.

"I never fucked with her, but yeah, what about her?" Iman asked.

"Just letting you know I got the goons on her head. I got a bone to pick with her, so if you hear word about her let me know," Cinco said, changing the context of his conversation.

Bleu heard Cinco end the call and he smiled sinisterly. "Glad we're on the same page."

"What if Iman is there? He can't get hurt. I won't be a part of any plot where something might happen to him. He isn't going to just lie down while we run in his house. It won't be as easy as you're trying to make it seem," Bleu protested. "Just think about this for a minute.' Bleu knew that no amount of reasoning was going to change Cinco's mind.

"We'll do it when he goes out of town in a week. He's meeting with my father in Mexico. It'll be the perfect time," Cinco replied.

It was then that Bleu realized that smoking dope would lead to her downfall. If she was willing to betray Iman, what else would she be willing to do? Sienna flashed in her mind and suddenly she felt guilty for harboring resentment toward her mother. What morals had Sienna sacrificed in order to smoke even a morsel of crack? Was this desperation the same feeling Bleu's father had that fated day he had committed the bank robbery that led to his death by police? It took her living a little, messing up a little, to understand her parents' plight. She had no idea what had occurred that led up to those moments. Bleu could see herself falling victim to the flip side of the game, but she couldn't stop herself from craving the glass dick. She was too far gone. It was no longer fun because now she felt like she needed it. It was what she used to keep herself from feeling everything. Hurt, anger, neglect, pain, and lately the most prevalent emotion that overcame her was guilt. The guilt of not being who everyone had expected her to be, for not being perfect, and for turning out just like her parents. She loved and hated them all in that one moment. She hated them for exposing her to a life of drugs, but she loved them because she now knew that every wrong thing they had done they hadn't meant to do. Perhaps they hadn't even wanted to do them. Her parents had loved her the only way they knew how, but love from a dope fiend only went so far, because no matter how much they loved Bleu, they would always love something else greater . . . dope. It was the way she felt about Iman, and as a tear slid down her face she knew that even after she got Tan out the way she would never be good enough for him.

She looked at Cinco and sniffed as she wiped the tear away. "After I get the money from this safe I'm done. We're done with this," she said, pointing between them. "I'll buy my shit like everybody else." She stormed out of the living room, letting him know that the night was over. "And leave a couple bags on the countertop before you leave!"

13

Bleu stood staring at herself in the mirror. Black gloves, black mask. She hardly recognized herself.

"What are you doing?" she said aloud, hoping that the good angel sitting on her right shoulder could outweigh the devil sitting on her left. The only thing that could be seen was her eyes and even she didn't recognize the look of desperation reflecting back.

She pulled the ski mask off her face and stuffed it into the front of her black hoodie and she hurriedly walked outside. Cinco waited curbside for her. She paused when she saw him, even turned to go back inside, but he flashed his headlights directly on her, halting her midstep.

Bleu sighed and joined him in the car, knowing that he could make life hell for her if she did anything other than cooperate.

"Get your mind right," Cinco said as he passed her a crack-laced blunt. It wasn't her preference, but she didn't turn it down. She hadn't smoked all day. Bleu had been trying to clear her mind long enough to talk herself out of this insane dilemma. She knew her involvement was wrong, but the thought of Cinco telling Iman who she really was made her feel as if she didn't have a choice.

"Whose car is this?" Bleu asked.

"Don't worry about it. It's stolen," Cinco said.

The long ride from L.A. to Calabasas was silent. Bleu was lost in thought. Her gut instinct told her to turn around, but she was in it now, she had agreed, and Cinco was taking her whether she wanted to go or not.

When they pulled up to Iman's mansion Bleu felt sick. Iman had welcomed her here, and now she had come to bring terror into his home.

"I can't do this. You can tell Iman whatever you want. I'm not going in there," Bleu whispered as she grappled with the notion of her betrayal.

Cinco was on her before she could even reach for the door handle. He smashed her head against the window.

"Agh!" she screamed. She saw stars as she tried to fight Cinco off.

"Calm your ass down!" Cinco growled as he forced her head down between her legs. She clawed at his hands, trying to loosen his grip on her, but the car was too small for her to put up much of a fight.

Cinco pulled his pistol and placed it point-blank against

her head. "Get out of the car. Let's handle this business. You do what we discussed or I'll leave you leaking out this, bitch," Cinco threatened. "Now put on your mask."

They climbed out of the car and Cinco pushed her forward, keeping the gun on her back so that she couldn't turn back.

He walked her up to the door. "We'll use the extra key that's hidden in the flower bed to get in. You know the security code. As soon as we step inside, turn the system off," Cinco instructed. "We'll put the key back and make it look like a break-in on the way out."

Bleu nodded and fought the urge to cry as she retrieved the key. *Ain't no point in crying now. I did this to myself,* she thought, ashamed. Not even the effects of the laced blunt made this easier. She wished she could turn back the hands of time. She would have rather not ever met Iman than cross him in this way.

Bleu used the key and then slid into the home. To both of their surprise, the alarm hadn't been set. Bleu heard the sound of music coming from the second floor and Cinco pushed her forward in that direction.

She paused when she came to the master bedroom door. She opened the door. The sound of the shower running could be heard as they crept inside.

Cinco walked into the bathroom calmly, barely making any noise. Bleu couldn't see this part. She couldn't make her feet move to join Cinco, so instead she sat on the edge of the bed and covered her ears. She squeezed her eyes closed. She couldn't bear witness to Tan's murder. It was cruel. Bleu felt like she would be sick.

Cinco stood watching Tan as she hummed a melody while holding her head under the stream of water. Her eyes were closed and Cinco was glad that she didn't see it coming. He lifted his arm and didn't hesitate.

Psst!

He sent an almost silent bullet crashing through Tan's forehead before she ever had a chance to react. Her body crashed through the glass shower and Bleu rushed into the bathroom. Bleu's hands flew to her mouth as she saw Tan's body hanging halfway out of the basin of the tub. Blood and water spilled everywhere and the steam from the shower seemed to suffocate Bleu. She couldn't breathe. It felt like there was a ball in her throat, stopping air from getting in. Bleu couldn't stop the bile from rising from the back of her throat. She rushed to the sink, pulling off her mask before she vomited on herself. "This isn't going to work. We aren't going to get away with this!" Bleu cried as she paced back and forth in a worried frenzy as she watched Cinco bend over Tan's body to make sure she was dead. "Why did I do this? What the hell was I thinking?" She gripped the sides of the sink as she shook her head in disgrace. This was the single most terrifying moment of her life. She had wanted Tan out of the way, but to contribute to her murder? Bleu couldn't believe this had ever sounded sane to her. The mixture of jealousy and the drugs had clouded her judgment. She wanted Tan's life and now she had done the unthinkable to get it.

"What about your father? He's going to find us and kill us." Bleu was hyperventilating as thoughts of the repercussions flooded her. Everything done in the dark eventually came to light. This sin would not be a secret for long. Tan was too connected, too important, for her death to be swept under the rug.

Cinco pulled Bleu by the hair. He was regretless as he forced Bleu to gather herself. "Get your ass up! Put your ski mask back on and get your shit together. Where's the safe?" Cinco asked urgently. Aggression fueled him. Hatred. Jealousy. Those were his motives, but pure fear was the only thing that made Bleu move her feet toward Iman's study. She just wanted to get out of there. One foot in front of the other, she rushed in a daze. It was like she was running through a matrix. She was high and afraid and anxious all at the same time. It was a Molotov cocktail of emotions. *Please just let this be a bad dream. This isn't real. Please don't let this be real. How could I be a part of this?* she thought. Now none of the reasons she had come up with before seemed to make sense. How had she ever convinced herself that she should do this?

"Where's the fucking safe?" Cinco barked. He pointed the gun at her. "I'm not playing with your ass. This shit has to look legit. Snap out of it."

"It's under the f-f-f-loor," she stammered. Bleu bent over and pulled up four wooden boards from the floor to reveal a large steel fireproof safe.

"Hurry up and open it," Cinco said. He walked over to Iman's desk and turned on the computer as Bleu punched in the numbers to the safe. She had only seen Iman open it one time, but that was all it took for her to commit the numbers to memory. She had never imagined that she would come back to rob it later. Her hands shook as she pressed each button. There was no undoing this. She had crossed the ultimate line.

"What are you doing? Come help me!" she shouted.

"I'm erasing the security footage from tonight and shutting down the cameras. It'll be like we were never even here," Cinco said.

She opened the safe and discovered bills in different denominations all banded neatly. It was more money than she had ever seen, even during her hustling days, and still she didn't even want it. It was dirty money. This entire setup was wrong. No amount of money could buy her a new soul.

I've taken this too far, she thought.

"Fuck is you doing? Where is your head, shorty? Stuff the fucking bag and let's get out of here," Cinco snapped.

Bleu began stuffing money into a black duffel bag.

The sound of a car door slamming caused Bleu to freeze in terror. "Who is that?" Bleu whispered in panic as she rushed to the window. As soon as she saw Iman getting out of the car tears filled her eyes. "It's Iman!"

Cinco rushed to the window. "Fuck!" he exclaimed.

"I thought you said he would be in Mexico?" Bleu said.

"He was supposed to be," Cinco said. "I'll pop that nigga too. Fuck it."

"No!" Bleu said as she lunged at Cinco. His gun flew across the room as he stumbled into Iman's desk. Bleu scrambled to pick it up and Cinco froze.

"Tan! I'm home!" Iman's voice carried throughout the entire home as Bleu stood there, shaking, aiming the gun at Cinco.

Cinco gritted his teeth as he climbed out of the second-story window, leaving Bleu to face the music alone. She ran over to the window and looked down to find Cinco half-running, half-limping away from the crime scene. There was no way she was going out the window. She turned around and headed toward the door only to be halted when Iman stepped into the doorframe.

Shock revealed itself in his eyes as he looked at Bleu, then at his open safe on the floor. She was so grateful for the mask in that moment, but the way he stared at her, almost heartbroken, it was like he knew exactly who she was just by looking in her eyes. Bleu was frozen in fear as she waited for his reaction. She could barely breathe, her chest was so heavy. Her entire body was tense as she stared at him desperately. His eyes lowered to the gun in her hand. She aimed it at him. She wouldn't pull the trigger, but she needed him to think she would.

"Shoot your shot," Iman said.

Bleu wanted to tell him to move, but she couldn't speak. He would recognize her voice. Instead she nodded her head, motioning for him to walk down the hall. He did, and she pressed her gun point-blank to the back of his head.

"You might as well kill me, because if you let me live I'm going to murder you," Iman stated.

She pushed him forward up the stairs and into the master bedroom. As soon as he saw Tan, he raced over to her body.

"Tan!" he shouted. "Tan, baby, wake up!" He picked her up in his arms as he cried over her.

He was distraught, like a man should be after finding his wife murdered in cold blood, but the hurt in his voice made Bleu weak in the knees. *He loves her,* Bleu thought. She didn't know why she was surprised. Tan was his wife. Tears soaked the ski mask Bleu wore.

I can't watch this, she thought. She ran full speed out of the house and didn't stop running until she felt like she would collapse. She keeled over, gripping her knees as she sucked in air. Vomit spewed everywhere and Bleu pulled off the mask as she sobbed. The things she had seen tonight were too much. The things she had done tonight were the devil's work. She had completely lost herself in this world and she wanted nothing more than to just pack it up and go home.

Bleu started the long walk home as sirens filled the air. She knew where they were headed and she put pep in her step, finding the wind to run again until she found a convenience store where she could clean herself up.

The clerk looked at her skeptically as she walked in, sweating. "You've got to buy something," he said.

"Is there a bathroom I can use?" she asked, fidgeting and antsy. She was paranoid and terrified. She needed a moment to gather herself.

"It's for customers only," the clerk mouthed off.

Bleu ignored him as she went to the back of the store and locked herself inside the dirty closet-sized bathroom. She completely broke down. She covered her mouth, stifling her cries as she tore up the bathroom. She beat her hands against the wall, kicking herself with regret. She tore off the black hoodie and dumped it in the garbage, along with the ski mask.

Bang! Bang! Bang!

"Lady! I said the bathroom is for customers only! Buy something or get out!"

Bleu rolled her eyes as she screamed back, "Just give me a minute! Damn!"

She looked in the mirror and for the first time she noticed how bad she looked. Her hair was disheveled, her eyes were red and dilated, and she was soaking wet with sweat. She was doing bad. She had thought she was managing herself, smoking dope low-key, and that no one would notice. She was wrong. She was down bad, and just because she was living off of Iman's dime and hidden away in his expensive condo didn't mean that she was better off. Without him she would be on the streets, because she was strung out on crack cocaine and tonight proved just how far gone she was.

Bang! Bang!

"I said give me a fucking minute!" she shouted as she snatched open the door.

She toned down instantly when she saw the uniformed police officer looming over her.

"Ma'am, is everything okay in there?" he asked. He frowned skeptically as he took in her appearance. "Can you step out of the restroom, ma'am?"

Bleu tried to squeeze by him. "I was just leaving."

The officer grabbed her wrist and turned her around until he had her in the assumed position. "Do you have any weapons on you? Any drugs in your pockets?" the officer asked.

"No!" Bleu exclaimed as she felt him handcuff her. He clenched them a little too tightly, pinching her skin as she grimaced. "Ow!"

"What did you smoke tonight?" the officer asked. "What are you high on? Coke? PCP? Heroin?"

Bleu lowered her head in shame as she was walked out of the store. He put her in the back of his squad car and she rested her head against the glass. She had no idea what would happen to her next. Her life had taken one too many turns for the worst and she wasn't sure if she would ever get back on track. She had come to L.A. with dreams of conquering the world, but it had conquered her. Now nothing seemed more comforting than going back to her tiny town.

14

Iman stood stoically, brooding silently as he watched the coroner roll his Tan's body out of his home. The white sheet that covered her hid the gruesome sight, but it was an image that he would never get out of his mind. A numbness took over him. He had grown up with Tan. She had watched him grow from a boy to a man. Divorcing her had been one thing, but having someone snatch her out of his life infuriated him. She was his wife. He didn't know if her murder was directly connected to him or if it was repercussions from a beef that Sandoza had acquired, but either way, somebody owed Iman a debt. It was one that had to be paid in blood. He had moved in and out of the game for years without drawing attention to himself. Now within the blink of an eye there were cops crawling all over every inch of his home. He had already covered up his floor safe, but just the fact that he was young and black and now a murder had been committed in the posh, upscale neighborhood put the police on high alert.

As he watched the police move in and out of his house the image of the intruder haunted him. It had been a woman and her eyes had been so familiar. *She reminded me of Bleu—*

"I'm tripping," he said as he shook his head and headed to his car. There was no way he would ever feel right sleeping in the house again. Someone had violated him and until he figured out who he would have to adjust how he moved. *What if it was Bleu?* he thought. He shook the thought from his head almost as quickly as it had formed. It had been a long night and his mind was playing tricks on him. He hadn't seen or spoken to Bleu in weeks, so he was manufacturing her wherever he went. She had been constantly on his mind. Depriving himself of her had proved challenging. Even now at the most inappropriate time he thought of her. He wanted to go to her because he knew he would find comfort in her arms. She was the one person he could show his vulnerability to, but it would be cruel to mourn over one woman on the bosom of another.

As he pulled away from his home he picked up his phone. He had to deliver the news to Sandoza. He knew it wouldn't be received well.

"What's going to happen to me? I've been in here for three days," Bleu said. The waiting had been torture.

"There is a warrant out for your arrest in Flint, Michigan. The LAPD called it in and Flint P.D. wants you. They are sending someone all the way here to escort you back to Michigan.

You will be turned over to them first thing in the morning," the court-appointed lawyer said.

"Warrant?" Bleu asked. "Warrant for what?" Bleu was terrified. She kept waiting for the officers to come in and tell her they knew she had been at Iman's house that night. She bit her nails, a nervous habit that she did when she was coming down from a good high.

"Felonious assault," the lawyer said. "Once the chain of custody is transferred back to Michigan, I will have the charges here dropped against you. Good luck, Ms. Montclair."

An officer came and handcuffed her as they escorted her back to a holding cell. As she sat trapped behind the metal bars of the county jail she felt disgraced. *Felonious assault?* She had no idea what she was wanted for, but she would rather be back in Michigan than out here waiting for the police to catch wind of her involvement in Tan's murder.

Morning came so slowly and she was tortured by the overwhelming urge to get high. She was irritable, her stomach was upset, and she had sunk into a deep depression as her body begged for more. She hadn't realized that she had been using so much that even a day without it was driving her insane.

"Montclair, on your feet!" an officer yelled as he unlocked the door. Bleu stood and turned so that the officer could cuff her. He snatched her roughly down the hall to where a black woman in a trench coat and cheap high heels stood next to another armed cop.

"You must be Bleu. You're a hard girl to track down," the woman said.

"She's all yours," the officer said.

"Bleu, I am Tori Nixon. I'm the Assistant District Attorney in Flint, Michigan. This is Officer Williams. I'm going to have him remove the cuffs. I don't think it's necessary to make you board a five-hour flight with your hands bound. If you run, he will shoot you. Is that understood?"

Bleu nodded.

"Looks like California hasn't been so good for you," the D.A. said as she took in Bleu's appearance. "I'll have to clean you up before you take the stand."

"Stand? What are you talking about? I thought I was under arrest?" Bleu asked.

"No, Ms. Montclair. I need you to testify in the murder and armed robbery case that you were a witness in before you left Flint," the D.A. informed Bleu. Bruno's face flashed in her head. "The warrant was just a way for me to locate you, but I can't put you in front of a jury like this. I thought you were a college girl. What drugs have you gotten involved in?"

Bleu lowered her eyes, embarrassed.

"Crack?" the D.A. pushed.

Bleu nodded.

The D.A. looked at Bleu sympathetically and then placed a hand on her back as she guided her out of the precinct.

"I'm willing to do whatever you need me to, but I have to do one thing first," Bleu said. "Can you take me somewhere before we leave town? That's the only way I'll testify."

Iman was eerily silent as he sat in the backseat of the Rolls-Royce with Cinco and Sandoza on each side. His brooding demeanor left no room for conversation on this solemn day.

As their driver followed the processional of cars in front of them, Iman's hand rested on his hip where his 9mm pistol was concealed. His gut told him that today's event could bring trouble. He still had no idea that the person who had committed Tan's murder was sitting directly next to him. Iman was blinded, thinking he was surrounded by family when there was a snake in his grass. He was paranoid on this day. *Whoever did this is still lurking. They could be anywhere!* Sandoza was heartbroken over the loss of his daughter and Iman was remorseful, wishing that he and Tan had been able to experience more good days than bad. Today felt empty. Yes, he was burying his wife, but he hadn't loved her the way that he should. Their love had been missing something and he hated that he was sending her off before he had gotten the chance to see her happy with someone who could love her the way that he loved Bleu. As Iman looked out of the window he felt exposed, as if whoever had violated him was just waiting to strike again. One gun didn't feel like enough to protect himself. Iman wouldn't be caught lacking. He already had some of his L.A. goons in the pews at the church just in case. If bullets started flying Iman had guns ready.

"We are sending one of God's angels home today," Cinco said. He was a master of manipulation. The tears he shed were so believable that they were Oscar worthy. "Whatever you need today, fam, I got you."

Iman didn't respond at first. "I appreciate that, bruh," he finally replied. He was anxious to bury Tan because once the dirt hit the casket a part of his life would be dead as well. He was paying his last respects to a woman he had grown up with, a girl whom he had turned into a woman, and in turn she had helped him to become a man. It would be a long, gloomy day indeed.

The car rolled to a stop as it pulled up outside of the Catholic church. "She was baptized in this church," Sandoza spoke solemnly as he looked out his window. "I almost don't want to go in. Once I step in, it will be real. It will the last time I see my baby girl."

"I know everything is fucked up right now, Papa, but Tan is laying in there. We both know her spoiled ass wouldn't give a damn about any of these mu'fuckas coming today to say good-bye, but if there is one person she would want to see one last time it's you. She's waiting on you, Papa. She won't rest well until she hears you say good-bye," Cinco said. His voice was strong, calm. He remained in control because he knew that Sandoza was watching his every move. "Have you heard anything about who's behind this? I don't know how this happened right under your nose," Cinco added, throwing a cheap insult and placing subliminal blame on Iman's shoulders. Cinco knew that Sandoza would resent Iman for not protecting Tan. He had let his queen be touched and that was rule number one: always protect your bitch.

"Now's not the time or the place," Iman answered sternly.

Iman stepped out of the car. He buttoned his Gucci suit jacket. It was like a celebrity had arrived. Iman knew half of the attendees were there just to watch the family crumble. They wanted to see if he would fold under pressure. If there were chinks in his armor, his enemies would attack, so he showed no emotion as he entered the sanctuary.

Hundreds of people packed the church. The scent of flowers filled the air and muffled cries could be heard as he made his way to the front of the church. Iman was uneasy, but as he made eye contact with his shooters who were meticulously placed throughout the room his tension eased a bit. He was almost positive that the heads of the other cartel families were in attendance. Everyone had come out to pay respect. Iman had love in L.A. He had expected the crowd, but he didn't know where the hate was coming from and that made him uncomfortable. It wasn't all love in the church. Someone harbored malice; Iman just had to figure out who it was.

He walked toward the beautiful gold casket that sat up front and placed one hand on Tan's chest. "Rest well, beautiful," he said. This wasn't Iman's scene. There was something about being around death that made him feel like the Grim Reaper would knock at his door next. He went to the front pew and took his place next to Sandoza and Cinco as the doors to the cathedral closed and the service began.

Bleu watched as the people spilled out of the church and her heart skipped a beat when she set her sights on Iman.

"Make it quick," Nixon said as she stepped out of the unmarked cop car and allowed Bleu to get out of the back.

Bleu walked sheepishly over to Iman. She fidgeted the entire way. She knew she looked a mess. After four days in lockup she even smelled horrible, but there was no way she could just leave L.A. without saying good-bye.

They locked eyes and Iman placed a hand over his heart as if the sight of her wounded him. She tucked her messy hair behind her ears, trying to tame it, but it did little to improve her appearance. When she saw Cinco exit the church and stand next to Iman she stopped walking instantly. Terror took over her and she turned around, running across the street so fast that she forgot to look. A car horn blared as the car barely missed her.

"Bleu!" Iman called after her.

She turned and waited as he caught up with her, but she could feel Cinco's eyes burning into her from across the street.

"Bleu," Iman said sadly once he reached her. "No, ma." He choked up more at the sight of her in this condition than he had inside the church. "Tell me it ain't so."

Tears filled her eyes as she cleared her throat. She was so embarrassed to be standing in front of him like this. "It just got too hard," she admitted.

"I was coming back to you, ma. I just needed time," Iman admitted. "You should have given me more time."

"There is no more time," she said. "I'm going back home."

"Stay," he said. "I'll be here this time, ma. I can get you clean."

Bleu shook her head. "No, Iman. I can't. I just didn't want to leave without telling you bye," she said. She wiped the tears from her face. "I have a police escort and everything. District Attorney of Flint, Michigan, came all the way here for little old me." She smiled, but Iman knew she was putting on a show, trying to make him feel better but he could see the fear in her eyes.

Her eyes, he thought as he frowned.

"Where were you four nights ago?" Iman asked.

Bleu froze. *Does he know it was me?* she thought. "Locked

up . . . for possession," she said. Her voice was so low that he could barely hear her, but he recognized her shame.

He exhaled in relief. Her answer was enough for him to erase the notion that she had been in his home the night Tan was murdered.

"The D.A. is going to take me home, get me clean. I'll be all right," she said. "I just wanted to let you know that I'm sorry and I love you. I love you so much."

Iman sniffed away his emotion and looked away from her. He wasn't big on displaying his sentiments. He was a straight shooter, but he never wore his vulnerabilities on his sleeve. Bleu seemed to have a different effect on him than any other person in his life as he said, "I love you too, ma. I was gon' get right back, Bleu. I just needed you to hold on for me." He pinched the bridge of his nose.

She could see his struggle. "I couldn't!" she cried. Bleu jumped into his arms and she hugged him so tightly. Like a little girl hugging her father she tucked her face into his neck and sobbed because she knew this would be the last time she saw him. He held the back of her head as he bit his bottom lip to stop himself from letting his emotional levees break. No one had ever exhausted him in the way Bleu had. She brought out every single emotion in him, ones that he guarded carefully. She was the key that unlocked his heart and he was being forced to let her go. It hurt and he wished he had nurtured her a little more. Maybe God would have let her grace his life a bit longer had he appreciated the gift of her affection.

"You take care of yourself, Bleu. You ever need me, you call. No hesitation. Get yourself clean, Bleu. If I could do it for you

I would. If there was a price to pay for that, it would be financed, but you've got to do it. You've got to want it. Go back to the girl I met at Picante. That girl was strong. She was perfect," he said. "You're a masterpiece, ma."

"We've got to go!" Dixon said.

Bleu let him go and it felt like he took her air with him as he pulled back.

"Good-bye, Iman," Bleu whispered, giving him a weak smile.

He reached into his pocket and pulled out his phone and handed it to her. "I'll keep it on for you. I want to be able to reach out to you and make sure you're straight."

He kissed her forehead but couldn't bring himself to say good-bye. Bleu climbed in the back of the car and turned to watch him as the car pulled away. She touched the back windshield as tears streamed down her face. Leaving him was the hardest thing she had ever had to do.

15

Bleu never thought she would see the day when going back home felt good. She had been so busy trying to escape her hometown that she didn't realize that the familiarity of it all was comforting. There were no shiny lights, no skyscrapers, no fancy foreign cars on the streets, but it was home. The distance she had put between herself and L.A. felt good. As dangerous and grimy as Flint streets were, she had never felt safer. There was security in knowing the hood. She knew the way these people thought; she knew the mentality; she knew the streets and the neighborhoods. She had come up on these blocks. There was comfort in the familiar. She had been clueless in la-la land, playing by other people's rules because she was a stranger to the city. Even with its toxic water and boarded-up houses on every block, Bleu had grown to appreciate where she had come from. The city was going through a massive crisis, but the people who called it home were among the strongest in the world. Flint was resilient; Flint was strong. Flint was home and it took her leaving to value all that it meant to her. She wished she were coming back in a better way. The small-town girl turned Hollywood should have come back with degrees and accomplishments. The expectation of her had been high. Coming back cracked out was sure to disappoint.

"There is a contract in the streets for your murder. So I will put you up in a motel until it's time for you to testify. I am preparing the state's case now against the shooters," Nixon said as they drove through the north side of Flint. "We will begin prep tomorrow. We'll go through the questions I'll ask and also questions that the defense will throw at you to trip you up."

"You didn't say anything about a hit on my head!" Bleu exclaimed. "Are you trying to get me killed?" Bleu knew that the wolves in Flint weren't going to pass on a payday. Every shooter in town would be gunning for her head.

"We can assign police protection," Nixon informed her. There was no way that Bleu was walking around with a walking bodyguard. If it weren't for the respect she had for Bruno she wouldn't even consider testifying. He had looked out for her by giving her a job and making sure she ate while her mother ran the streets. He had become like family, so the least Bleu could do was help put the goons who had killed him away. She didn't need to place the word "snitch" on her forehead however by walking around with a cop as an accessory.

"I can take care of myself," she said as she rolled her eyes and focused her sights on the streets that she had thought she left behind.

"So don't I get some money or something for getting on the stand?" she asked. Bleu had come back with nothing, no clothes, no money. She didn't even have a change of panties. She had fled L.A. with the stuff on her back, and after spending four days in jail she wanted nothing more than to burn everything she was wearing.

"The state can't pay for your testimony," Nixon replied. "I have some connections with the Michigan Work First Program, but you have to be clean, Bleu. You would be drug tested each week to ensure the integrity of the program. We don't take drug addicts."

Bleu didn't respond. She didn't like that she was this transparent. She hated the look of condemnation that she saw in the D.A.'s eyes. Everyone looked at Bleu like that now. It was like she couldn't go anywhere without someone judging her. She was see-through. There wasn't even a point in lying about her habits anymore because she looked the part. "That's all right," she whispered in embarrassment. "I'll figure it out." Just that quickly her mood had changed and she was already regretting coming back here.

They pulled up to the Red Roof Inn and Bleu stepped out of the car. She was used to penthouse suites at the expense of Iman. Despite the fact that she was using drugs, she had lived at a high standard on his dime. She had wanted for nothing. Coming back home would take some adjusting. She only had herself to depend on, and the downgrade made her frown in disgust.

"This is where you're putting me up?" Bleu asked as she turned up her nose.

"You're a junkie that I just pulled from a jail cell. Beggers can't be choosers," Nixon reminded Bleu.

Bleu climbed out of the car and waited while Nixon checked her in. When Nixon handed her the key she said, "I'll be by tomorrow to begin prep for trial. We'll go over some of the questions I'll be asking you at trial," Nixon replied. "Until then stay out of trouble, and no drugs."

Bleu nodded, but in her mind she was already thinking of how to cop something to make her feel good.

She took the key from the D.A. and walked out to find her room. She entered the room and stood in the doorway surveying the furnishings. This would be the new normal for her. She wasn't in Hollywood anymore.

Bleu tossed and turned on the itchy sheets, unable to sleep. She was restless. It had been too long since she had taken her last hit and she was feigning for just a little taste. Sweat covered her as her body's temperature rose, then fell as her anxiety changed with the passing minutes. She felt panicked. Her heart was beating too fast one moment but then felt like it wasn't pumping at all the next. It had been five days since she had smoked dope and every part of her craved it. It was like having sex with a man who couldn't quite get you over the top. Her body knew how good it would feel to just wrap her lips around the cool glass of a pipe and pull all of that smoke into her lungs. She wanted that orgasm, but she just couldn't get it. She was dead broke, and on top of that, Nixon had put a squad car on her, so there was an officer watching her every move. Bleu was so frustrated that she felt like crying . . . like screaming . . . like hurting somebody . . . or maybe even herself. She sat up in the bed and clicked on the TV, hoping that there would be something on to distract her, but she knew it was pointless. She was restless and nothing would occupy her until she got her feel-good.

That's what my mama used to call it, she thought, and now she knew exactly why. *I thought she was the meanest person in the world sometimes, but she was spazzing when she couldn't cop. God, why does it feel so bad?* she thought. She was at a point where she couldn't even imagine herself without drugs. She didn't want to be clean. There was no point. The world had beaten her up for the past nineteen years. It had been so hard, so unbearable, living up until this point. Bleu had finally found a release, something to bring happiness into a life so void of anything close to it. She had almost had fulfillment with Iman, almost . . . had she been his priority and not his option she was sure she would have felt it. Almost didn't count, though, and she had found her heart's substitute in the form of a tiny rock. Crack wouldn't abandon her. It wouldn't put her last or throw her shit on the curb. It wouldn't disappoint her. It wouldn't play with her heart. Bleu could rely on it to make her feel all the things that life hadn't. As long as she was faithful to it, it would be faithful to her. She didn't care how toxic the relationship was. She would ride until she died as long as it kept feeling so amazing.

Bleu was in despair, and if she didn't get out of this hotel room soon she would lose her mind. She went to the window and pulled the curtains back just enough to see that the police were posted outside. *I told that stupid-ass bitch I didn't need* *protection*, Bleu thought. She picked up the cell phone Iman had given her and looked up the number to the hotel. She pressed *67 before dialing.

"It's a great night at Red Roof Inn. How can I help you?"

"I'm a guest at the motel and I heard gunshots from the room next door. I'm in the back building, room four-one-four," she said. "Please. Oh my God, someone is screaming. You need to call nine-one-one."

Bleu hung up and darted to the window to see if the officer assigned to guard would react. She knew that the clerk would call it in and the officer would be the first to respond to the scene. She needed him distracted so that she could get out of her room without him noticing. She waited anxiously until she saw the red and blue lights flash on the top of the cop car. He pulled off in the direction of the back of the property. Bleu grabbed her cell and slid out of the room, running down the stairs and away from the motel as fast as she could. Relief flooded her as she slowed down to avoid suspicion from people passing by. She didn't know who was serving in Flint, but she did know exactly where to go to find out. When Bleu was little, her mother had dragged her all over the city, going from one dope spot to the next looking for somebody to throw her a bone. If it was one thing Bleu knew, it was where to cop from and, more important, where to find hustlers who would give her something for next to nothing. It paid to be a pretty girl on the streets, and as much as Bleu wanted to get high, she would do just about anything for it.

16

Standing in front of the abandoned apartment building was like déjà vu for Bleu. A lot had changed over the years. The complex was now run-down and dilapidated and there was no one in sight, but from the dirty needles and used crack pipes that littered the parking lot she knew that other aspects of this place had remained exactly the same. She had been here so many times before. The complex sat in the middle of one of the city's busiest streets, but the dilapidated building in front of her was a place where only the scum of the city dared to roam. Its boarded-up windows were tagged in gang signs and doors kicked in. The winter winds whipped through the hallways so briskly that a whistling sound could be heard coming from inside. Some of the walls had holes big enough for the homeless to just walk right through, roaming from apartment to apartment. A shiver went down her spine as her mind drifted back to the last time she had wandered inside.

• • •

It was dark. Bleu hated the dark. It was always in the pitch-black that the bad things happened, and as she sat at the kitchen table waiting patiently for one of her parents to walk through the door she shivered slightly. The last time she had been in the dark, she had been asleep when she woke up to fingers that didn't quite fit in between her legs. Occurrences like that were common in her household. Her mother would often tell her she was sick, make her drink medicine that made her feel sleepy, only to wake up too groggy to fight off the predators who came into her room at night. Bleu still hadn't quite figured out if it was all a dream or if it was really happening, but either way, she had hated the darkness ever since. Bleu saw the other apartments out her window. Their lights shone brightly as if perfectly normal people lived inside, and jealousy filled her. She wished she lived in one of those houses where paying the light bill was a priority over smoking dope. She wished for a house like Noah's, which was filled with love and sometimes fussing but never fear. She stood to her feet and walked over to the kitchen, pulling out the junk drawer. She knew they had a lighter. They had those all day, but finding a candle proved more difficult. Her hands finally landed on a round wax candle and she lit it, sighing in relief as it cast a small glow. It wasn't much, but she could see in front of her now and that made her feel slightly better.

Bleu pulled out her homework and laid it out on the kitchen table as she focused. She squinted but kept going, despite the fact that she was working under the hardest of conditions. Bleu felt like her schoolwork was the only thing in her life that she could control. No one could take the things she learned away from her, and she valued that. Coming up in a home where everything came up missing, she made sure that she had one thing that no one could ever steal away. Her smarts. Her father could pawn TVs, her mother could turn in jewelry, and the local hustlers who served them both could come take a piece of Bleu's body, but no one could take her mind.

She didn't stop until the growl in her stomach grew too loud to ignore. Bleu knew then that it was time to go find her mother. She stood and checked the refrigerator just for good measure, but nothing but condiments and baking soda was inside. Nine-year-old Bleu was starving. She hadn't even eaten at school, because her mother had smoked up all her lunch money. She thought about going to Noah's to hang out, but Miz Monica would know that she had only come to eat. The last time, Bleu had scarfed her food down so fast that Ms. Monica had sent Bleu home with a plate for later. When her mother saw the food to go, she had given Bleu the worst ass whopping. "Don't put my muthafuckin' business in the streets. That bougie-ass bitch Monica sending you home with plates like I can't feed my own child," she had said. Bleu had learned her lesson. She hadn't accepted a dinner invitation from Noah since. Bleu walked out of her apartment, headed to the hangout spot where Sienna and Wayne went to get high.

The apartments were alive with music and boisterous shit talking as the local dope boys stood outside, some enthralled in a craps game while others sat on the hoods of their nice cars. It was a party. They were living hood rich as their customers came to cop from them and then took their guilty pleasures into the basement of the building to use in private.

Bleu's young eyes bounced from face to face in search of her mother. Even Bleu's father would suffice, but he usually got high in private, so she didn't anticipate finding him. It was Sienna who liked to be on the scene. She was a beautiful woman with zero inhibitions, and whenever she showed up she smoked for free . . . or rather for fucks. She might not have dealt in cash, but she dealt in pussy, and each time she made a transaction she lost another piece of herself.

Bleu walked around to the back, not wanting anyone to notice her, but as soon as she rounded the corner she froze. The scene in front of her made her feel sick to her stomach. No child should have to witness her mother doing such things. Bleu didn't even understand or process what she was seeing. Her mother was bent over, her knees digging into the concrete so badly that they bled, as one man pounded into her from behind and her mouth wrapped around the length of another in front of her. A small crowd of young men cheered her on.

"Damn, she working for that shit. That bitch can smoke with me for free anytime," one of the onlookers heckled.

Bleu was too horrified to do anything but run. What she had seen, happening outside, in front of everyone, frightened her. She ran all the way back to the projects, but instead of going home she went directly to Noah's door. She was crying, snot and tears mixing on her face as her small fists beat on the door frantically.

"What in the world . . ." Ms. Monica opened the door and Bleu ran into her arms, bawling her eyes out.

"Oh, baby," Ms. Monica whispered, her own eyes misting as she held Bleu tightly. Ms. Monica was aware of Bleu's circumstances and could only imagine what Bleu had been through that had brought her there.

Noah came up behind Ms. Monica. "What happened to her?" he shouted, angry and emotional from seeing his best friend so distraught. "Ma!"

"Just go to your room, Noah!" Ms. Monica shouted as she held Bleu in her arms.

"But Ma—"

"Noah, now," Ms. Monica snapped.

Noah gritted his teeth and stormed off, enraged, because he had never seen Bleu so hurt. The thought alone made him want to kill something.

Bleu cried her eyes out, for hours, unable to get the images of her mother out of her mind. They were burned there and would forever change the way she felt about not only Sienna but herself as well. Sienna was worthless, and because Bleu was her daughter she wondered fearfully if she was worthless too.

A tear slid down her face as she shook her head to clear her thoughts. Bleu had always been embarrassed by her upbringing. Thinking about it only allowed ghosts of her past to come back and haunt her. Her gut churned as she stood on the sidewalk outside the gate. She knew once she stepped inside she would never be able to save herself. Many souls had been lost inside these walls. Guilt filled her because as a little girl she had judged her mother for her choices. On the nights when Bleu had to rescue her mother from these raggedy halls she had felt nothing but hate and resentment, but she now understood. The monkey on her back urged her feet forward despite the fact that her mind was screaming no. She remembered her mother's words: *I'm sick. I can't help it, Bleu.* When Sienna had said those words, Bleu had dismissed her. It had sounded like nothing more than an excuse all those years ago, but today as Bleu stood, waiting to walk into hell on earth, she knew it to be true. Bleu had caught the sickness. Apparently it was contagious. The demon of addiction ran in her family. Two addicts had raised her and she had doomed herself to repeat the mistakes of her parents.

Bleu noticed that the habits of the local hustlers hadn't changed. They stood outside, popping big shit and laughing, carefree, as if the poison they peddled didn't ruin the lives of little girls looking on.

Bleu walked up to the guy who sat on the hood of his Benz AMG truck. He wore a Detroit baseball cap low over his eyes as he kicked shit with the men around him. Bleu knew this was his block. She could tell just by the way he carried himself. Bleu knew there was no point in approaching the others; he was the one who called the shots. She walked up to him, jittery and scared, not completely comfortable being back in the spot her mother had scoured for her next high. "You working?" she asked.

"Nah, shorty doo-wop," the guy replied with a charming smile. "I don't know what you talking about."

"Look, can you just front me something?" Bleu said, shifting from foot to foot as she ran her fingers through her hair. "I'll work for it. I'll do whatever you want. I just need a break, real bad." Bleu had desperation in her eyes. Even thin and rundown she was still an attractive girl. It was just in her DNA to stand out. It was the one good thing she got from Sienna.

"What you doing out here?" the dude asked.

"Don't give me no shit. I'm out here buying what *you* selling. If there weren't niggas like you, there wouldn't be people like me. You feed the hood your poison. So are you really that much better than me?" Bleu shot back in frustration. She was tired of niggas acting like drug dealing was better than drug using. They were all trapped in the same game, in love with the same high; only difference was the dope boys got high off the power that they got from it. Bleu got high off the superpowers she felt when she used it. They all were hooked, Bleu just wore her addiction on her sleeve whereas the guy in front of her hid his inside.

"Not better, just different," the guy said. "What's your name?"

"Bleu," she said. "Who are you?"

"Messiah," he replied.

"Now that the introduction has been made," Bleu said, "you gon' help me out or what?"

"I don't want none of that dopehead pussy, doo-wop," he said. "I'll look out for you, though. Pick your poison. You want H or C?"

"I ain't into shooting up," she replied.

Messiah stood to his feet. "It really is a shame, doo-wop," he said as he licked his lips and eased up off the truck. He got into his car, then hollered across the lot, "Yo, Tip! Bless lil' mama. Her credit on me."

"Yup!" the young hustler called back.

Bleu stepped back, feeling the weight lifting off her slightly because she knew within a matter of minutes she would be back right. Messiah drove off and Bleu rushed over to pick up her package. No conversation was needed. Tip served her and Bleu walked around the back of the building as she looked for a place to enjoy herself in peace. As she passed the spot where she had seen her mother sell her soul Bleu's mind flashed back to that day. She shook the memory from her mind. The thought of it still caused a pit to form in her stomach.

Bleu walked inside, her heart sinking lower and lower with each step that she took. This was rock bottom. She knew it and somehow she still couldn't stop herself. She made her way inside, pulling back one of the boards that covered one of the apartment doors to squeeze through. The smell of trash hit her immediately. Rat droppings and dirty needles were scattered throughout. Her eyes were wide as adrenaline pulsed through her. She made her way to the back of the apartment and down the stairs that led to the basement. All the apartments connected to a shared space beneath the building. Bleu called it hell. It was where her mother used to come to party with her friends. Time had changed nothing. There were people everywhere, huddled in corners, some alone, others together, all chasing their own escape. The sound of broken glass crunched beneath Bleu's feet as she made her way inside. She grasped the dope in her pocket, holding on to it tightly. She was so anxious to smoke. She wanted to feel the euphoric rush so badly that it drove her crazy. She walked back toward the storage room where she used to find Sienna passed out. Time had caused the tables to turn. Instead of rescuing Sienna from a place she used to hate, Bleu now sought refuge there. There was something so devastating about the irony of it all. She found the room and entered one of the jail cell–sized spaces. Closing the door tightly, she sighed in relief before sitting Indian-style on the sticky floor. Her hands trembled as she loaded the straight shooter. The sound of the lighter flicking and the dance that the flame performed on the dark wall was hypnotizing. She got lost in the flame as she lowered her head. It was a process she had done so many times before that she no longer had to think about it. She barely even felt any pain as she took her first hit. The sensation hit her instantly, dulling the burn as the heat from the glass pipe sizzled her lips. *Fuck trial. Fuck rehab. Fuck Iman and California.* This was exactly where she wanted to be.

Bleu stayed up on a three-day binge. She hadn't been free to smoke like this since her days of bumming on skid row. Even when Cinco was serving her, he had spoon-fed her, giving her just enough to get her hooked and keep her in control. With Messiah's word as her credit she was free to cop as much as she wanted, and Bleu was taking advantage of the offer while the getting was good. She was like a chimney.

"You smoking real good over here, but you ain't giving up no money. No pussy. No nothing," an older black woman with a matted blond wig said as she walked over to the storage unit where Bleu had been squatting for the past few days.

"Mind your business," Bleu said.

"You look just like your mama. You Sienna's baby, right?" the woman said.

Bleu froze and she looked up at the woman in surprise but didn't answer.

"If I didn't know any better I would have thought it was Sienna herself that came walking through that door. Yeah," the lady said as she entered the unit and took a seat against the wall facing Bleu. "You're her daughter. Red, right? I never forget a name or a face," the woman said.

"Oh yeah?" Bleu asked, being facetious, finding the old woman funny but knowing that there was truly nothing humorous about her current state. Bleu had no right to laugh. They were in the same position. Iman had elevated her so high that she had become a little bourgeois, not realizing that at the end of the day she and this woman were both just two women addicted.

"Why don't you go over there and cop again since they just giving it to you? Let me have that little bit you got left," the woman said. "Come on, baby girl. Me and yo' mama good friends. I used to look out for her all the time."

"And what that got to do with me?" Bleu asked.

The woman waved her hand at Bleu dismissively. "Shit, if you ain't gon' ask him, I'ma go ask him for you," the woman said as she climbed up.

The woman stood and Bleu went to the doorway to watch the shenanigans unfold. She was feeling good and in the mood for a good laugh. She already knew the local D-boys were about to make a spectacle out of the woman.

"Hey, playboy, you holding?" the lady said, her decaying gap-filled smile turning the young boy off.

"What your old ass want? You ain't never got no money. I ain't Visa. I don't give out credit," he said, causing his friends to chuckle.

"Come on, man, you gave baby girl a freebie. Let me just get a little bit," the woman said.

"A'ight, you want a little bit?" the hustler said. "I'ma let you earn it. Fuck it, I'm bored. You about to entertain me."

"I'm good at entertaining, young buck," the lady flirted, poorly.

The hustler dusted her off, flicking her hand away as if she were a pestering insect. "Man, if you don't get your old ass off me. I don't want nothing you got." He stood. "Yo' want to smoke for free on me? All night?"

A few random fiends looked in his direction. "We about to have a contest!" he announced, smiling devilishly as he tapped his friends to get them to join in on the fun. He stepped into the corner of the basement and grabbed a bag of dog food.

"Get in a line. Who want to smoke for free?" the hustler called out. "You too, girl," he said as he looked toward Bleu. "Gravy train's over. You want to get high for free you better get cha' ass over here with the rest of these mu'fuckas."

Bleu hesitated and he snapped his fingers at one of the younger workers. "Drag her ass over here. I got a nice pile just for her," he said as he poured a large portion of the dog food on the floor. He made seven servings. "Now, whoever finishes their food first wins."

Bleu stood wide-eyed, not wanting to participate. "Get cha' ass on the floor," he said, this time without humor in his voice. There was malice in his eyes and Bleu reluctantly got down on both knees as five others lined up next to her in the same position.

"Let's go. Eat! Eat that shit up!" the hustler shouted as he walked around them. The other workers laughed as the fiends dived in, doing anything to win that grand prize of an unlimited high for the night. Most of them had hung around trying to bum off the users who actually came with money. Bleu had already been smoking for most of the evening. She was still floating on cloud nine, so she was reluctant as she bent over. "Come on, girl! Eat up!" the hustler antagonized her as he pushed her face so hard into the pile of dog kibble that she hit her face on the cement. She tasted the blood as her lip busted and the tears stung her eyes and she began to eat the food. She closed her eyes, disgusted with herself as the men around her pulled out their cell phones and recorded the contest. They were in stitches as they walked around laughing and filming.

"I won! Un-uh! I got this!" the old lady called out proudly as she stood up.

The hustlers fell out in hysterics as the rest of the addicts climbed to their feet.

"Yeah, a'ight," the ringleader said as he pulled out a bag and tossed it on the ground. "Yo, we out!" he called to his friends.

"You out?! You said all night!" the lady protested. "This ain't even my thing! I don't do heroin!"

The hustler tossed a couple more bags at her before disappearing from the basement. Despite the fact that she didn't do boy, the lady still scrambled to pick up the bags before any of the other fiends in the basement got their hands on them.

Bleu gathered herself and sucked her bottom lip into her mouth, nursing her wound. She prepared to leave, unsure of where she would go, knowing she couldn't go back to the room.

"Where you going, Red? You ain't on this with me?" the old lady said.

"You sharing?" Bleu asked.

"Hell yeah. I don't really fuck with this shit. I don't want to do it by myself," the lady said.

Feeling humiliated, Bleu really just wanted to flee, but it was the insatiable urge and a bit of curiosity that made her follow the lady back into the storage room.

"Aw-w, Red, don't let them young boys fuck with you. The universe has a way of paying 'em back. It's all fun and games until it's one of they mama or sister or daddy. This shit here can happen to anybody." The lady was speaking nothing but truth. "Wait right here. I got to go get my friend. She do this shit. She'll be able to set us up."

Bleu felt an inkling of fear fill her belly. Her intuition was trying to tell her that she was taking this thing a little too far. There was a difference between wanting to get high and having to. Bleu felt she was teetering on the line, threatening to cross it.

"Come on, girl. You can go first," the lady said as she came back with a jittery young white girl. Bleu didn't even bother to get her name, figuring she wouldn't remember it after the night anyway.

"Why am I going first?" Bleu asked.

"Cuz it's my shit and my rules," the lady said. "Come on now. Give me your arm." Bleu stuck out her arm and the white girl wrapped a belt around Bleu's biceps.

"You got good veins, girl," the white girl said, marveling as she pulled out a metal spoon.

"What will it feel like?" Bleu asked.

"Like God came down from the clouds himself to kiss you," the white girl said. "Especially the first time."

"How old are you?" Bleu asked. Her pulse was racing. She felt like she was out of breath, her anxiety was so bad.

"Seventeen," the girl said, and Bleu gasped in shock. This girl was too young to be caught up so bad. What was this white girl doing in the middle of the hood? White girl didn't belong there, but truth be told, neither did Bleu. She watched the girl place the heroin in the spoon and light a flame beneath it. The heroin melted.

"Grab one of the cotton balls out of my pocket," she instructed. Bleu did it. "Place it in there." The white girl motioned for the old lady. "Come hold the spoon."

The white girl took a syringe out of her pocket and stuck it in the cotton ball, drawing the heroin up until the syringe was full. Bleu shivered slightly as the white girl placed it in her arm. Her arm burned and then seemed to freeze as the heroin traveled up her arm.

"I can't feel my arm," Bleu said. Suddenly her heart felt heavy, as if it just took too much effort to keep beating. She heard it in her ears, heard it slowing, felt the sharp pain in her chest as her eyes rolled up inside of her head. She was trying her hardest to gain control of her body, but suddenly she was shaking uncontrollably. The last thing she saw was the white girl running off just before Bleu's eyes rolled in the back of her head, turning everything white.

"Fuck is going on?" Messiah asked as he and Noah pulled up to the apartments just as a rush of degenerates who hung out in the bowels of the building came running out.

"Where the lil' niggas that run the block?" Noah asked as he stepped out and slammed the door before heading toward the commotion. He grabbed one of the fiends who were hightailing it out of there. "Yo, what's the problem? What's going on?"

"O.D. in the basement. Don't nobody want no part of that. Police will be all up and through here now. Gotta find a new spot to get zooted," the toothless man said. Noah let him go and shook his head as he and Messiah headed toward the basement.

"If these the lil' niggas you vouching for, we in trouble. They can't even run this shit right. One of these dopehead mu'fuckas die from our shit and it's gon' be bad for business," Noah scolded as he entered the basement. "Get them on the phone so they can come clean up their mess. Can't have the police pulling bodies out of these buildings, G," Noah instructed, highly upset that aspects of his operation were being run inefficiently.

He went down the stairs to see that some of his customers didn't even flinch at the notion of one of their own overdosing. *They really like zombies down here,* he thought as he shook his head.

"Damn, man. This little shorty don't even look like she supposed to be out here like this!" Messiah called out. "She approached me the other day straight, G, checking a nigga. I put her on credit just of G.P., now this."

Noah made his way over to Messiah, and when he reached the girl she was slumped in a corner of the musty basement; her sweaty, greasy hair covered her face.

"See if she still breathing, man. I can't fuck with no dead bodies," Messiah said.

Noah looked at him sideways. "As many niggas as you done laid down?" Noah questioned.

"That's different, my g. I ain't waiting around afterward, checking pulsing and shit either," Messiah defended himself.

Noah smirked as he bent down. When he moved the girl's hair out of her face his heart sank. He couldn't breathe, as all of the oxygen in the room seemed to be sucked out as the walls caved in on him. His eyes widened in horror and his gut twisted in absolute fear.

"No, no, no, no, no," he pleaded urgently as he frantically picked the body up from the ground. "Come on, B; this can't be you," Noah said, practically begging as his voice cracked from the flood of emotions that were drowning him. He couldn't believe this was happening. How had she ended up here? "No, B. No! What did you do to yourself? What did you do?!" he asked as tears came to his eyes. "You ain't supposed to be here. This ain't for you."

"Fuck is up, bruh? You know her?" Messiah asked.

"Get the door!" Noah shouted as he carried her through the basement. "Hurry!" There was so much emotion in his voice that Messiah halted all lines of questioning. He ran ahead of Noah, opening doors for him so that he could carry Bleu's body out to his Range.

He climbed into the backseat and cradled her in his arms. "Drive, man! Get me to the crib as soon as possible and get Khadafi on the line. Tell him I need a doctor ASAP."

The ride to the outskirts of town had never felt so long. Bleu was out of it from an apparent drug overdose and Noah was going crazy at the thought of her not coming out of it. He had had no idea she was even back in town, let alone that she was in trouble. His heart ached at the sight of her.

"Come on, Bleu; don't do this to me. Wake up!" he screamed as he rocked her back and forth. He gripped her chin, shaking her head slightly, trying to shake her as if she were simply asleep. "Get up, B. Get up."

Messiah didn't know what to say. He wasn't even aware of how Noah knew Bleu, but the bond they shared was apparent. Messiah had never seen any man grieve over a woman like that. The amount of sorrow that filled the truck was palpable. For a lack of knowing what to say he said nothing; he just did as he was told and put the calls in to make sure there would be help when they arrived.

Noah hopped out before the truck even stopped moving, carrying her effortlessly as he rushed her into his home. He took notice of the amount of weight Bleu had lost. She was nothing in his arms.

A woman hopped out of an SUV and rushed up to him. "Khadafi sent me. I'm Simone. I'm a nurse. I can help," she said as she followed them hastily up the walkway. "What happened?"

Messiah opened the door and they all rushed inside.

"I don't know. I found her like this. I think she overdosed," Noah said, unable to wrap his mind around the fact that Bleu was using drugs.

"Overdosed on what?" the nurse asked as she immediately

went to work. She placed rubber gloves on her hands and pointed to the couch. "Put her here for now."

"I don't know; crack, heroin. I'm not sure," Noah replied. "You've got to get her to wake up. That's my life right there."

He was in such a frenzy that he had completely forgotten that Naomi was home. He looked up to find Naomi standing in the hallway, her mouth hanging wide open as confusion resonated in her eyes.

"What the hell is all this?" she asked. "Who is this dirty bitch you got ruining my fifteen-thousand-dollar couch?"

Noah stepped over to Naomi and looked her dead in the eyes. "That's my couch. This is my crib. You don't decide who I bring here, and watch your mouth when you speak about her," he said.

Naomi was stunned to silence. Noah had never spoken to her that way. This was a side of him that she had never seen.

"How about I just leave *your* crib then?" she said sarcastically. "You and your little crackhead girlfriend over there can do whatever you want."

Naomi stormed out, slamming the door so hard that it rocked the frame. Noah exhaled and rubbed the top of his head. His life felt like it had turned completely upside down.

Messiah stepped toward him. "Don't worry, fam. I'll go after her and get her to cool down. You know she a hothead," Messiah said. "Who is this girl, though, my g?"

"She's a friend. Somebody I used to know," Noah answered sadly as he watched the nurse work on Bleu. He pinched the bridge of his nose as he sniffed away his emotion.

"Damn, must be a good friend," Messiah said, knowing

there was more to the story. With that he left and Noah focused on Bleu.

"Is she going to be okay?" he asked.

The nurse stood. "Will she wake up from this? Yes, but she has a bad drug addiction," the nurse informed him. "The tracks in her arms say heroin, but the corroded bone up her nostrils says cocaine. The darkness of her lips says crack cocaine. She's a full-blown addict. I don't even think she has a preference as long as it gets her high. That's the most dangerous type of substance abuser. She needs to be in rehab. I've done all I can. She has an IV to replenish her fluids. After she rests a bit, she will come out of it. Then maybe you can clean her up and convince her to get help." Noah nodded, but he couldn't respond. Words snuck past the lump in his throat. He let the nurse out and as soon as she was gone he slid to the floor. He rested his forearms on his knees and allowed himself to cry. Bleu had always been his weakness and today he feared that she might break him.

He sat by her side for hours watching the rise and fall of her chest.

"Hmm," she groaned as she blinked her eyes open slowly.

"Relax, B," Noah said as he helped her sit up.

She looked at him in shock. "Where am I? How did I get here?" she said more to herself than to him as she squinted in disbelief. She reached out to touch his face and gasped when her hands actually felt him. She had thought she was hallucinating. "You're here."

"I'm here," he confirmed as he touched her hand and then kissed it. "What did you do to yourself, Bleu?"

Bleu's lip trembled as she replied, "It just got so hard."

Noah pulled her into his arms and hugged her so tightly that she began to sob. "It's okay, B. Everything is going to be fine. I'm going to help you," he whispered. He rocked her back and forth. She felt so comforted in that moment. So loved. So valued. It was the first time in a long time that she felt like she meant something to someone. They stayed like that for an hour, just holding on to each other with him whispering reassuring things in her ear. He was giving her hope, letting her know that she was worth saving.

"I've done so many bad things. If I tell you, you're going to throw me out. You won't want me here," she whispered.

"I swear I'm not going to give up on you, B. Not ever. I don't give a fuck about nothing that you've done," Noah promised.

He kissed the top of her head and said, "There is one thing that might make me kick you out."

She pulled back, her eyes filled with worry. "Please, Noah," she said.

"Your ass stink, B. I'm going to need you to wash your ass if you gon' be in my crib," he said with a sly smile.

She hit him in the chest before giving him an embarrassed laugh. She knew that she was a mess. She couldn't remember the last time that water had touched her body.

"Come on," Noah said. "Let me clean you up and get you something to eat." He slowly pulled the IV out of her arm and grabbed a Band-Aid off the table, fixing her up. He held out his hand for her and as she stood she wobbled slightly.

"My legs are so weak," she said as she reached out one hand to catch her balance on his shoulder.

Noah scooped her into his arms and carried her up the stairs to the master bathroom. She felt safe with him, and although she was embarrassed, she didn't feel judged. He set her on her feet as he bent over to run her a bath in the Jacuzzi-sized tub. He grabbed some of Naomi's soap and poured it into the water, then added a few drops of peppermint oil.

"You can take your time, and when you're done I'll have food waiting for you, a'ight?" Noah asked.

She nodded. "Thank you."

"Don't thank me, Bleu. You don't never got to thank me for looking out for you," Noah responded. "Towels are in the linen closet."

Bleu waited until the door was closed before she shed her clothes. She opened the linen closet, but her heart skipped a beat when she noticed the prescription pills that sat inside. She reached for them and then pulled her hand back as if she were about to touch a hot stove. Her pulse picked up and she closed her eyes as temptation tortured her. *Don't fuck this up,* she thought. Bleu couldn't help herself. In her heart, she wanted to do the right thing but still she grabbed the pills off the shelf and read the label. *Vicodin.* She would have to take a lot to feel a comparable high to that of the heavy stuff she was used to. Bleu poured the entire bottle out into her hands and stuffed them down her throat. She dipped her head under the sink and washed them down. She climbed into the water and let the bubbles soothe her skin as she leaned her head back, waiting for the pills to take effect.

Noah knocked at the door. "Yo, you a'ight in there?" he shouted. "It's been almost an hour. I ordered Chinese. It's been here for twenty minutes. It's going to be cold by the time you get out."

Noah frowned when Bleu didn't respond, and he reached for the doorknob. "Bleu! Unlock the door." She didn't answer and a pit formed in his stomach. He knocked harder. "Open up, B."

When she didn't answer he rammed his shoulder into the door, knocking it down. "Bleu!" he shouted as he saw her slumped in the bathtub, her nose barely above the water.

He noticed the pill bottle on the floor. "No, no, no, no, no," he uttered as his heart dropped. He instantly pulled her from the water. He didn't know if she was trying kill herself or if she was just that desperate to get high, but he was terrified of this version of Bleu. This wasn't her. He didn't know what demons she was battling that made her want to be out of her mind, but he wasn't letting her give up. Her body was like noodles in his arms as he put his back against the tub and held her head back against his shoulder as he stuck his fingers down her throat. Vomit spewed everywhere as she spat the pills up and awoke in a choking fit.

"What did you do?" Noah asked.

"I'm sorry!" she cried. "I'm so sorry. I can't stop. I need help," she admitted.

Noah wiped his hand over his face, overwhelmed by the complexity of this disease. He knew there was more to it than just lack of self-control. He had been there during the years when her mother and father were strung out. Shit, Noah still saw Sienna running around the hood, selling her soul just to get mercy from the local D-boys. These demons were generational for Bleu and it killed him to see her like this. He never thought it would be her.

"Okay, okay," he whispered as he helped her back into the tub. He ran her a new bath, but this time he washed her body, being gentle with her as she hugged her knees, crying the entire time. He washed her hair, conditioned it, cleaned the dirt from beneath her fingernails. When he got to her chest he noticed the scar from her shooting. He traced it with his finger briefly before rinsing her body.

He was so focused on her that he didn't hear Naomi enter.

"Really?" she said.

He turned toward Naomi as Bleu tried to cover her breasts with her hands.

"It's not what it looks like. Just give me a minute to pull her out of the tub. We'll talk in a few," Noah said assertively.

Naomi frowned as she looked at the vomit and noticed the smell. Clearly there was nothing sexual going on, but she still didn't like the fact that Bleu was in her bathroom, using her shit, and having her man catering to her every whim. Naomi stalked out of the bathroom and Noah pulled Bleu out of the tub.

"I'm sorry. I'm causing problems for you," she said.

"You're not a problem; don't worry about it," Noah stated as he put her in his bed. He dried her, lotioned her entire body, and then pulled some of Naomi's clothes out of the drawers. "You're smaller than her, but this is all I've got for now. I'll get you some clothes tomorrow," he said. "You hungry?"

Bleu nodded.

"Stay here while I clean up the mess in the bathroom and then I'll bring you up some food."

Noah tucked her in and then went into the bathroom, his stomach turning at the sight. He cleaned up the mess, disinfecting it all and tossing her old clothes. By the time he emerged from the bathroom Bleu was asleep, restlessly, but at least her eyes were closed.

He took the trash downstairs and, sure enough, Naomi was waiting for him. She sat, livid, her anger written all over her face as one eyebrow rose, demanding answers without even speaking.

"It's Bleu," Noah said.

"That's Bleu?" Naomi said with a frown. "That crackhead-ass bitch—"

"Watch your mouth," Noah said. It was the second time he had to warn her. "She needs to stay here for a while. I'm going to help her out. Get her on her feet. Get her clean."

Naomi looked like she smelled something that stunk. "What? That includes you bathing this bitch too?" Naomi was steaming and Noah knew that this had taken her by surprise. It had thrown him for a loop as well, but there was no way he was throwing Bleu back in the streets.

"I don't trust anybody when it comes to her. This is something that I just got to do. She's my—"

"Your life. Yeah, I heard," Naomi interrupted.

"Don't be fucking selfish," Noah said, raising his voice. "I keep you laced; everybody knows you're my woman. You don't want for nothing. You don't ever hear about me out here tricking off on none of these bitches. I'm all about you, all the time. I'm just telling you I need to focus on a friend for a little while. Not everything is about you. Just play the position I put you in and have my back on this. Stop with the jealousy shit. She's my best friend; before all of this street shit she was there. She just needs some help."

Naomi was amazed at how quickly he had turned the tables. He had her feeling bad, like the scum of the earth. "Fine," she said, conceding. "Help your friend." She tried to walk past him, but he grabbed her and kissed her softly on the lips.

"Thank you for understanding," he said.

She cut her eyes at him. "Hmm-hmm," she said. "I'm going back to the apartment for a few days."

"You ain't got to leave," he stated.

"Just call me when your company is gone and when shit is back to normal," Naomi snapped.

"You don't want to put me in a position where I have to choose between you and her," Noah stated firmly.

Naomi scoffed, "Why? Because you won't choose me?" His silence was answer enough and she stormed toward the door. "Fuck you, Noah!"

He didn't go after her. He knew the best thing would be to let her cool down before he tried to remedy the situation. He was conflicted. On the one hand, he felt strongly for Naomi. She had held him down when the rest of the world had forgotten about him. Some of his roughest days when he was locked away had been made brighter by her. She saw something in him when he had nothing to offer her. The belief of a woman in a man was worth more than gold, and while he wouldn't say he was in love with her, he did care a great deal for her. Bleu, on the other hand, well . . . Bleu was Bleu. His Bleu. She was the girl he had spent his childhood years laughing with. The same girl who knew his mama, whom he had walked to school with, whom he had crushed on when she went from looking like a flat-chested tomboy to a blossoming young woman. She was the girl he defended when the entire hood laughed at her for her parents' mistakes. She was the girl who mourned on his shoulder when her father died and the girl whom the entire city knew Noah would fight for whenever she needed him. They had discussed their hopes and dreams, talking about what they would do when they made it out of the hood. Bleu was his soul mate in every sense of the word. Despite the fact that they had never been together in a romantic way, she was the woman he envisioned standing beneath a white veil when he finally decided to man up and choose a wife. He loved her with every fiber of his being. Their friendship was the most valuable thing he had in his life. From the most innocent aspect to the most complex, Bleu was his very best friend. He would go to the ends of the earth for her. He had proved that before when he had done a bid for her. He would prove it again now by digging her out of this grave that she had put herself in. Even without any romantic dealings with Bleu, he was still connected to her. She was family. Their friendship transcended labels. It was deep and there were depths of it that just couldn't be explained. Like the ocean, it was so massive that it drowned you.

Noah walked back to the bedroom. He climbed on top of the covers and she moved her head to his chest as he watched her sleep. He was afraid to close his eyes, in fear that when he awoke she would be gone. So he stayed up all night, listening to the cadence of her breaths until the sun came and nature woke her up.

"You've been up all night?" she asked as she yawned and looked up at him.

"Yeah. Been thinking. Seeing you got me fucked up," he admitted as she sat up and sat Indian-style across from him. "Tell me how it came to this, B?"

"I honestly don't know how I let it get this bad. It just started as me taking a couple pills to stay up and study for finals. Then it was meth, then coke, then . . ." She stopped speaking, too embarrassed to say it aloud.

"Crack?" he finished for her. "Then H?"

She nodded.

"You know how fucked up I feel, knowing you was in them apartments getting high off my shit? That's my product you smoking? My shit you shooting in your veins," Noah said. "Makes me feel like this ain't the right move. Like for real, Bleu. It's messing with my head."

"Don't let it. This ain't on you. If it wasn't you, it would be somebody else supplying the streets. Trust me. When I want to get high, I get high. It doesn't matter who I'm copping from. I don't put my troubles on the nigga that serves me because even if one D-boy refuses to there is always another that will. You're in it for the money. You don't feel guilty for getting your paper. It's me. I chose this life," she admitted. "Enough about me, though, boy, look at you!" She threw her hands up, motioning to all the luxury that surrounded them. "You're living, Noah. Like really living."

"I do a'ight for myself," Noah said humbly.

"I'm proud of you," Bleu said. "You went from pissy-smelling hallways and six hundred square feet in the projects to a mansion in Grand Blanc." Noah heard her changing the subject, deflecting attention off herself, to speak about something else, anything else other than the elephant in the room.

"Let me help you, Bleu," he said.

"It's not your responsibility, Noah," she replied as she shook her head. "Besides, it is not going to work. I've tried. Don't you think I want to go back to the person I used to be? This wasn't supposed to be my story. I don't know how to shake this shit. It seems like every time I try I fail and it just gets worse." She held out her arms. "Look at this. I'm shooting dope, Noah. I'm killing myself and the bad part is I don't know if I want to stop. If I get clean, I have to deal with all the shit that I've done while high. It's too much." Her tears were endless. He was her priest and she was giving confession. She had put her worst fear out into the world. She had finally told someone what really prevented her from getting better.

"It's too much for you, but it ain't too much for me, Bleu," Noah said. "I don't care if I have to lock you up in this mu'fucka, you're not going back to the streets. You're staying here until you kick this shit. You got to promise me one thing, though, Bleu," he said.

"What's that?" she asked.

"That you'll trust me," he said.

She nodded. "I trust you."

Noah nodded. "Good. Now get up and go choose which

room you want to sleep in. Then we'll go shopping for some of the things you need."

"That girl that was here last night. That's your girlfriend?" Bleu asked. Noah nodded. "How is she going to feel about me staying here?"

"I'm on her shit list right now, but she'll come around. You let me handle her," Noah said. He shook his head as he smirked. He knew that making up with Naomi would cost him a pretty penny. She wasn't a gold digger by far, but there was a price to pay to have a bad bitch on his arm and it went up when he pissed her off. He would have to splurge on a Chanel bag or two just to get back in her good graces. It was the cost of having a high-maintenance type of woman. Roses and apologies just didn't do. "Hurry up so we can shake."

Bleu headed out of the room but stopped when she got to the doorway. She ran full speed over to Noah and hugged him tightly. He was such a good friend. He was seeing her at her worst, but he wasn't leaving. He wasn't running away from her, and she appreciated his loyalty. She wasn't even loyal to herself at the moment. She couldn't look out for herself, but she knew that he would hold her down until she was strong enough to rely on herself.

They said nothing as he held her close and the feeling of her heart beating against his, at the same rhythm, soothed her. This was genuine love from one person to another. No matter how hard it got, or how many times she messed up, or how much she sabotaged the process, Noah wouldn't leave her.

Noah felt himself becoming emotional. Bleu was the only person who made him tap into that forbidden part of himself that he kept hidden. While he had always been her strength, she had always been his weakness. He couldn't allow that this time. He had to be there for her without allowing her to distract him. He cleared his throat and pulled away, disconnecting from her. Whenever he touched her the energy he felt was so intense it left him with bated breath. "Hurry and get yourself together. I'll be waiting."

She walked out and he sat on the edge of the bed, perplexed by the way Bleu made him feel. He put his hands on top of his head and blew out an anxiety-filled sigh because he knew that Bleu had just come raging back into his life like a category 5 hurricane. He just hoped that she didn't blow down all that he had built.

17

When Noah pulled up to the old projects where they used to live, Bleu looked at them timidly. Memories came flooding back to her. It was as if he were asking her to go into a haunted house. In a way, he was. A lot of ghosts dwelled inside and she feared that if she was forced to enter they would come back to haunt her. It looked the same as she had remembered. Same struggle, same people, same everything. Absolutely nothing had changed. No matter how much money Noah made, he couldn't seem to let go of his humble beginnings. Usually he and Messiah would convene at Noah's old apartment, politic, drink, and bullshit. This time, it was Naomi who had taken refuge there after their disagreement. She wasn't from Flint, however; she didn't know just how dangerous his old stomping grounds were. He had allowed her to cool her top for one night, but anything longer would have him unsettled.

"You coming in?" he asked.

"No, um-m, I'm good right here," she said.

"You scared of your own people?" he asked with a frown.

"No, I just . . . I'm good," she responded.

Noah looked skeptical and said, "I'll be right back."

He was like a star as he walked through the hood, dapping up the young lieutenants in his operation and stopping for a moment to throw up a basket with the kids playing hoops with a milk crate tacked up to a tree.

Noah made a mental note to bring a rollaway basketball hoop by when he got a chance and then made his way up to his third-floor apartment.

He entered and found Naomi sitting on the couch with her feet propped up as she painted her toenails.

"What you doing here?" she asked as she sucked her teeth.

"I take it you're still mad," Noah stated.

Naomi didn't answer as she concentrated on the work of art she was doing.

"Look. I need your help. Bleu needs clothes and I'm not good with the girl shit. Can you play nice and take her to the mall? It'll give you a chance to get to know her," Noah said.

Naomi frowned. "Do I look like I want to be seen with that girl? We are on two different levels," Naomi said unapologetically.

"She's down bad right now, Naomi. I've seen a lot of sides to you, but I would love to see you think of somebody else beside yourself. I know most of the time it's all about you. I've made it that way, so it's my fault that you're spoiled, but you got to show me a different side. For real. A pretty face ain't shit without a pretty heart to match."

"I'm not friendly, Noah. You know that," Naomi sighed.

"Do it for me. I'll eat that pussy real good for you later to thank you," Noah said as he moved closer to her, kissing her neck as she whimpered at his touch.

"You're not playing fair," she whined.

Noah smirked and pulled back. "Hurry up. She's in the truck. We'll be parked out front waiting for you," he said.

Naomi purposefully took her time getting ready. *Little Miss Bleu is going to learn her place if she's going to be around. Her ass can wait,* Naomi thought. It took her an hour to shower, dress, and apply her makeup to perfection. She didn't feel bad about it either. She stepped out of the apartment and looked like a million bucks as she strutted down the stairs. When Naomi got outside she knew Noah would have an attitude. He hated to be left waiting, but Naomi didn't care. She had a point to prove to Bleu: *I come first in his life and shit don't move until I move.*

When she got outside and noticed Noah buying ice cream for all the kids in the neighborhood and Bleu passing it out Naomi grimaced. It was like they hadn't even noticed that she had taken all day. Bleu's smile was electric as she handed the soft-serve cones out. When Naomi saw Bleu offer the last cone to Noah she gritted her teeth in disdain. Noah shook his head and Bleu mushed it on his lips anyway, forcing Noah to eat some of the sweetness. They both were in fits of laughter by the time Naomi reached the truck.

She stood with her arms crossed, one hip cocked, and her eyebrows raised in aggravation.

"See, the wait is worth it. You coming out here looking like a million bucks," Noah said in a jovial mood that irritated Naomi to her core. *All of a sudden this nigga is carefree. She come around and he all smiles,* Naomi thought bitterly.

She gave him a tight smile as he walked over to kiss her cheek. "Bleu, this is my girl, Naomi. Naomi, this is Bleu," he introduced them.

Bleu waved but didn't speak before climbing back in the truck.

Naomi frowned. "You can move to the back," she said as she held open the door for Bleu.

Noah quickly diffused the situation as he tossed the keys to Naomi. "I got a few things to handle with Messiah. Can't text and drive. I'll take the backseat."

Naomi knew he was being diplomatic but she held her tongue and walked over to the driver's side.

The ride was filled with awkward silence as the threesome hit 75 South.

"Where are we going?" Bleu asked.

"I don't shop in the city. Detroit has a better selection. Although for you I guess anything will do. You're not into high fashion clearly," Naomi said.

Bleu scoffed and shook her head as she surveyed Naomi's outfit. *This bitch thinks just because she wearing every brand in the world she knows fashion. Her gaudy, tacky ass,* Bleu thought. Naomi had no idea that Bleu was a fashion-scene killer. She was down on her luck, but back in L.A. she had everything from Céline to Tom Ford lacing her closet and she knew how to pair it with vintage and low-end stores so that she didn't look like a walking label whore. She wasn't trying to butt heads with Noah's girlfriend, though. Bleu knew that whatever static she made with Naomi Noah would have to suffer for, so instead of creating conflict she just let the insults slide off her back. She didn't have time for catfights. She had bigger problems. While Noah was a great distraction, she could feel the monkey beating on her back. Even in this very moment she just wanted to sneak off and score a quick high.

"Clearly," Bleu replied. "I'll follow your lead. Maybe you can help me put a few looks together."

Naomi looked at Bleu out of the corner of her eye, surprised that the girl didn't snap back at her. "Yeah, maybe."

"Just go to the Valley," Noah said, referring to the local mall. "You on that Hollywood shit."

"I thought your girl was Hollywood," Naomi said snidely.

"No, Noah likes me regular . . . like the hometown Flintstone I am," Bleu said in a low tone as she looked out of the window. "Of course you know what he likes. I mean it's obvious you're not from Flint, but you know what I mean. He prefers for his girls to be simple. The extra shit isn't necessary."

Noah sat in the backseat, perplexed as he watched the nicest nasty exchange of words he had ever seen. Women didn't need to fight with their hands; their words flew like bullets. He reached around the side of the passenger seat and gave Bleu's arm a reassuring squeeze.

The truck felt too small for the three of them. Being around

Noah was one thing, but hanging out with him and his girlfriend made Bleu uncomfortable. Considering the fact that Naomi was gorgeous and had her shit together, Bleu felt insecure in her own skin. *I'll never let this bitch know that,* Bleu thought. Facts were facts, however. Bleu couldn't say anything to Naomi. She was sitting here in Naomi's clothes accepting charity from Noah. Bleu didn't have a pot to piss in or a window to throw it out of. She couldn't touch Naomi and they both knew it.

"So Bleu, how long have you two known each other? You have to excuse my behavior last night. He's never mentioned you," Naomi said as they arrived.

"Since we were kids," Bleu responded.

They climbed out and made their way inside. She looked back at Noah, who trailed behind the women as they walked. He was distracted, his attention was buried in his iPhone, and Bleu really wished that he had just taken her shopping himself. She wasn't with the game of twenty-one questions that Naomi was playing.

"You just moved back from L.A., huh? Looks like the city was pretty rough on you," Naomi said.

"I guess," Bleu replied vaguely.

Bleu turned to Noah and noticed he was frowning. "Hey, are you okay?" she asked.

Noah looked up, his face fixed in anger. Bleu noticed it instantly.

"Yeah, yeah, I'm good," he said. "You two stay here and finish shopping. Messiah's going to pick me up. I've got to shoot this move. I'll meet you both back at the house tonight."

Bleu nodded, feeling put on the spot, because there was no way in hell she wanted to be left alone with Naomi. "Oh, okay," she said.

He noticed the look of uncertainty in her eyes. "You'll be fine," he promised. He turned to Naomi. "Let me talk to you for a minute."

He pulled her to the side. "I need you to keep a close eye on her for me. I've got something important to handle," he said.

"What? I can't babysit a grown woman," Naomi protested under her breath.

"Just take her shopping and bring her back to the house. You ain't got to do nothing major. Just keep her under you for the day," Noah instructed.

Naomi sighed but nodded her head. "Okay," she agreed.

He peeled off a knot of hundred-dollar bills. "Get her whatever she wants," he instructed.

Naomi wanted to protest, but she didn't. She took the money and gave him a quick kiss before he rushed out of the mall.

Naomi turned back to Bleu. She peeled off three hundred dollars. She knew that she was being petty. Noah had left five bands for Bleu to get some of the things she needed, but Naomi wasn't comfortable with her man giving another woman so much dough.

"You can get what you want and meet me back here in an hour. I'm going to the nail shop," Naomi said.

Bleu took the money. "Okay, that's cool," Bleu replied. She watched Naomi walk away, ensuring that she was out of sight before she walked hastily out of the mall. She hadn't had money in her hands in so long that she had forgotten how it felt. All she wanted to do was score. It was like her body turned to autopilot as a growing grumble grew in her belly. Gas filled her as anxiety grew in her heart. As she climbed on the city bus she knew she was making a mistake, but still she didn't stop. The day had been overwhelming. Naomi's probes, Noah's expectations, her own guilt. She was a ball of emotions and it had her spent. There was only one sure way to ease the tension and erase it all, and she had a pocketful of money. Bleu was about to get high all night. She would deal with the consequences in the morning.

Messiah was waiting curbside as soon as Noah stepped out of the mall. He hopped into the passenger side.

"Now what was you saying on the text?" Noah asked.

"The niggas that Bleu was supposed to testify against upped the price on her head. Word spread the streets like crazy too. You got a problem on your hands," Messiah said. "Might want to think about sending her back to L.A."

"That's not an option," Noah said firmly.

"Then you know what you got to do," Messiah said. "I know where them niggas be. I can send the goons through. Clean that up real quick," he said.

"Yeah, put the call in," Noah said.

"Time to heat up the city?" Messiah asked.

"Absolutely," Noah replied. He was livid at the fact that the hit on Bleu had been revived. It was the reason that he had sent her away the first time. She had come to him confessing her love for him, and Noah had told her to go to Cali. She had no idea she was even wanted in the streets. It was a decision that he now regretted and he wouldn't let anyone else force his hand to get rid of her. As long as he wanted her around, she would be around . . . he would have to make niggas respect it.

It was a pitch-black night. Only the sounds of crickets broke through the silence as Noah and Messiah pulled up to the one-story house. Nothing moved inside. Noah exited the car and the sound of the slamming car doors seemed foreign in the stillness of the night. The two cars that followed him were filled with men who would kill for him at the drop of a dime. They were about to get their hands dirty tonight, but it was Noah's soul that was about to turn black. He didn't even like to move like this. He only took these measures when it was absolutely necessary, but when Bleu's safety came into question it would play out this way every time.

Noah nodded his head and his goons approached the house carrying gallons of gasoline. Noah never stepped away from the curb. He and Messiah stood back as their men poured gas all over the porch, around the sides, on the windows . . .

"No women and children, right?" Noah confirmed.

"I play by the rules. I snatched them up just like you said. Had the baby mama call home and tell her nigga she was staying the night at a friend's house. I'll go back and cut the bitch loose once it's done," Messiah answered.

"She see your face?" Noah asked.

"Come on now, my g," Messiah answered, reassuring Noah that it had been done correctly.

Noah didn't need the screams of women and children on his conscience. The deaths he was about to deliver would rock the entire hood. The Snell brothers would feel the fires of hell tonight. Noah walked up to the porch and pulled a matchbox from his pocket. The old Noah would have hesitated. He wasn't afraid to kill, but he hadn't believed in grandstanding. But being head of his own team, he knew that sometimes he had to show the hood exactly how he could get down when pushed. Bleu's face popped into his mind and he struck the match against the box, watching the flame dance briefly. He knew that once he committed these murders he would never be the same. It was too heinous of an act to come out on the other side of it alive. He tossed the match onto the porch and like a cat chasing a mouse the flame spread across the wood swiftly.

The bars that had been placed on the windows were supposed to be for protection. They were supposed to keep the dangers of the neighborhood out, but on this day they trapped them inside. Noah waited until he heard the screams before he turned and headed back to his Range. They were bloodcurdling and put a sick feeling in his belly, but Noah disregarded the guilt, citing the greater good of his heart. With the Snell brothers dead, Noah didn't have to worry about the hit on Bleu's head or think about the state forcing her to testify in open court. She was free. Now he just had to help her break her mental chains so that she could go back to being the girl she used to be.

Naomi paced back and forth as she waited for Noah to come home. She was terrified. *How did I lose this bitch?* she thought as concern filled her. She didn't care about Bleu's well-being, but she did care about Noah finding out that she didn't really give a damn at all. *He shouldn't have put this on me in the first place. That damned girl is not my responsibility. I am not her keeper,* Naomi argued with herself, trying to develop her defense and get her story together before he even walked through the door.

It was close to two o'clock in the morning when Noah's headlights pulled up to the house. Naomi's breath caught in her throat.

"Just act worried," she told herself aloud.

Noah entered and Naomi could see by the look on his face that it had been a hard day. He was serious, his forehead creased in brooding. Noah had put in work tonight. Naomi could always tell because the look in Noah's eyes changed whenever something heavy went down. They turned coal black as if he had seen something so evil that they had been stained in darkness.

"Bleu's gone," she said, just blurting it out as soon as he laid eyes on her. She wrung her fingers nervously.

"Fuck you mean, she's gone? Do you know what I just did for her?" Noah barked. "You were supposed to keep an eye on her for me. What happened?"

"I don't know. We were shopping," Naomi started, realizing that she was about to lie to save her ass. "Then we decided to get our nails done. She told me she had to go to the bathroom, but when I realized she was taking a super long time I went to check on her and she was gone."

Noah wiped his face in frustration as he took a seat on the

couch. "And you just now telling me? Why you ain't hit my line as soon as you realized she was gone?" Noah shouted.

"I did!" Naomi lied. Truth was, she wanted Bleu gone. *Hopefully the bitch took that three hundred and got ghost.* "Your phone kept going to voice mail."

Noah gritted his teeth in frustration. "She ain't got no paper; she couldn't have gone too far."

"I think she stole some money from my bag before she left. There was a couple hundred dollars missing when I went to pay," Naomi added.

Noah closed his eyes to hide the sorrow that swept through him. He knew exactly where Bleu had gone. Noah stormed out of the house and hopped into his Range, headed back to the abandoned apartment building where he had first found Bleu. He couldn't get there fast enough. Fear and dread filled him. He was terrified for his friend. He hoped that she hadn't smoked anything yet, but he knew the possibility of finding her sober was unlikely.

He pulled into the apartment complex and around to the back, parking wildly as he hopped out of the truck. The hustlers who manned the block were out, each competing for sales, and they all nodded, showing him respect as he made his way inside. His blood boiled, but he didn't know exactly who to blame. He understood that addiction was an illness, so he couldn't blame Bleu. She had just gotten caught in the trap. It was like quicksand: the harder she fought it, the deeper she sank. It couldn't be Naomi's fault. She wasn't responsible for Bleu. Then he realized that it was his fault; maybe not directly but indirectly he was contributing to the problem.

He was flooding the streets with shit that was corrupting the next man's wife or daughter or the next kid's mother. *It's niggas like me that poison the hood. I'm damaging my own people,* Noah thought. It was all in the pursuit of the almighty dollar. Society had him thinking that this was the only way for a black man to get rich. He had grown up looking up to the dope boys and kingpins. The legit men had been considered squares, but those squares took care of their families without fear of repercussion. They didn't leave their families to sit behind steel and concrete. Noah didn't want to be one of those men, but as he entered the abandoned apartments he knew that he was responsible for each one of the brothers and sisters sitting in there getting high. Bleu just happened to be the one he loved.

He felt a rage that he had never experienced before. He was mad at himself for playing right into society's hands. He had been a little black boy who grew up to be exactly who they told him he would be. They hadn't expected much of him and he didn't disappoint. He had become exactly who they wanted him to be . . . nothing.

Noah found Bleu sitting in the corner of the basement, grasping a crack pipe in her hands. He could tell by the look in her eyes that she was gone. He was too late. She was already on a cloud.

"Noah!" she exclaimed when she saw him. "Hey, boy!" Her excitement was induced by the drugs that flowed through her system.

"Hey, B," he said as he bent down, tears clouding his vision.

She pouted playfully when she noticed his tears as she held his face and wiped them away.

"What you crying for? I've never been better. I love you so much. You're my best friend, boy. You know that?" she asked.

He composed himself as he stood. "Yeah, I know that, B," he replied. He stood up and held out his hand to her. "Come on. Let's get home," he said.

Bleu followed him willingly.

"Come show me who served you. I want to know. Where did you get the shit from?" Noah said seriously, his tone flat as he pulled her from the basement.

When they entered the courtyard at the back of the building Bleu pointed her finger to the opposite side of the yard. "That's him," she said.

"Wait right here," Noah said, feeling heat expanding in his chest as his temper flared. He didn't know if he was mad at himself or mad at the little nigga moving twinkies across the way, but it was too late to contain it. Noah left her where she stood. "Yo, my man, let me holla at you," he said as he walked over to the hustler. "You served homegirl right there?" Noah asked.

"Hell yeah. I low-key wished Shorty ain't have no paper. I would have let her pay in pussy with her fine ass," the hustler stated pompously as he eyed Bleu from afar. He was none the wiser of Noah's anger. Noah pounced on him like a lion on prey as he pulled his pistol and grabbed him by the back of the neck simultaneously.

"Get cha' ass out of here," Noah growled through gritted

teeth. The four other dope boys who worked the complex grew weary as they noticed Noah pulling their comrade to the middle of the courtyard.

"Aye, man. What the fuck?" the hustler protested.

"All you niggas hear me and hear me well. You see Shorty right there? That's me. If any of you mu'fuckas serve her, this is what happens!" Noah barked. Bleu looked on in horror, her eyes wide as she watched Noah put the pistol to the man's temple.

Bang!

The .40-cal pistol was so loud that the entire hood seemed to echo as the body fell to the ground.

All the blood drained from her face. This was a side to Noah she had never seen. Noah didn't even give a damn about the life he had just taken. He had caught three bodies since Bleu had been back in town. He had always known that she brought out the best and the worst in him, but her addiction was bringing out a completely new beast.

"Let me go," Bleu whispered as Noah grabbed her up and practically dragged her to the truck. "Noah. Why did you do that?" she cried.

"I'm not playing anymore, B. You are responsible for that nigga losing his life. You have to stop this shit. You've got to get better, because every time you cop from anybody in this city I'm putting the burner on 'em and it's only so many times I can pop a nigga before I get caught. I just murdered a nigga in broad daylight, Bleu, over you. His death is on you, and when I go back to prison behind some dumb shit that's gon' be on you too!" he shouted. "You want that?"

He fussed at her all the way until they got to his truck before tossing her inside. She didn't speak. Her eyes just filled with tears as she sat back and let him drive her home.

They didn't say one word to each other the entire drive. She was mad at him for blowing her high. He was mad at her for being so reckless with her life. Even when they arrived in the driveway they sat there, silent, brooding in anger.

"Do you trust me?" Noah asked.

"You know I do," she said, staring out her window and refusing to look in his direction.

"Good, because I'm about to do something that you won't like, Bleu," Noah said. "I just need you to remember that I love you. What's coming next is going to be hard, but I'm going to fight for you because you can't fight for yourself," he said.

"What are you talking about?" Bleu said, confused.

"Don't worry about it. Just remember that I'm doing this for you, not to you," Noah said. It was him who couldn't look her in the eyes now. "I want to ask you something. Did you go in Naomi's bag and take the money out to cop the drugs today?"

Bleu frowned. *This bitch told him I stole from him,* she thought, enraged.

Bleu shook her head, slightly offended that he had to ask her. *He should know me better than that.* She didn't realize that in her current state she was foreign to him. He didn't know her at all.

She didn't have the energy to defend herself. *For what?* she thought. *If he had to ask, he already believes her,* she thought.

"Yeah I took it," she lied.

She watched him breathe a sigh of relief as if he were glad.

As if the thought of her being a thief was more believable than the thought of Naomi being a liar. It wounded Bleu and she got out of the truck, slamming the door as she stormed toward the house.

He picked up on her attitude. "Bleu!" he shouted as he ran after her. Forcing her to stop and look at him, "You mad? Fuck you mad for?" he hissed. "You know what you got me out here doing?"

"Just forget it, Noah," Bleu said as she walked inside. Bleu rolled her eyes when she saw Naomi.

Noah could see that she had been waiting anxiously for his return.

"Hey," Naomi said as she stood to her feet. "I'm glad you found her."

"My bad. For stealing the money out of your bag and all," Bleu said sarcastically as she gave Naomi a knowing look.

Noah turned to Bleu. "Go upstairs and rest. We can talk in the morning. I can't look in your eyes when you're high," Noah said, sounding injured.

Bleu saw the pain in him. She felt it and suddenly she felt guilty for taking Noah through so many changes. She opened her mouth to speak.

"Noah—"

"Just go upstairs, Bleu," Noah said.

Bleu didn't push him and Noah sighed in relief when he heard her climbing up the stairs.

He approached Naomi, falling into her open arms as he sighed loudly. "You're so tense," Naomi said. She was thankful that Bleu hadn't spilled the beans and exposed her in a lie. *Maybe the bitch ain't that bad*, she thought.

"Maybe you should go. Just for a few days. Shit is going to get worse around here before it gets better and I don't want to be barking at you, taking the shit out on you, like I did earlier," Noah said.

Naomi nodded. "Are you sure that you can handle this, babe?" she asked. "I mean, she's fucked up out here. She needs real help. Rehab, doctors—"

"She'll just run. If I got to lock her in the bitch until she's clean, that's what I'm going to do. It's going to get ugly, but I can handle Bleu. I've been saving her since we were kids," he said. He could see the skepticism on Naomi's face and he kissed her lips, providing reassurance.

"She's just my friend. I'm one hunnid. You can trust me," he said.

"I know." Naomi nodded. "I'm going to head home. Take care of your friend."

He walked her to the door, and when she was gone the silence of the house seemed daunting. Usually he liked his peace. The quiet gave him time to think and plot his next move, but with the demons Bleu had brought into his life the silence seemed to be filled with negative energy.

He picked up his cell phone and reluctantly dialed his mother's number. He hadn't spoken to her since he found out Khadafi was his father. She had lied to him for years about where his father was, and once the truth had come out Noah hadn't been able to look her in the eyes without harboring resentment. They had been distant, but right now he needed his mother. Bleu needed help or she would die, and he didn't know what to do.

He held his breath as the phone rang in his ear.

"Noah?" Miz Monica answered.

"Hey, Ma," he said, slightly emotional as he sniffed, trying to compose himself before the floodgates opened. He had never loved anyone the way that he loved Bleu. Seeing her down this bad made him weary. He was losing his mind worrying about her. "I need your help," he said, breaking down. "I just killed a nigga over her, Mama. I don't know what else to do. . . ."

Hearing her son so distraught and hearing him talk about murder and violence with such disregard caused goose bumps to form on her arms. This was the exact reason why she had hidden his father from him. She didn't know exactly what was going on, but Miz Monica knew that the gangster in him had been inherited directly from Khadafi and if she didn't step in now she might lose her son to the streets forever.

"Stop talking. I'm on my way," she said before hanging up the phone. She got on her knees and held her head up to the sky. "God, please help my son." It was the only thing a mother could do in this position. She just hoped Noah hadn't sinned to the point of no return. She had to save him before it was too late.

18

Noah waited for his mother on the steps of his massive home. He sat with his head bowed in angst at the thought of the desperate measures he had been forced to take. When she pulled up into his driveway she stepped out of the car and rushed up to him.

"Are you okay?" she asked. "What's wrong?"

"I've got to show you something," he said as he stood and walked into the house. The look on his face was so solemn that Ms. Monica feared what she would see once inside.

He climbed the stairs and walked into his room, where Bleu sat on the edge of the bed, her own eyes red and puffy from the tears of guilt she had just cried.

"No, please take the handcuffs off. I'm not a fucking prisoner here!" she shouted, enraged as she pulled at her wrist that Noah had bound to the bed.

Noah stepped aside and let his mother enter the room.

"Oh my Lord," Ms. Monica gasped when she saw Bleu, sitting there. She rushed over to Bleu and wrapped her in a hug. "Oh, Bleu." Her heart broke. Bleu was like a daughter to her. She had watched Bleu grow up and had been so proud when she had escaped the perils of the hood. Nobody had it tougher than her. Ms. Monica had been surprised Bleu had made it out in the first place. She certainly had not been given anything. Ms. Monica had been so proud when Bleu graduated from high school and moved to L.A. She had no idea how Bleu had come back here or how she had sunk so low, but Ms. Monica now understood the devastation she heard in Noah's voice. "You locked her up in here?" Ms. Monica turned to Noah.

"If I don't, she's going to run right back to the hood and get high, Ma. I don't know what else to do. I have to keep her here, at least until she detoxes some of that shit out her system," he argued.

"Please, tell him to take these off, Ms. Monica. I promise I won't get high. I promise!" Bleu cried.

Ms. Monica was overwhelmed as she looked at a desperate Noah and an even more desperate Bleu. She didn't know whose side to take, so instead of getting in the middle she simply hugged Bleu tightly and whispered, "Sh-h-h. It's okay, Bleu." Ms. Monica knew that Noah would never do anything to harm Bleu, but still, seeing a woman held against her will didn't sit right with Ms. Monica.

Bleu melted in the warm embrace of her arms. Ms. Monica was always like the mother she never had.

"What did you do to yourself, Bleu?" Ms. Monica asked with sympathy.

Bleu didn't respond as she cried on Ms. Monica's shoulder. Bleu had no answer. There was no explaining why she had made the choices that had led her here. She only remembered the logic behind her very first time using drugs. She had wanted to stay up to study. Everything after that point had just snowballed out of control.

"Give me the key and leave us alone, for a little while," Noah's mother said.

Noah handed his mother the key and retreated from the room.

"Bleu, you know that I love you very much. Ever since you were a little girl. Noah loves you. We both just want what's best for you. If you keep using drugs you're going to die. Now I know the things you've been through. There were so many nights that I fought with myself about sending you back to that house. Any child growing up the way you did will have demons. You had the odds of the world stacked against you. You have emotional scars, honey, and they are deep. You thought running off to L.A. was going to fix everything, but running never does. Your pain is in here," Ms. Monica said as she touched Bleu's chest with the palm of her hand. Bleu lowered her head in shame and Ms. Monica lifted her chin. "Uh-uh, you hold your head high, Bleu. That's been the problem. You've always felt like you had something to be embarrassed about. So you wanted to go somewhere new, where nobody knew who you were or what you came from. You isolated yourself and left the people who love you. You've done some things that aren't so good. You've pushed Noah to do some things that aren't so good, but you can change for the better. You're young, baby girl. It's not too late. It's never too late. We are going to start dealing with the inside, healing what ails you in your heart so that the outside world can't affect you. You won't need to get high and check out from reality, because you're built strong. You're tougher than you think," Ms. Monica said.

Bleu couldn't say anything. She just listened, all the while thinking how lucky Noah was. She wished she knew what it felt like to have a mother like Ms. Monica. There were so many things that Bleu had missed out on, so many lessons that only a mother could teach her growing daughter. Bleu became what she had seen. Her mother hadn't been a role model; she hadn't nurtured Bleu or shown her a strong example of what a woman should be. There had been no lesson on the power of her femininity, no uplifting of her spirit, or building of her self-confidence. Hell, Sienna hadn't even shown Bleu how to insert her first tampon. Bleu had navigated her way through the world as a motherless child. Her mother might not have been dead, but she had been so disengaged. The drugs had made her selfish and had caused her to leave Bleu to figure it all out on her own. *Now I'm stuck in the same cycle,* Bleu thought.

"I just wish I could start over," she said.

"No one can do that. You only get one chance to get this life thing right," Ms. Monica said. "But it's not too late for you, Bleu. But we have to go back to where this all started. I want you to speak with your mother. I think she may be able to help you."

Bleu shook her head. "She can't even help herself. I've never been her priority."

"You've been gone a long time, Bleu. A lot of things have changed. People can change. What do you have to lose? You're already at the bottom. You can only go up from here," Ms. Monica said. "I think she needs to see you this way because you are a product of her. You also need to tell her exactly how you feel. After all these years it's time that she hears your voice. You held it in for so long and look at what it has done to you. It's time to break this generational curse. Noah and I wouldn't do anything to harm you, Bleu. You just have to trust us. You aren't capable of taking care of yourself right now, so we have to do it for you, and I know that seeing Sienna will help."

Bleu mulled it over in her mind before saying, "I don't even know how to reach her."

"You let me worry about that," Ms. Monica replied.

Bleu nodded and Ms. Monica reached down to remove the cuffs.

"No, leave them," Bleu said.

Ms. Monica looked at her in surprise.

"Noah knows me and he's right. If you take these cuffs off, first chance I get I'm going to run. As soon as I get antsy and that tingle comes back to me, I'm going to want to get high. I won't be able to stop myself, but these will," she said, holding up her chained wrist. The clang of the metal against the bedpost rang out loudly, making her feel like a caged animal, but in all honesty an animal was exactly what she had become. She just wanted to feel normal again, to be a better version of herself, and if speaking to Sienna was what Ms. Monica thought she needed then Bleu would oblige. She only hoped the reunion didn't send her down an even darker path.

The dancing smoke from the Virginia Slims cigarette rose in the air as Sienna sat at the small booth in the back of the diner, enjoying a smoke. Her feet hurt, she smelled like fried foods and cooking grease, and her apron was dirty, but still she couldn't complain. She was alive and it was the first day of gainful employment. As she filled her lungs with the nicotine she recalled the days that a different type of smoke would have put her on cloud nine. Her eyes glazed over slightly as the memory sent a chill up her spine. She shook it off and snuffed out the cigarette, not wanting to even crack the door open to Pandora's box. Busying herself every moment of every single day was the only thing that had kept her clean these past ninety days. Even the little smoke break was too much free time. It gave her mind time to wander, and when that happened she usually got lost. She couldn't afford to forget the Ls she had taken during her drug days. She was a recovering addict, and if she lost focus even briefly she would stumble back into the darkness. She stood to her feet and tucked the cigarette behind her ear as she started to get back to work. The ring of the bell caused her to look up.

"Hello, Sienna."

"Monica," Sienna said, greeting Noah's mother snidely as she walked around her and behind the high counter. Sienna grabbed a pitcher of water and went to the only customer in the place and filled his glass. She then tried to appear busy, as she picked up a towel and began to wipe down a table. "You can sit here if you want to order."

Ms. Monica stood, her hands clasped in front of her as she replied, "I came to talk."

Sienna grabbed the spray bottle and towel before moving to the next booth. It wasn't really dirty; she just wanted to avoid Ms. Monica. *This holier-than-thou-ass bitch,* Sienna thought. She had always resented Monica. From the very first day their kids had become friends, there had been animosity between the mothers. *I'm not in the mood for her shit today. Fuck we have to talk about anyway?*

"I'm busy. I'm on the clock," Sienna commented.

"Look. I know you don't want me here, and frankly, I don't want to be here. You and I have never seen eye to eye. Believe me, if I could have turned anywhere else I would have, but unfortunately, I'm here," Ms. Monica stated.

"Girl, what do you want? Just spit it out. I don't have all day," Sienna said.

"I'm here about Bleu," Ms. Monica revealed.

The mention of her daughter's name made Sienna freeze. She stopped working as she sat down in the booth. It had been so long since she had seen her daughter's face. Even before Bleu had left town, Sienna had been absent from her life. Sienna had been too consumed with drugs to even care about what was happening in Bleu's life. When Bleu had been shot, Sienna had been on a weeklong run. By the time she came out of her high Bleu had already checked out of the hospital, but Sienna couldn't even use that as an excuse. She didn't really try too hard to find Bleu and make sure she was okay. Truth was, Sienna had been a bad mother to Bleu and nothing made her realize that more than being sober.

"She's out there in Hollywood, right? Living the grand life," Sienna said as she blinked away tears. She pushed the initial stun to the back of her mind and continued to clean the booth.

"She's here in Flint and she needs you. She's in a bad way and I don't think there is anyone else who can help her but you, Sienna. She needs her mother," Ms. Monica stated.

Guilt weighed on Sienna. "I ain't never been much of a mama to that girl. Ain't that what you were trying to be all this time? Take my place. I'm sure you can help her out," Sienna said.

"No one can ever take your place, Sienna. That girl has wanted you to step up and nurture her for as long as I can remember," Ms. Monica said. She was disgusted at Sienna's disinterest. "Do you hear me? Stop cleaning these damn tables and listen to me for a minute. Your daughter needs you, damn it."

It wasn't that Sienna didn't want to be there for Bleu; she just didn't know how. There were so many things she had done to endanger her child, so many mistakes that Sienna had made, so many sins she had committed against her own seed. Sienna didn't know if she could look Bleu in the eyes. How could she face Bleu? Sienna feared that reconnecting with her flesh and blood would put so much pressure on her that she would resort to smoking dope. The guilt and remorse of all the things she had put Bleu through would eat her alive as soon as she set eyes on her child. It was best to just not think about Bleu at all.

"That girl stopped needing me a long time ago. She's big-time. I'm sure whatever is going on, she can work it out," Sienna said.

Sienna started to walk away, but Ms. Monica grabbed her arm. "She's on drugs, Sienna, and while I showed her how to comb her hair, taught her what a period was, and helped her with her homework when things got too hard, I can't help her with this. Nobody can. She's on crack and only you can help her with that."

Sienna snatched her arm away from Ms. Monica. "Just get out of here," Sienna said. "Go!"

Ms. Monica shook her head and grabbed Sienna's pen and order pad out of her apron. "Here is the address where Bleu is staying right now just in case you want to be her goddamn mother for once in your miserable selfish life," Ms. Monica said with disgust. "That girl deserves so much better."

"Everybody can't be a saint like you!" Sienna shot back. She rushed to the back, hiding in the kitchen out of sight of judging eyes. She broke down immediately, sobbing. The news of Bleu's addiction made Sienna feel so guilty that she instantly thought about going out to get high. Her heart felt heavy, as if it would fall out of her chest and rip right through her other organs. Nothing had ever felt this bad. The overwhelming urge to wrap her lips around a pipe hit her, causing her mouth to tingle. Since she had gotten clean the urge to do wrong had never hit her this hard. *Fuck this,* she thought as she snatched off her apron and rushed out of the back door. *What do I have to lose?*

Noah sat on the side of Bleu's bed. "You can stop mugging me, B. I don't care if you're mad," he said as he picked up the pieces to the Scrabble game and placed them on the board.

"*B-r-a-t*," Noah spelled.

"Ha-ha, very funny," she said as she pushed the Scrabble board away. "Why do you care so much about what happens to me?"

"You know the answer to that," Noah replied.

She didn't say another thing, because he was right. She did know, and at a time like this when she was at her worst she was reminded just how lucky she was to have a friend like him.

"In a day or so, when it gets unbearable, promise you won't judge me," Bleu whispered. "I've always used before I allowed myself to see the monster in me."

"I won't ever judge you," Noah answered.

The doorbell rang and Noah stood.

"I'll be right back," he said as he made his way out of the room. He pulled open the door and he didn't know if there was an angel or a devil in his presence.

"I should have known that Bleu was here with you. You have always been her knight in shining armor, I guess. Can I come in?" Sienna asked.

Noah knew that the relationship between mother and daughter was a strained one and he wasn't sure if he should allow Sienna entry into his home, but what right did he really have to refuse her?

He stepped to the side as she passed him. He scanned her, taking in her appearance. He had never seen her clean before, so the sight before him was almost like a mirage. It couldn't be real, but he had to question her, because if there was even the slightest chance that Sienna was still getting high he wasn't letting her near Bleu.

"No disrespect, but for as long as you've known me I've been fucking with your daughter. That's all I'm about right now, making sure she is taken care of, and I can't let you see her if you are still on drugs," he said.

"I'm not on drugs, Noah," Sienna assured him. "But I hear Bleu is. Can I just see my daughter?"

Noah nodded and led her up the stairs.

He walked back into his room and Bleu was focused on the Scrabble board. "*L-o-s-e-r* . . ." She looked up from the game and her face fell in a mixture of shock, disgust, and fear as her mother entered the room behind Noah.

Suddenly it felt like Bleu couldn't breathe, as the walls seemed to close in on her. Time stood still as mother and daughter faced off for the first time in years. Tears filled Bleu's eyes as she stared into Sienna's. Neither of them spoke, but an energy pulsed between them.

"What is she doing here?" Bleu shouted to Noah. "Get her out of here! What is she doing here!" Bleu shouted as she pulled at the handcuff she was anchored by. "I hate you! Get out!" Her cries were so shrill as she tried to get free, and Sienna bolted from the room. Noah had never seen Bleu spaz out in this way. She was panicking as anger and years of hurt threatened to bury her. "Why would you bring her here?"

Noah went to her side and knelt on the side of the bed as he rubbed her back.

"Sh-h, calm down, B," he soothed. "It's okay. It's okay," he repeated. Bleu cried, ugly tears, tears that spilled pain that she had buried for decades, tears that made snot run down her nose and had her heaving for air. "You wouldn't be hurting this much if you didn't care. Just breathe for me, B. I promise you it's going to be okay. You've waited years to see her like this. She looks clean. That's a start. Now you can tell her everything you been holding in since we were kids. She can hear you now. Just calm down. You can do this. You can face her, B, and if you're not strong enough to do it by yourself I'm right here with you."

Bleu was holding on to Noah for dear life as he knelt over the bed in a praying position while holding his hands over Bleu's.

"I've imagined this moment for so long, but now that it's here I don't know what to say," Bleu whispered.

"Just say what you feel," Noah said.

Bleu nodded. He kissed her forehead and Bleu sat there waiting with bated breath until Sienna reentered the room.

"I'm sorry to just show up like this," Sienna started, and then paused to clear her throat as nerves took over her. As she surveyed Bleu in the bed, her frame too thin for comfort, her eyes sunken in, her eyes wild from drug lust, Sienna felt sick. *I did this to my baby,* Sienna thought. She thought back on all the years she had neglected to parent Bleu, all the times she had sent Bleu to the block to cop for her, and all the times she had let grown-ass men fondle her daughter to pay for drugs and Sienna wanted to die. Of course Bleu had ended up here. She was doomed from the beginning.

"What do you want?" Bleu asked while wiping her eyes. It was almost like she didn't know her mother well enough to let Sienna see those tears.

"I want to ask how did you get here? My smart girl, with the big dreams, and the brains to match. You weren't supposed to end up like this, but I know exactly how it happened," Sienna said. "I only have myself to blame. I could have done things differently."

"Let's not sugarcoat this," Bleu said, steaming as she looked Sienna straight in the eyes. "You never gave a single fuck about me. I was your daughter and you just didn't care."

"Then why do you want to be like that? Because that's what you're becoming. You're becoming the selfish cracked-out bitch who doesn't care about anything or anyone except getting high," Sienna said. "You don't know how happy I was when I found out I was pregnant with you, Bleu. It was the best day in my life and I was pretty good at the motherhood thing too, at first. But then I started feeling tied down. I started having too much time on my hands. My homegirls were out partying and bullshitting while I was stuck in the house raising you. So I started to bring the parties to me. Me and your father were the only kids our age with our own place, so no rules, no parents. It started with weed and just escalated from there. It was supposed to be fun, but the next thing I knew ten years had passed and I was on my knees in alleyways sucking on real dicks for glass dicks."

"And when you became washed up you let grown-ass men rub their hard dicks against me, and suck on my tender breasts, all so that you could smoke for free," Bleu said. "I hated living in this city. I hated being here because everybody knew what you were. All my friends, my classmates, the teachers!"

"I know," Sienna admitted. Bleu was screaming so loud that she was shaking. Sienna moved closer to her daughter, drawn to her like a magnet. The pain that Bleu felt Sienna felt, and she climbed into the bed with her baby as Bleu laid her head on Sienna's chest and cried. "I know, baby girl, and I'm so sorry. I had no worth, so I couldn't teach you to value yourself. You are so worthy, Bleu. Worthy of every single thing you ever wanted. I know you did a lot of dreaming because reality was so bad, but you deserve nothing but good. It hurts me to know that you're doing the same things that destroyed me," Sienna said, her voice cracking as she held Bleu.

"It hurts so bad that . . ."

"It feels good now," Sienna finished for her.

Bleu sat up looking at her mother in shock. She had never thought anyone would be able to relate to the backward logic, but it was something that Sienna knew all too well.

"I felt everything you are feeling right now, Bleu," Sienna said. "I know how tightly the devil has a hold on you, but you are not his to control. You're one of God's loveliest angels, Bleu. You're supposed to soar. The devil can only hold on to you if you hold him back. Let go."

"I can't," Bleu admitted.

"*I* did," Sienna said. She pulled out a circular coin and held it up. "It's been three months for me. This is my ninety-day chip," she said as she placed it in Bleu's palm. "I had years on the street, I did every drug that there was to do, and if I can do it you can. You are so much stronger than me. You just have to feel the hurt that you're suppressing, Bleu. Let it out. Hate me, hit me, curse me out, but just get it out. I can take it. I deserve it. This life that you've stumbled into . . . the drugs . . . the addiction . . . it isn't for you, Bleu, and I can promise you that if you don't get your life together it will kill you."

Bleu held on to Sienna as she closed her eyes while her mother stroked her hair. This was the love that she had been missing. It was the bond that she had craved for so long and the connection that she had searched for everywhere she went. She had wanted to feel like she belonged to someone. She wanted Iman to claim her as his and his always, but the only true person whom one ever really belongs to is their mother. Sienna had never made Bleu feel loved until this moment, and as she felt the rubs of her mother's hands on her scalp she felt soothed, protected, and cared for.

"You have so many people who love you, Bleu. That boy out there. He's special. You only get one love like that in a lifetime," Sienna said. "As long as he is behind you holding you up, you'll never fall," Sienna schooled Bleu.

"It's not him. He isn't my one," Bleu said dismissively as her thoughts drifted to Iman. "My one is in L.A."

Sienna chuckled. "Trust me. If it's one thing I know, it's men. You're young and you think that you met someone out there who you want to be with. He's different from what you're used to because you're not from where he's from. He's handsome, probably charming, and he is probably a great man for somebody . . . but you found the soul that your heart wanted a long time ago in Noah, and no matter what happens, you'll always find your way back to him. You just have to get clean, baby. We have to get the poison out of your system so you can go after everything you deserve. It's not too late for you; I promise."

Bleu was left speechless. She felt the wetness of Sienna's tears as they fell and mixed with her own.

"I'm so sorry," Sienna said.

Bleu had become what Sienna had shown her a woman should be; now Sienna had to help Bleu in her quest for redemption.

For the first time, Bleu felt like she could bounce back. It was like the fifteen minutes of love that Sienna had bestowed upon her was the real euphoria that she had been chasing. The feeling she felt in this moment was incomparable to any drug she had put into her body. It was a different level of satisfaction. This feeling didn't just trick her senses temporarily; it resonated in her heart. The love of her mother, the love that Bleu had wanted her entire life, made her feel whole.

"It's going to get worse before it gets better," Sienna said. "You just have to be strong. You can do this. You're so much better than me."

Bleu wanted to stay angry at Sienna. Bleu wanted to tell her about every single moment that she had needed a mother but had been let down. She wanted to rub in the fact that Sienna had failed her over and over again, but she knew that she would be hypocritical. Bleu was now in her mother's shoes, and although she had no child, she had done her fair share of damage to people's hearts . . . Iman's and Noah's in particular. Although it had never been her intention, when people walked away from her they walked away with emotional scars. That was her impact on Iman and she was sure it would be her impact on Noah as well. She dreaded it, but such was life for a young woman addicted to dope. Who was she to hold grudges and place judgment when she was ruining lives herself?

"I'm going to show you why you should get clean, Bleu. You're my daughter and I have so many regrets. There are so many things I wish I could go back and do differently. I'm going to motivate you to get clean. This isn't what I wanted for you. I'll show you why you need to stay away from the drugs. I promise you. After it's all said and done you won't want to touch it ever again," she said.

Bleu clung to Sienna until her tears turned dry and exhaustion forced her to sleep. Sienna lay there, holding her child, praying to God, for hours. When Sienna finally decided to get up she planted a kiss on Bleu's forehead. "I love you, my smart girl," she whispered before leaving the room.

Noah sat outside of the door, his back leaned against the wall as his elbows rested on his knees. He looked up when Sienna exited.

"How is she?" he asked.

Sienna sniffed as she wiped her emotional eyes. "She's in a bad way, but she'll be okay. She's going to crash, for days probably, and when she wakes up is when the hard part begins.

She's going to see why she has to kick this. I have to show her," Sienna said. "I've been so selfish. I have to be selfless in order to save my daughter."

Noah stood, confused by her ramblings but grateful that she was on board to contribute to Bleu's recovery.

"You take care of her," Sienna said as she walked by him, heading for the door.

Noah nodded. *I always have,* he thought as she disappeared from sight.

Sienna went back to the hole-in-the-wall motel room where she lived. It was all she could afford on the waitress's paycheck that the diner provided. She couldn't complain. It had four walls, running water, and a bed. She had slept in much worse places. She had made a plan for the next six months of her life that centered around staying clean. She went to meetings faithfully, she read the Bible nightly and prayed religiously to God to deliver her. Sienna had worked hard to stay away from the life, but when she had seen her daughter she knew that what happened to her no longer mattered. She was heartbroken, her emotions spent by the mere thought of her Bleu being more like her than she would have ever wanted. Bleu never knew, but Sienna had bragged on her daily. *My baby out in la-la land kicking ass and taking names,* Sienna would tell her friends as they all sat around enjoying a good high. She knew the people whose ears she sang Bleu's praises to could care less, but still Sienna gloated anyway. Bleu was a representation of Sienna, so the fact that she had made it out was fulfilling for Sienna.

She had to get that smart shit from somewhere. That's me in her, Sienna would say.

Sienna was devastated to find out that Bleu was more like her than she thought. Bleu had gone all the way to California and brought home a la-la land addiction. Sienna knew that it was all her fault.

She sat down and pulled the twenty-dollar rock out of the front of her apron and then rolled the brand-new glass pipe between her fingers as her vision misted with regret. Her heart raced as she struggled with her decision. She pulled the needle out of her apron. *Fuck smoking it.* In order for it to hit her quickly she needed it in her veins. She wanted it to happen fast and quick. She knew it would be the best high of her life. She picked up her phone and sent Ms. Monica her home address.

Sienna wanted to be strong, to stay the course of her journey as a new woman, but seeing Bleu had left her feeling so empty. This was the only way to rectify the many wrongs she had committed against her daughter. Sienna had cherished the moments that she had spent with Bleu in her clear mind. It was the first time she had looked at how beautiful Bleu was through sober eyes. Sienna wished that she hadn't taken it for granted before. She had missed so much. Ripping and running through the back alleys of Flint had robbed her of all credibility as a parent. She hoped she could make up for that now. She hoped Bleu would appreciate her one day.

Sienna picked up a piece of paper and pen. These would be her last thoughts as a clean woman, so she wanted to document them before she put the needle in her arm.

My beautiful Bleu,

I don't know if you know how you got your name; in fact, I'm pretty sure that I never told you. We never had the mother-daughter heart-to-hearts, but the day you were born I saw the clearest blue sky. You were about to bust out of my pussy and rip me from front to back and the only thing that took the pain away was gazing at that sky. I can still remember the hues of blue and white. I had never seen anything more beautiful until I set my eyes on you, and so Bleu Montclair was born. I wish I had tried so much harder to get to know you, because knowing you and truly being loved by you is a blessing. It is a privilege that I missed out on because of my foolish ways. I'm less than a woman because I failed to love my child. That was the one job I was put on this earth to do and I failed. I am so sorry. From the bottom of my being, I regret every day that passed that I neglected you. I'm sorry for every man I let hurt you. I was chasing the devil's tail and being so stupid. I was a bad mother and a selfish person. God trusted me with you and I ruined you. I tore you down before the world ever got its hands on you, so you were equipped with nothing to defend yourself with. I never told you that I love you, but know that I do. As I write this my mind is as clear as that blue sky on the day you were born and the thing I know most in this moment is that I love you, my daughter.

I hope you don't judge me after you read this, because what I'm about to do next is for you. You have to see what will happen to you if you continue to abuse drugs. You have to know that it will kill you. That it will destroy you as it is about to destroy me. Do not end up like me, Bleu. I have the will to stay clean. Before seeing you today I would have stayed clean. I'm getting high today to show you that if you continue to smoke dope, or shoot poison in your veins, or even just do a quick snort to pick you up from time to time you will die. You will end up dead, soul first, but your body will inevitably follow. Get clean for me. Do it to prove that you are nothing like me, you are better than me. I'm sorry for the love I never showed you, because despite my actions I always felt it. I know you will never understand, but I'm doing this now to be the sacrifice that will make you wake up and get you to fight for your life. Get clean, Bleu, and when it gets hardest and you think you can't take the pain just look up into the sky. I'm sorry, Bleu. My heart will forever hold you in it.

Your mother,
Sienna

Sienna folded the letter and addressed it, then set it on the nightstand in the room. She picked up the crack rock. This time felt different from all the other times she had done this same routine. She knew it would be her last taste. She had purchased a hot shot from one of the local dealers. The bag of bad dope would kill her certainly, feeling good momentarily before sizzling in her veins and going straight to her brain. She was afraid, but most of all she was ready. Ready to leave this life of pain and regret behind. More so, Sienna was ready to show Bleu what her reality would be if she stayed on this reckless path. Sienna hoped her death wouldn't be in vain, but in her gut she knew that as Bleu mourned her dead body it would give her the strength she needed to get back on her feet.

Sienna tied a belt around her arm, then melted down the dope. She drew in a sharp breath as she stuck the needle in a bulging vein. A tear slid down her face as bliss overtook her. Somehow the last high felt just as orgasmic as the first, probably because each of them was the last of their kind; she would never feel this way again. Her first hit had birthed her and the final one would put her to rest. A burning sensation ran up her arm and Sienna's mouth fell open in an O of excruciation before her body seized and she fell out of the chair. Her head hit the floor with a sickening crack, blinding her as everything turned white before her eyes. Sienna had once heard that when you were a child of God death would be painless, euphoric in fact, as God welcomed his angel into heaven. She knew exactly where she was going. The amount of pain she felt was immeasurable, and as every second ticked by she knew she had earned a one-way ticket to hell. It was too late to repent. She just prayed that her death would save Bleu's life.

19

Ms. Monica stepped out of her car and looked up at the motel. She wasn't sure who had texted her the address in the wee hours of the morning, but something had drawn her here. At first she thought it might have been Noah sending her a message through someone else, but when he had called her this morning to thank her for assisting him with Bleu last night she knew that he hadn't sent the message. She approached the room and knocked on the door. She wasn't frightened but more wary of what she might be walking into. No one answered and Ms. Monica frowned, deciding to walk to the front office.

"How can I help you?" the front-desk clerk asked.

"Who is in room nine A?" Ms. Monica asked.

"I can't tell you that, ma'am. I have to protect our guests' privacy," the clerk responded.

Ms. Monica sighed and pulled a hundred-dollar bill out of

her purse and set it on the countertop. "I really need to know who is in that room," she insisted.

The clerk slid the money into her pocket before typing into the computer.

"Looks like a Sienna Montclair is checked into that room."

Ms. Monica frowned. "I need you to open the room for me," she said as an ominous feeling of doom filled her.

"I can't do that."

"Listen. Sienna is a recovering drug addict and she sent me this text late last night. I'm afraid she might be using in that room. Now if you don't let me in I can call the police and I'm sure they will be more than willing to kick in the door," Ms. Monica said.

The clerk made a copy of the plastic key card and then handed it to Ms. Monica.

She hustled, half-running, half-walking, as she rushed back to Sienna's room. "God, please let this woman still be clean," Ms. Monica whispered before opening the door.

She didn't even have to walk inside to see the tragedy that had occurred. Ms. Monica gasped as she covered her mouth in horror. Sienna's body lay contorted, with her eyes wide open. There was white residue and blood dried around her nose. The needle that had killed her was still protruding from her arm.

Ms. Monica knew that it wasn't a coincidence that the day after seeng Bleu Sienna had gone back to drugs. She would never know the true motive, but she was well aware that Bleu's addiction had pushed Sienna off the wagon. Ms. Monica noticed the envelope that was addressed to Bleu and grabbed it. She placed it in her purse before picking up the phone to call 911.

Knock. Knock.

Bleu heard the faint sound of someone knocking on the door, but she was so tired. She could barely even open her eyes. She was crashing from the high and it made her want to sleep endlessly. Everything just felt too hard. Even breathing took too much effort. She lay in Noah's plush bed as she struggled to open her eyes. She wouldn't mind the rest under normal circumstances, but this kind of sleep felt like misery. It was like she was spiraling in an endless black hole. The nightmares that haunted her were inescapable, because she didn't even have the energy to just wake herself up. So instead she lay there, stuck between life and death, writhing in her sleep as she went through the first twenty-four hours of withdrawal. The demons that dwelled beneath her closed lids were terrifying, and although her body was still, her heart raced as she battled internally for her soul. Bleu didn't know if she was hallucinating or if there were really angels and demons at war around the bed, but each time her eyes lazily drifted open she saw the shadows around her, battling. She could only get a glimpse of them before drifting back into the depths of sleep. The hours of the night passed her by, but she didn't wake when the sun arose. She was on God's time, and until one side came out victorious she wouldn't wake up. She tossed and turned, her eyes shed tears, and she whimpered in agony as her body sweated profusely, all the while she never awakened fully. It was the most terrifying thing she had every experienced. While the angels around her were beautiful—they had wings that were the most brilliant color of white she had ever seen—the demons were horrifying. Their faces contorted in darkness as their bodies flew over her like shadows in the night.

God, please give me another chance, she thought. Her mother's face appeared before her eyes. Sienna was crying; so was Bleu as she tried to reach out to her. Suddenly she was chasing after Sienna, running full speed, but Bleu could never catch her. The harder Bleu tried, the farther Sienna got from her. Bleu knew it wasn't real. She knew that she was dreaming, but the pain she felt in her heart was like nothing she had ever experienced before. She would rather go back to the nightmare about demons and angels than feel this. Suddenly everything went blank and her exhaustion pulled her into unconsciousness. She stopped fighting; she stopped battling, she stopped struggling. It was time to let God do some of the fighting for her, because this was a battle that she couldn't win without him.

"How do I tell her that?" Noah asked as he looked his mother in the eyes. "That news can't come from me."

"You're the only one it can come from, Son," Ms. Monica said.

"She's been asleep for three days," Noah said. "She's crying and screaming in her sleep. She's already got too much on her. This is gon' break her. I know it."

"Probably so, but sometimes you have to be broken all the way down before you can build yourself back up," Ms. Monica replied.

"What about the arrangements?" Noah asked. "Can you handle that part? I'll cover everything. Money isn't an issue. She didn't live the best life so give her the best death. If she ain't do nothing right, she did one thing that's worth something."

"What's that?" Ms. Monica asked.

"She gave birth to the best person I know," Noah said seriously.

Ms. Monica caressed her son's cheek and looked at him sympathetically. "She will get through this," she reassured him. "I've got to go get the funeral arrangements together, but if you need me you know how to reach me."

Noah kissed his mother's inner wrist. "Thanks, old lady."

She snatched her wrist and swatted him. "Old lady my ass."

He chuckled at her chagrin and walked her to the door and before she left she turned to him.

"And keep that girlfriend of yours away from Bleu. I know a jealous woman when I see her. She don't want to see Bleu prosper. She means her no good. It would be best if you kept them separated, especially while Bleu is so vulnerable," Ms. Monica advised.

"Naomi's loyal. She got a little jealous streak, but she rocking with who I'm rocking with. She just has to get to know B. They'll be all right," he replied.

Ms. Monica wanted to say more, but she refrained and walked out.

Noah went back to Bleu's room and walked inside as she lay there. He was surprised at how still she was. For days she had been fighting herself in a comatose-like state, but as he looked at her now she seemed at peace. He bent down and put his face to her nose to make sure she was still breathing, then sat in the chair in the corner of the room, waiting for her to wake up. Naomi called him, but he sent her to voice mail. Messiah called and he got the same result. No one was getting through to him because his entire focus was on Bleu. Nothing had ever bothered him this much. He waited hours until finally she began to stir.

He went to her bedside as she began to sit up. "I've got to throw—"

Noah hurriedly picked up the small garbage pail and held it up for her as she vomited.

"Oh-h!" she cried as she collapsed back onto the bed while gasping for air. "Take me to the bathroom, please," she moaned weakly.

Noah put down the pail and picked her up, hurrying into the bathroom and barely placing her on her feet before she erupted again. It came from everywhere. Out of her nose, her mouth. She couldn't even control her body as her bowels let go from the force of throwing up. She was pathetic. She was disgusting and embarrassment filled her as she mumbled, "I'm sorry," between her vomiting fits.

Noah had never seen anything like it. She had no control over her bodily functions as she sat in her own soils. The sight made him emotional and he had to bite into his bottom lip to stop himself from losing it. He was a grown man watching someone he loved battle addiction. He couldn't imagine how traumatic it had been for Bleu as a little girl to have to watch her parents go through this. *No wonder it fucked her up*, he thought.

He didn't give a damn about the mess. He stood over her, holding her hair back in a ponytail as she got the garbage out of her system.

"It's okay, B. Just get it out," he whispered as he rubbed her back with his free hand.

"I can't do this. I just need some more. It'll make all of this go away, Noah, please. I know you sell it. I know you can get me some!" she cried while gripping the porcelain seat.

"No, Bleu. Just fight it. You're going to have to fight it," he said as he watched her bury her face in the toilet again and again. They sat there, bathroom stinking, a mess everywhere, for hours until there was nothing left for Bleu to throw up. She was sweaty and spent by the time she started dry heaving. Noah picked her up, placed her in the tub, and bathed her again before cleaning his bathroom.

Bleu sat in the water, her eyes puffy from crying. She shivered slightly from the water that Noah poured on her hair as she held her head back.

"I'm weak," she whispered.

"Yeah, well, I'm strong, B, and I got you," he replied. She was so thin. To the average eye her weight would be no big deal, but he knew that she had had the hips and ass of a stallion, she wasn't naturally thin, but the drugs had made her drop to a model's size while a small bulge settled around her midsection. She looked unhealthy, and even worse, her eyes shone unhappiness. He just wanted to help her get better. Noah struggled with whether or not he wanted to inform her about Sienna, but he knew that it wasn't his place to keep something like that from Bleu.

"I've got to tell you something," Noah said.

She bent her knees and rested her head on top of them as she wrapped her arms around her legs. Her eyes pierced his as a look of inquisition told him to keep talking.

"Your mama—"

"I can't believe she came by here," Bleu said. "And she was clean. I don't even think I can remember a time that I've ever seen her clean."

"Yeah, that was three days ago, B. You've been knocked out since then. Something happened. . . ." Noah was struggling with his words and Bleu sat straight up. He wasn't one to get tongue-tied, so watching him choose his words carefully made her stomach clench in anticipation.

"What? What is it? Just say it," she urged. "She's using again? That's no surprise. So just spit it out. . . ."

"She overdosed, B. She's gone."

Bleu went deaf. No. Seriously. She lost all function of hearing as her eyes widened in horror. Suddenly she felt herself hitting Noah. Naked as a newborn baby she pounded his chest as he pulled her from the tub and held her as she cried. Bleu bawled like she never had before.

"Oh my God! Why!" she screamed as she clung to Noah as he carried her into the bedroom.

He set her down and rocked her gently until she had no more tears left. *I've really got to get her some clothes,* he thought as he pulled Naomi's things out of a drawer and dressed Bleu once more. She sat there, looking completely drained. "I don't even know why I'm so fucked up over this. It's not like she was even a good mother, but for some reason it just hurts."

"It don't matter if she was good or bad. If she was fucked up or Clair Huxtable, B. She was yours. She was your fuckup of a mother. To tell anyone that they can never see or hear from the person that brought them to this earth . . . that's painful. Don't try to dull that pain, though, Bleu. You got to feel the pain to know that you need to heal," he said as he bent down and placed socks on her feet.

"When did you get so smart?" she asked.

"When yo' ass started acting dumb!" he shot back with a smirk. She smiled weakly because she knew that although he was joking there was truth behind his words.

"She wrote you a letter," Noah said before reaching into his back pocket and holding the letter out for her.

Bleu was almost afraid to read it. She reached for it and then pulled her hand back as if it would burn her. "Can you read it to me?" she asked.

Noah sighed and sat down next to her on the bed, not feeling right about reading the last words of Sienna.

"Please," Bleu pushed.

Noah opened the paper. "'My beautiful Bleu . . .'"

Bleu closed her eyes as she soaked in her mother's last words. There was something comforting about Noah's voice being the method of delivery. *She wrote this like she knew she would die. She O.D.'d on purpose to teach me a lesson,* Bleu thought, and that revelation sent silent tears rolling down her face. She sniffed as Noah folded the letter and handed it to her. It was the deepest thing he had ever read.

"I guess she did love me," Bleu said, feeling overwhelmed. She wanted to smoke something so badly that it made her antsy and her leg began to bounce. "You're going to have to handcuff me back to the bed because right now I just want to run out of here and get high," she said aloud. "But then she would have died for nothing."

Bleu stood to her feet and when she did the room spun. "Noah, I don't feel so—" Bleu crashed to the floor, passing out as her world went dark.

When Bleu woke up, her head felt like it had been split in half. She thought she was dreaming. It was the same scenario that had happened two years ago when she had been shot before leaving for college. Noah sat at her bedside, with the same look of worry.

"Hm-m," she moaned. "What happened to me?"

"You were suffering from dehydration," Noah said. "It's a symptom of the withdrawal. They're running blood tests and everything now to make sure everything else is okay."

"Is she really gone?" Bleu asked. "Was I dreaming?"

"No, B, you weren't dreaming, but you've got to learn how to deal with reality. I swear to God, I will murk every nigga who even think about serving you, so you got to fight this shit," Noah whispered.

"It's going to be hard," she whispered, completely terrified of the days to come. She already felt defeated.

"Everything that's worth something always is," he replied. "You're fighting for your life."

Noah reached over and grabbed her hand. "It's a lot on you right now, Bleu, and I'm here. Whatever you need. Twenty-four-seven."

A doctor entered the room wearing a white lab coat. "Ms. Montclair, glad to see you're awake," the woman said as she pulled up a rolling stool and took a seat. She pulled out her stethoscope and checked Bleu's vitals. "How are you feeling?"

"A little queasy, weak . . ."

"You have a nasty disease. We found traces of crack cocaine and heroin in your system, but I don't have to tell you that," the doctor said. "I want to show you something."

The doctor pulled out a monitor and then looked at Noah. "I have to examine her. You may want to wait in the hall."

"No. He can stay," Bleu said quickly, reaching out for his hand. She didn't know what the doctor was about to tell her but she was terrified. Had the white girl used a dirty needle? Did Bleu have HIV? Or hepatitis? Had she fucked herself up with the constant crack use? She didn't know what was about to come out of the doctor's mouth and gasped as the woman squirted a cool jelly on Bleu's abdomen. The doctor then placed a handheld machine on Bleu's skin and pressed down, moving it around.

"You see that image right there on the screen?" the doctor asked.

Bleu gasped.

"That's your baby. You are pregnant. About twelve weeks,

I would say," the doctor informed her. "That needs to be what you think about the next time you have the urge to use drugs. Your baby is taking in everything that you put into your body. There is no telling the damage that has already been done. You have to have a flawless pregnancy from this day forward, and even then you have to pray that your drug use didn't cause any birth defects," the doctor said.

Bleu couldn't tear her eyes from the screen as she looked in disbelief. She sniffed back her emotions as she looked toward Noah. "What have I done?" she asked.

The news had placed a weight on his heart that he couldn't hide. Noah was speechless. "It's not about what you did in the past. It's about what you gon' do now, B. I got you," he promised.

"Are you the father?" the doctor asked as she cleaned the gel off of Bleu's belly.

Oh my God, Iman, Bleu thought. She didn't know how she had gotten here. *Or is it Cinco's?* That thought was even scarier and Bleu immediately felt like she would lose it. Both of them had been inside her without protection and Bleu had no idea which one had fathered her child. She did the math inside her head. *Twelve weeks ago it could have only been Iman.* She remembered the night that Cinco had refused to pull out of her, and that was more recent. *Or was it?* She didn't know. The endless nights of getting high had all run into one another. She hadn't been in her right mind. She couldn't tell if it was night or day, let alone who she had let cum in her three months ago.

"No, I'm a friend," he replied. "Can you give us a minute?" Noah asked.

The doctor printed the ultrasound picture. "Sure. I'll let you have some privacy. The nurse will bring some rehab pamphlets in for you in a little bit." She handed Bleu the picture. "Here is your motivation."

The doctor left the room and Bleu looked at Noah. She was completely lost.

"Is that nigga out in L.A. the father?" Noah asked.

Bleu just nodded her head, not wanting to explain to Noah all of the unthinkable acts that she had done. "You want to go back to him?" he asked.

Bleu would love to be with Iman, but to tell him that she had endangered their unborn child or, worse, to find out that the child was in fact Cinco's would destroy him. It was in that moment that she decided to raise this baby on her own. She shook her head no.

"Then you'll stay with me. I'll help you out," Noah said.

"You have a girlfriend and a life and—"

"It's nothing to talk about, Bleu. The only deal breaker is the drugs. You can't use, B. I can't watch you become Sienna. As long as you're clean and you're doing the right thing for this baby, we're good. I'll take care of you and I'll take care of this baby like it's my own," he promised.

"How did I get so lucky to have a friend like you?" she asked rhetorically.

Noah kissed her forehead and stood to his feet. "I've got to go make this right with Naomi. I'm trusting you to be here when I get back," he said.

"I'm not going anywhere," she promised, this time really meaning it.

He turned to leave.

"Noah?"

He stopped.

"My mom?" she said. "I'll never be like her. I'm going to get clean. For her, for this baby, for you . . ."

"For you, B. Do it for you," Noah said before walking off.

Bleu leaned back against the pillows of the hospital bed and looked up at the sky. "Help me, God." All she could do was pray.

Noah walked into his old apartment and saw Naomi sitting in her panties and bra counting up the money from his latest drop. She was sexy, confident, and strong as she nodded her head to the J. Cole album that played softly in the background.

"Yo' put that up for a minute. Let me talk to you," he said, causing her to jump. He smirked. "You ain't even on point, baby. I could have been a nigga coming to rob you."

Naomi stood and walked into his arms. "Shut up. Give me a kiss," she whispered as she greeted him sensually, jumping up on him, forcing him to catch her by placing his hands under her ass.

"Wait a minute," he said seriously as he lifted her off him. "I need to talk to you about something. It's important."

Naomi frowned and motioned for him to sit down as she grabbed her short silk kimono robe off the back of the chair. She slid her arms into the soft fabric, then had a seat next to him.

"What's up?" she asked.

"I know Bleu showing up is awkward for you, but she's

going to be around. She'll be staying with us for a minute," he said.

"Excuse me?" Naomi asked.

"She's pregnant and she's strung out. There isn't anything you have to worry about. I just need you to ride this out with me. When she's on her feet she'll get her own spot. It's only temporary," Noah said. "Can you handle that?"

Naomi was seeing red. She wanted to tell Noah to choose, but she had seen the bond between Bleu and Noah. Naomi was afraid she would lose if she left it up to him. "Yeah, okay. You should help your friend."

Noah pulled her on top of him and kissed her deeply. There was no way Naomi was just going to let Bleu come to town and take her spot. She didn't care if they were friends or not; the only woman Naomi was playing second to was Noah's mama. This affection that Noah had for Bleu was more than irritating Naomi. It was too intimate. As Naomi untied her robe she thought to herself, *I'm going to get rid of this bitch one way or another.*

20

"I can't do this. I can't . . . it's too hard," Bleu whispered as she gripped the sink in the guest room of Noah's home. Her doctor had warned her about this feeling, about the pain and the inevitable depression that would hit her in the days following her release. Her body was going through detox, and because she was pregnant they couldn't give her medicine to help with the extreme changes her body was going through. Bleu had been using for so long that she had changed the dopamine levels in her brain. Dopamine helped manage pain, emotional and physical. It was what made an orgasm feel so good and what made a splinter in a finger feel like no big deal. Without it in her system everything was magnified. From emotional wounds to physical bumps and bruises, Bleu felt it all. She had to purge her system of its impurities, and doing it cold turkey was proving to be unbearable.

"Yes, you can, Bleu," Noah said as he came up behind her

and placed his hands on her shoulders. She cringed at his touch; even her skin hurt.

"Stop saying that! You don't know! You have no idea what I'm going through!" Bleu shouted. She was taking her frustration out on him, but he wasn't taking it personally. He knew life had beaten her up. She was facing an uphill climb and getting to a place of healing wouldn't be easy. He reached around her body and placed a hand on her stomach. "Just think about why you're doing this, B. It's important. Remember how you felt when Sienna used to run the streets instead of taking care of you? How you used to feel being the daughter of two crackheads?"

Bleu looked at him through the reflection in the mirror. He could see by the look in her eyes that she remembered it vividly. Pain resonated within her.

"Remember that feeling. You don't want this baby to feel like that," Noah said.

Naomi came into the room with a plate of food and halted uncomfortably, as if she had walked in on an intimate moment between lovers.

Her face fell. She scoffed as she rolled her eyes, set down the plate, and walked out. Her anger was apparent and Noah removed his hand.

"You better go deal with that," Bleu said. "I'm sorry. I'm not trying to complicate things between y'all. Maybe I should just go to a rehab center."

"You're not complicating anything and you ain't going nowhere. I don't want you worrying about anything except getting better," he said. "It'll get better. Y'all just have to get to know one another, because nobody is going anywhere. You're here and she's here and I'm here. We just got to make it work." He nodded toward the plate of food. "She ain't ever even cooked for me. She's jealous, but she is trying. Just give it time. Eat and get dressed. You've got to say good-bye to Sienna today."

Bleu nodded as she watched him walk out of the room. She walked over to the plate and picked it up. "Bitch probably spat in it," Bleu said before throwing it in the trash.

It didn't matter if Naomi tried or not; in truth it didn't even matter what Noah did to Bleu right now. Everyone pissed her off. She was mad at the world. Everything irritated her. The world around her seemed dismal. She felt like she was drowning in front of everyone and no one could swim well enough to save her. She didn't know how she would survive the day. All eyes would be on her as she put her mother in the ground, and she didn't want to be in the spotlight. Not like this. Not when she was most vulnerable. Bleu had lost control of her life. She was terrified that she would end up just like her mother. With a kid who hated her because she loved dope more than she loved her own seed. It was so much easier to just stay in the clouds than to face the consequences of reality.

She turned and looked at the black dress Noah had purchased for her.

It was a pretty way to cover up the ugly person she had become.

She snatched the dress off the rack and rushed into the en suite bathroom to try to clean herself up as best she could. She didn't want to be the focus of today. She wanted to blend in with everyone else who attended and let Sienna be laid to rest without making a mockery out of her memory.

If the goal was to blend in, Bleu failed miserably. As she stepped out of the bedroom, she glowed. She may have been going through her own personal hell, but with her face made up to perfection, the Fendi dress, six-inch heels adorning her feet, and her hair pulled back into a sleek chignon, she looked like she had stepped straight out of heaven. She was thin but still beautiful, and seeing her took Noah's breath away. Bleu didn't look like what she had been through. God had kept her through it all. Naomi felt like someone had punched her in the gut when she saw the awestruck look on Noah's face.

"I'm not ready for this, but I guess I have to be," Bleu said, just above a whisper.

"Let's go bury your mother, B," Noah said.

The three of them were silent on the way to the church. Bleu didn't feel comfortable speaking about her feelings in front of Naomi, so she opted to say nothing at all. Instead she looked out the window as the city passed her by. When they passed the apartments where Noah had found her, she tensed. Bleu closed her eyes as the stress of the world rested on her shoulders. It was that same stress that made her want to get high because she knew that it could all just go away with one little puff.

She bit her inner cheek, drawing blood as she listened to the sound of her heart beating. She was in the middle of her detox period. *It only takes ten days to flush the immediate drugs out of your system,* the doctor had said. *After that your body will begin to feel normal; it's your mind that will make it hard for you to stay detoxified after that.* The doctor had warned her. Bleu had to get her mind right. Once she trained her brain to function independently of the faux happiness that crack gave her, she would be able to find true joy without the aid of any stimulant. She couldn't wait for the day.

When she, Naomi, and Noah arrived at the church Bleu couldn't bring herself to get out. Her angry stomach twisted violently and she didn't know if it was a part of the process or if it was her nerves. She took a deep breath as Noah held open the back door for her.

"I need a bathroom. I feel like I'm going to throw up," she told him. She rushed inside the church.

"I'll check on her," Naomi said. "You get seated. I'll get Bleu together and we'll find you in the front."

Noah looked at her in shock, and as she walked away he grabbed her hand, spinning her back toward him. He kissed her lips, giving her a quick peck. "Thank you."

"Anything for you," she said with a wink before turning on her heels and going after Bleu.

When Naomi entered the bathroom she could hear Bleu inside one of the stalls. Naomi frowned as the smell of vomit filled the small room. "You good in there?" Naomi called out.

The toilet flushed and Bleu cleared her throat before coming out. The last funeral she had been to had been her father's, and she knew from the hole in her heart that this one would be no easier. It had been a week to the day since Sienna had killed herself and Bleu was six days into a lifetime sentence of recovery. They had been the most excruciating six days of her life.

Bleu bypassed Naomi and bent over the sink to rinse her mouth.

"Here," Naomi said, handing her a stick of gum. "You fucked up your beat," Naomi added, referring to Bleu's makeup job. She pulled a compact out of her Chanel bag. "Here, let me fix you up. That woman popped you out her pussy. You can't come to her funeral looking crazy. Let's get you all the way together before you step out there. Better adjust your crown, girl." Bleu stood still as Naomi grabbed a paper towel and wiped the tears from Bleu's face before fixing her running mascara and smudged foundation. "You know, I'm really sorry about your mom," Naomi said. "I can't even act like I know what you're going through. Then with the withdrawal and everything I know it's tough." Bleu fanned herself, feeling abnormally hot as Naomi continued. "I mean look at you. Your body is all fucked up. You can't even control your temperature. You're sweating like you ran a marathon." Naomi put the compact in her purse and then reached inside and pulled out a vial of cocaine. "Look. I know you need a little pick-me-up. Just for today to make it through this funeral. It's not like it's crack or H. It's just a little powder for you to balance you out. It'll be our little secret. It'll make you feel so much better. Handle your business and Noah and I will meet you up front."

She placed the vial in Bleu's hands and gave her a tight-lipped smile before walking out. Naomi knew that once Noah discovered Bleu was getting high again she would be out on her ass. Naomi was tired of babysitting and watching Noah give all of his attention to Bleu. If Naomi had to sabotage Bleu's recovery in order to get rid of her, then so be it.

Bleu's hands shook as she rushed to lock the bathroom door behind Naomi. She sighed in relief as she looked at herself in the mirror, knowing that this was exactly what she needed. *It's just a little coke,* she thought. Bleu had forgotten that it was that same logic that had gotten her started on this horrific journey in the first place and she was about to succumb to the same thing that had led to Sienna's demise.

21

"You all right? You was in there for a while," Noah whispered as Bleu took her seat between him and Ms. Monica. Bleu met eyes with Naomi, who sat on Noah's other side.

Bleu nodded as she sniffed and blinked away her tears. "Will you go up there with me?" she asked.

Noah stood and placed a hand on the small of her back as he led her up to Sienna's coffin. He had spared no expense. "She looks so pretty," Bleu said. "I've never seen her look so peaceful."

Bleu turned and looked at the handful of people who had shown up. The church was practically empty. Sienna had lived for fifty-one years and of all the people she had met only ten had bothered to come tell her good-bye. Bleu didn't want to be like that. She didn't want to die addicted and lonely, with a troubled soul. Bleu was terrified to leave behind a resentful, scarred child. Bleu wanted more and it wasn't until she saw her mother lying in this casket did she truly realize that this life wasn't for her. She had thought she would cry. She had thought that this day would be unbearably painful, but it wasn't. It was freeing. She had finally received the message that Sienna had meant to deliver. Her death would not be in vain. Bleu would use her mother as the motivation she needed to get clean. Sienna had set the example not to follow. Bleu leaned over Sienna's body and kissed her cheek; one tear fell onto her face. "Rest well, Ma. I forgive you. Thank you," she whispered in her ear.

Bleu turned to Noah. "I don't want to sit through this entire thing. I need to get out of here," she said. She hugged him tightly and slipped her hand into his inner jacket pocket. "Tell your girl thanks, but no thanks. I'm getting clean, Noah. I have to," she replied.

Bleu walked down the long aisle of the church and Noah frowned in confusion as he reached into his jacket to see what Bleu had placed there. When he pulled out the vial of cocaine fury took over him.

He was on Naomi's ass before he could even stop himself. He grabbed her up by the arm and snatched her down the aisle of the church.

"What the fuck is wrong with you? Let me go!" Naomi shouted as she snatched her arm away.

"You gave her this? You put this in her hands knowing what she's struggling with? You that jealous?" Noah asked. Anger blazed in his voice, scorching her with every word that he spoke. He jabbed a stern finger in her face as he checked her. He had to calm himself to stop him from flying all the way off the handle with her. He had never laid a finger on a woman in his life, but Naomi was pushing him. He knew at that moment that he couldn't be with her. This was a malicious side to her that he had not even met yet. Giving Bleu drugs was like giving a suicidal child a loaded gun. Naomi had tried to kill her.

"I don't know what you're talking about. Whatever that bitch told you—"

Noah flung her off of him before she could finish her sentence, sending her flying to the floor in embarrassment. Ms. Monica came racing down the aisle. "Noah, go after Bleu," Ms. Monica said as she bent down to help Naomi up.

"This shit is a wrap," Noah said to Naomi. "Being loyal to me means being loyal to the people I fuck with. She's my friend—"

"Friend?" Naomi scoffed as tears flooded her eyes and she dusted herself off. The entire church was watching the dramatic scene unfold and Noah wasn't feeling the theatrics. He walked out, but Naomi was on his tail. He had started the argument, so she was ready to see it through. "Nigga, who you fronting for? I got eyes. I can see the shit that's going on between you two. You got me fetching soup and you putting this bitch in my clothes while you praising the ground that her crackhead ass walks on!" Naomi shot back. "I ain't got no friends that I treat better than my nigga."

"You ain't got a nigga no more. No, you ain't got to be worried or jealous at all," he said, walking toward his truck.

Ms. Monica grabbed Naomi. "Let him go. When a man wants to leave, you let him," she said as Naomi folded like laundry in her arms.

Noah sped out of the parking lot and turned onto the street, looking for Bleu. He spotted her about a block away and pulled up on her recklessly. "Get in, B," he said.

Bleu followed his command without hesitation and he skirted off, leaving burnt rubber on the pavement as they rode out back to his home.

They didn't speak. They didn't need to. The fact that he had come after her without Naomi said enough. He reached over and grabbed Bleu's hand and she intertwined her fingers with his. There wasn't a person in the world who could make Noah let her go. She belonged to him, and as his heart pumped furiously as a reaction to their connection he began to realize that she meant more to him than what he would like to admit.

When they pulled up to the house Bleu pulled back her hand and they sat awkwardly for a moment. "I'm sorry she did that to you. I'm sorry I even had somebody around you that had malice toward you," he said.

"It's okay," she said. "You just fell in love with a crazy bitch." She smiled.

"Is she really that crazy, B?" he asked seriously. "Shit between us has always been complicated, and there's been so much going on since you got back. I know you're dealing with this baby news and trying to stay clean. I'm trying to be here for all of that. Every day—"

"You have been, Noah. You've done more than enough," Bleu interrupted him.

"With you, Bleu. I want to be with you and I'm tired of

playing the back, waiting for the right time. I fuck with you, Bleu. The long way, and it ain't poetic. I ain't no fancy nigga selling you la-la land dreams, but I do love you," he said.

"You don't want me. You don't love me. Like this," she said, her eyes tearing. After all Bleu had done she didn't think she was worthy of love.

"I love you at your worst and I want to love you back to your best," Noah admitted.

"No," she said as she opened her door and ran toward the front door.

"Bleu!" Noah called after her as he climbed out, following her.

"Just open the door, Noah," she pleaded.

"Why are you crying?" he asked, pinning her against the door as he looked down at her. She was so fragile, so insecure, and so broken. She had no idea how she looked through his eyes. If she did, she would love herself more.

"Your expectations are too high for me, Noah! I'm not perfect Bleu anymore. I ain't shit. I'm a girl who likes to get high. I'm a girl who isn't even excited about her own baby. I hate this baby because I can't smoke while it's inside of me. I hate the way you look at me . . . like I'm this prize . . . this dream girl. I'm nothing. I'm nobody and I'm never going to be anything more than what you see now."

"Stop crying," Noah said as he wiped her tears.

"I wanted to sniff that coke today, Noah!" she shouted. "When Naomi gave me the drugs, I was this close to stuffing it up my nose," she said, pinching her fingers together in front of his face. "I wanted it more than anything I've ever wanted in my life. So don't profess your love for me! Don't stop fucking with Naomi for me, don't change everything in your life for me, because I'm going to disappoint you. You don't know shit about loving somebody like me. I do. I loved my mother and she let me down every time!" Bleu was shouting, trying to get Noah to understand that she wasn't worth loving. "I have a baby inside me and I almost did a line of coke today," she said in a defeated whisper as if she couldn't believe it. "I'm so fucked up. I don't even know how to go back. It's like I might as well keep fucking up because it's too late to be anything better."

Noah squeezed his nose, struggling with seeing her this way. He looked to the side for a moment, gathering himself before he focused back on her. He grabbed her chin and forced her to stare directly into his eyes. "You almost sniffed that shit today, but you didn't. A week ago you would have done it without thinking twice. That's called growth, B. You have to acknowledge the small things you're doing right. It's not just about the end goal; it's about making the right decision every day, every step of the way, every minute, until you don't even think about putting another drug in your body. You're making progress and that's all you can do. I love you and I'm not going nowhere and you're not going nowhere. Not this time. We did that already. We let life take us away from each other. We staying here this time, with each other, no matter how hard it gets," he said. He kissed her and she melted into him. "You'll be okay. I'm going to make sure of it," he said. It was a promise that he would die before breaking.

• • •

Noah sat in his luxury basement, in front of a pile of money. The different denominations were stacked up so high that they were taller than him when he stood. He had sat there for hours, running the bills through a money machine, counting and recounting until he had come up with the total of $800,000. He wasn't rich, but he wasn't hurting either, especially considering the fact that his house was paid off; that money could last for a long time if he invested it wisely. The doorbell rang and he quickly covered the cash before heading upstairs. Bleu was sleeping. He didn't want to wake her. The past few days had been rough, but she was finally out of the detox stage. It was the first night she had rested without tossing and turning. He snatched open the door.

"Nigga, I told you to call when you pulled up," Noah said as he greeted Messiah.

"My fault, fam. You called me over here in the middle of the night. I was half-sleep when you called," Messiah said. "What was so urgent that it couldn't wait until morning?"

"I'm out," Noah said.

"You out of what? Bread? Sugar? Milk? My nigga? Cuz I know you're not saying what I think you're saying," Messiah said.

"I'm out of the game, man," Noah clarified as he rubbed the top of his head in stress.

"This got anything to do with that girl?" Messiah asked. "We just got started. You got the plug. It's so much money out here to make, bruh. We on our way to being legends, my g. You sure you want to give all this up?"

"I'll plug you and you can have everything we still got on the streets. I ain't trying to leave you dry. It just ain't for me," Noah said.

"Nigga, you took to this shit like a duck to water. What you mean, it ain't for you?" Messiah asked in disbelief. "This green money ain't for you?"

"This shit got a foot on my girl's neck, G. I can't ask her to give this shit up if I'm still out here knee-deep in it. The money is good. It runs through my hands like water, but the way I'm getting it . . ." He paused as he thought of Bleu. "It got to be a better way."

"I dig it, fam. That's one hunnid for real. You love your old lady. This her weakness, then you got to be her strength. That's what a real man do," Messiah said as he slapped hands with Noah.

"No doubt," Noah replied.

"But you know Naomi around town talking reckless. She knows a lot," Messiah said.

"Let birds chirp, my nigga. It's half my fault anyway. I should have cut shit off sooner than I did. She'll get over it when she meet the next made nigga to get under," Noah assured.

Bleu cleared her throat as she entered the room and Messiah stood.

"I'll hit you tomorrow," Messiah said. He nodded to Bleu. "What up, shorty doo-wop?" he said. "You getting your weight up. You look good. You never belonged out there anyway."

She smiled bashfully and looked at her feet as the men concluded their business.

When Messiah was gone, Noah turned to Bleu. "Come here," he said. She walked over to him and he pulled her into his arms. "I want to show you something."

He led her to the basement, and when Bleu saw the pile of money on the table she gasped.

"I trust you. That's why I'm showing you this. The combination to my safe is eleven, oh-eight, oh-seven, eighty-five. I just told Messiah I'm out of the game. I can't support you if I'm still selling dope, Bleu. So I'm done. For you, I'm done," Noah said.

Bleu rushed into his arms and held him so tightly that it felt like their heartbeats had synced.

"We still gon' take over the world, B. We just have to find our way. That's all," he said.

She looked up at him and suddenly just wanted to kiss him. Bleu wanted to feel him. She wanted to be with him. She couldn't use dope, but she didn't mind him being her drug.

He wanted her just as much as she wanted him. She could feel his strength pressing into her, so when he pulled back she frowned in confusion.

Lust filled the air, but embarrassment filled her as she said, "You don't want me?"

"I want you, but you're growing life inside your right now, B. Another man's seed," Noah said. She lowered her head. "Let's just wait until the time is right. When this baby comes,

I'll love it like it's mine. I don't feel no type of way about providing for you or about raising a baby with you. But doing this when your body is vulnerable and your mind is vulnerable doesn't feel right."

She nodded and walked upstairs, wondering how many more awkward moments they would have before everything just felt normal between them.

22

I ain't been right since you left L.A. I miss you.

—Iman

Bleu drew in a sharp breath as she stopped walking midstep. She hadn't heard from him in five months, and now out of the blue here he was, sending text messages of endearment to her. She was just starting to get her life back on track. She had been clean for six months. They had been the hardest days of her life, but she had fought for every one. It was like the world drew Iman to her. As soon as she had started to move on with her life with Noah, Iman shot her a text out of the blue. For so many nights she had thought of him, missed him, and wondered if she should save her love for him instead of going forward with Noah 100 percent. Reading Iman's words brought out so many emotions in her. It took her back to the intensity that he made her feel and brought confusion into her heart. She was pissed that this was the first time he had reached out since she left. Still she was excited that he was thinking about her at all. Even after his being absent from her life, she still got butterflies in her stomach at the thought of him. He had left an imprint on her life that was hard to erase. She knew that eventually she would have to call him. He deserved to know about the baby growing in her stomach. Noah had assured her that he would be there, but he still hadn't touched her in a sexual way. It was like Iman's baby stopped her from being loved fully by Noah. At least that's what it felt like. She couldn't help but think that Noah would get fed up one day and leave her. No man wanted to take care of a kid who didn't belong to him. Although Noah never gave her reason to doubt him, she felt like a burden . . . like a girl with too much baggage.

As she tucked her phone into her handbag she sighed. It was insecurities like these that made her want to go back to her old ways. Whenever her emotions began to overwhelm her it made her want to use drugs. She couldn't handle stress. She had relied on different substances to dull her pain for so long that she had to remember how to work through it without clouding her mind. She had to be very aware of the type of energy she invited into her life. The wrong person could send her spiraling back out of control, and Bleu couldn't afford that. She took a deep breath and thought, *Just focus on today. One thing at a time. One goal at a time. One day at a time.*

Bleu put Iman in the back of her mind and walked into the glass building in front of her.

"Welcome to Mott Community College. How can I help you?" the woman at the front desk asked.

It was a far cry from UCLA, but it was a step in the right direction. Bleu needed to find herself, and although she was stable now, she wouldn't truly go back to feeling like her old self until she was back in school.

"I'm here to enroll," Bleu said.

"Okay, you need to fill these out and then I'll send you upstairs for your placement tests and to see a counselor," the woman said.

Bleu exhaled deeply, blowing out the nerves that filled her. She filled out the application and then took the elevator to the second floor to take her test. She didn't realize how much she had missed something as normal as school until she was filling in the little bubbles, marking her answers on the scan sheet. This was her element. This was where she thrived when she was in her right mind.

By the time she walked out of the college, she had tested out of all the introductory classes and had been able to enroll in second-year courses. Bleu felt like a million bucks as she walked out of the building. But then she felt a sharp jab in her stomach. She paused, then smiled as she realized it was the flutters from her baby's first kicks. Bleu gasped in shock as it happened again. A smile spread across her face as she placed her hands on her growing belly. Her phone rang in her hand, interrupting the moment. *Iman,* she thought. He knew that if he was persistent enough she would answer. She had never been able to resist him for too long. She pressed the green button to answer his call, but before she could get the phone to her mouth she was hit with another feeling in her belly. This time it was stabbing and brought her to her knees as she dropped everything in her hands.

She took a deep breath, hoping that it was just body aches. She was out of the withdrawal stage, so it couldn't be from that. *Maybe the baby just kicked me in the wrong place,* she thought. Then she felt it again.

"Agh!" she called out.

A student coming up the steps rushed to her side. "Oh my God. You're pregnant. Are you okay? Are you in labor?" the girl asked.

"Please, call nine-one-one. I hope not. I can't have this baby right now. I'm only twenty-four weeks," Bleu gasped through gritted teeth. It felt like her insides were in a vise grip.

The girl grabbed Bleu's phone. "Hello? Hello?" the girl said when she realized there was someone on the line. "This girl is about to have her baby. I don't know what to do!"

"Baby? She's pregnant?" Iman whispered in disbelief. "Hang up and call nine-one-one. Tell her I'm on my way," he said.

"She's losing a lot of blood. We have to get her into the operating room! Stat!" Bleu was in and out of consciousness. Lying flat on her back as the doctors and nurses around her rushed her gurney through the halls of the hospital.

She kept trying to open her eyes, but she was so tired and her lids were so heavy. The fluorescent lights above her were bright and the faces around her fuzzy as she tried to focus on someone, anyone.

"Her blood pressure's dropping. We're losing her!"

Bleu could hear the panic in their voices. *Am I dying?* she thought. This couldn't be death. It felt too good, too comforting, too peaceful. Bleu wasn't afraid. In fact, she had never been calmer in her life. It was like she knew that if she just closed her eyes all her troubles would go away; that bright light would draw her in, and everything would be fine.

It wasn't until she heard Noah's voice did she begin to fight.

"What happened to her? Is she going to be okay?"

"Are you the father?" the doctor asked.

There was a pause and then Bleu heard Noah answer, "Yes."

She heard something that she had never heard from him before. Fear. It was like it was contagious, because suddenly she didn't want to follow the bright light. She was terrified of leaving him, of being without him and he without her.

She wanted to live. She wanted her baby to live. Bleu was finally getting her act together only to have life knock her down again. She could never understand why her journey on this earth was so hard.

The doctor polled Noah aside. "I have to ask you this. If it comes down to saving her or saving the baby . . . who do you want us to focus on?" the doctor asked.

This time there was no pause. "You save her. Whatever it takes," Noah said.

"Okay. One of the nurses will take you to sterilize so that you can come inside. We're about to perform an emergency C-section," the doctor informed Noah.

Bleu was wheeled into a sterile room. It was so cold inside that she shivered, and when they put an oxygen mask over her face it felt like she was suffocating. She was scared.

"Bleu. We need you to relax. Just breathe in and out," one of the nurses said.

"I can't. I can't breathe," Bleu said as she weakly reached up and pulled off the mask.

"You can; you can do it. You're just hyperventilating. We've given you something to calm your nerves and we've numbed you from the waist down," the nurse said. The doors opened and Noah walked in. The nurse waved him over. "Your boyfriend is here now. Just focus on him."

"Hey, B," Noah said, clenching his teeth as he tried to remain strong for her.

"I'm scared," Bleu admitted.

"Shit, me too," he said with a chuckle. "Everything is going to be okay. You've done the hard part. You did the work to be a better person, Bleu. Now you just lay back and think about how you want to decorate the nursery."

Tears rolled out of the corners of her eyes and slid down into the creases of her neck. "I don't even know what I'm having," she said. Bleu had been so afraid to find out. She didn't want to become too attached just in case she decided she wanted to give in to temptation one day and smoke. She figured if she didn't know, if she didn't choose a name, or know the sex, or purchase tiny clothes, then she wouldn't feel guilt. She had never slipped up, though, so she had deprived herself for nothing. Bleu had held strong from the day she found out she would be a mother.

"We're about to find out," he said. He placed the oxygen mask over her face. "Just breathe. Breathe, B." Noah got choked up and he sobbed a bit, having to turn his head away from her to check himself. He focused back on her, clearing his throat as she brought her hand to his face. He grasped it and kissed the back of her wrist.

"We're almost there," the doctor announced. "We are cutting into the uterus now."

Bleu felt so much pressure. It was like she was a car with an open hood and the doctors were the mechanics who were taking parts out and moving things around.

"And he's out. Congratulations. It's a boy," the doctor announced.

Bleu waited to hear the cries. "Why isn't he crying? Is he okay?"

Noah stood to his feet, and when he walked over to the area where they had carried the baby he froze. It was the most heartbreaking thing he had ever seen. The baby was so little. At only two pounds he was fighting for his life.

"Take care of the mother. We're going to take the baby and work on him. He was born too early. His heart is on the outside of his body. We have to get him to Cardiology immediately," the doctor said as an entire team rushed in and took the baby away.

Noah knew that he had to be strong, but his eyes had witnessed firsthand what the drugs he used to peddle had done. The damage that they had caused. It was something that every young, black boy coming up in the hood should see. If Noah had known, he would have never had a part to play in the destruction of his own people. He gritted his teeth to stop his emotional levees from breaking.

"She needs you. She's crashing!" the doctor called out.

Noah rushed to Bleu's side and watched in horror as her eyes closed and she gave in to the fatigue.

Bleu awoke and every part of her body hurt, but the first thing to come out of her mouth was, "Where's my baby?"

It was an instinct that only developed after a woman had taken her rite of passage into motherhood. The ability to care for another before you cared for yourself was something that couldn't be taught. It was a gift and Bleu had earned the right to open it.

Noah sat at her side. It seemed to be where he belonged, because every time she needed him it was where he was. "He's in surgery, Bleu. He was born really early. They're doing everything they can," Noah said, not wanting to be the one to inform her about the baby's heart condition.

"Oh God," she said as she leaned her head on the pillow and shook it from side to side.

"Noah, I did this. My baby is struggling because of me. I would have been able to carry him longer if it weren't for the drugs," she whispered. She was ashamed of herself. She had been so stupid and so selfish.

"You don't know that. Only God knows that. Let's just hope everything will be okay," Noah said.

A knock at the door interrupted them, and when it opened Bleu's heart dropped.

Iman was there, standing in front of her with pure agony

reflecting in his eyes. The scent of his Burberry cologne reached her before he did.

"Hey, ma," he said as he walked to the vacant side of her bed and leaned down to kiss her on the forehead.

Bleu was speechless. Iman had such a grand presence. He was omnipresent, filling up her mind, her heart, her body. He was the controller of her emotions as if he had a battery-operated handheld that allowed him to turn her on and off whenever he wanted. Bleu was completely wrapped up in him whenever he was around. Just the feel of his skin on hers as he caressed her made her quiver.

"What are you . . ."

She couldn't find her words as her heart beat erratically in her chest. She had to close her eyes and focus on her breathing just to gather herself.

"What are you doing here?" Bleu finally asked, her cheeks turning a slight shade of crimson as if someone had turned up the heat in the room.

"I heard my girl was in trouble. Can't have that," he said. "You were pregnant and you didn't call me, ma," he said, the tone of his voice letting her know that the news injured him. "Is this my baby, Bleu?" Iman asked, wrinkles of concern creasing his forehead as his eyes burned into hers.

"You don't owe this nigga no explanations, B," Noah said, becoming territorial.

"Yo, homie, don't with that rah-rah shit. You don't want it," Iman said, turning g real quick. He had a soft spot for Bleu, but he handled the rest of the world with an iron fist.

"Nigga, what?" Noah asked. "Look here, Hollywood. You

ain't in L.A. This my city and I'll send you back west in a pine box. You coming in here like you been here? Where were you when she was overdosing in the trap? You was ghost, so get ghost now before I turn you into one."

Bleu was conflicted as she looked at the men she loved, arguing over her, beating their chests over her. They stood each thinking they were protecting her from the other. How could she choose between two perfect specimens of men? They both had a part of her heart. She was in love with two men. They were more alike than they knew and in the streets they could have unified, but their shared love of one woman divided them. She was their Helen of Troy. To be loved by them was a luxury. Bleu's heart broke because she knew she would have to set one of them free.

Bleu looked to Noah, feeling conflicted. "I'm so sorry. Can you give us a minute to talk?"

"Yeah, nigga, take a walk," Iman said.

Bleu reached for Noah's hand and squeezed it reassuringly. "Please," she added.

Noah smirked as he shook his head in disbelief and stood to his feet. "Yeah, B. Whatever you want," he said sarcastically as he walked out, his temperament toward her suddenly turning ice-cold.

"You can't just show up here," Bleu whispered when she and Iman were alone. "You have no idea what I've been through."

"I know, ma, and I'm sorry," Iman said as he caressed her face with his thumb while wrapping the rest of his hand around the back of her neck. He pulled her face toward his and kissed her lips. She wanted to resist and she pulled back, but he pulled her back in as he kissed her eyes, her lips, her cheeks, the tip of her nose. "I missed you so fucking much, Bleu. Like crazy. I've been out of my mind without you, ma."

Bleu hated how weak she was for Iman. It was like he could do anything to her and she would just forget about it as soon as he opened his mouth to say, *I love you.* She was stupid in love with him. Her love for him defied logic and it was like a magnet, sucking her in and leaving no room for the power of resistance.

The doctor came into the room and Bleu looked at her, trying to gauge the expression on her face. "Where is he?"

"It's a boy?" Iman asked. Bleu gripped his hand so tightly that her own knuckles turned white as she waited for the news.

"Your son made it out of surgery. He is in the neonatal intensive-care unit. You can't touch him, but you can see him if you would like," the doctor said. "I don't want to mislead you. He isn't out of the woods. He was born very early. We have a lot of hard days ahead. He only has a fifty percent chance, but there is a chance," the doctor informed them. "And as long as he has that, we will do everything we can to get him healthy enough for you to take home."

"Can I see him?" she asked.

The doctor nodded and brought in a wheelchair. The nurses helped Bleu from the bed to the chair and Iman pushed her out of the room.

She had never been more nervous in all her life. She was about to meet a little person who belonged to her. The nurses covered her in a protective paper gown.

"Can I go in?" Iman asked.

The doctor looked at Bleu in confusion.

Bleu nodded. "This is the father," she said.

The doctor appeared shocked. Everyone in the operating room had seen Noah's interaction with her and had felt the love that circulated throughout the room. Knowing better than to ask questions, however, the doctor gave Iman a paper gown to put over his clothes and made both parents wash their hands before entering the sterile environment. Cubicles with premature babies filled the nursery and Bleu was instantly drawn to one in particular in the corner of the room. Her eyes landed on it before Iman could even ask which baby belonged to them.

When she laid eyes on her son, she fell in love. Guilt plagued her because of his size. He was underdeveloped and was hooked up to so many machines that she felt hopeless. He was the most beautiful thing she had ever seen and she wondered if the sky was blue today. He had ten little fingers and ten tiny toes, one little button nose that was smaller than the tip of her finger. Even the cap they had placed on his head was too big for him.

"I love you," Bleu whispered as she placed her face against the glass.

Iman squeezed her shoulder in support, but he had no words. He had waited for years to feel this moment. He had wanted a child of his own since the day that Tan had lost what would have been their first. Bleu had given him an unbelievable gift.

"I got clean the day I found out I was pregnant with him,

but I can't help but think that all the smoking I did before that is the reason why he is in this glass box!" Bleu cried. It was a burden that she would have to carry with her the rest of her life, and if he died she would never forgive herself.

Iman knelt down in front of the wheelchair. "Look at him, ma. If God was going to take him away, he would have done it way before he tasted his first sip of air. He's struggling right now, but he'll find his strength. You can't control what you did before you knew you were a mother. Forgive yourself for that. I do. I forgive you because I should have been right there with you. I should have protected you better. Look at him, Bleu," Iman said, lifting her chin and forcing her to look at their son. "He came from us. We made perfection and I'll take care of you forever for giving me that." He leaned in and kissed her lips. When Iman stood, Bleu looked up and saw Noah looking at her through the glass window. She could see the hurt in his eyes, and without saying anything he turned and walked away.

23

Noah walked into his house, brooding with anger, so much anger that he put his fist through a wall as soon as he stepped foot inside.

His mother came rushing from the upstairs of the house. "Noah! What's wrong, baby?" she shouted in a panic as she rushed to her son's side. His hand was swollen and knuckles busted up as he lowered his head onto his mother's shoulder. "Noah baby, you have to say something. I came here to put together a nice surprise for Bleu, and you walking in here, without Bleu, without a baby. Where are they, Son? Please tell me nothing happened," she said.

Noah felt like a bitch, choking up in front of his mother. Only Bleu could bring out this type of emotion from him. She was like kryptonite to Noah and today he hated her for it.

"The nigga that got her pregnant came to take her and the baby back to Cali," Noah said.

"Oh, Noah," Ms. Monica said, exhaling deeply. She could feel the pain emanating off her son. She had witnessed the love story of Bleu and Noah unfolding in front of her for the past fifteen years. From kids to teenagers to now they had shared a connection that resembled true love. She knew how much Bleu meant to Noah. He had given up everything for her. "Baby, I know that you must be hurt beyond my comprehension, but I also know that you love Bleu and that she loves you."

Noah sank to the floor and leaned his back against the wall and his mother knelt with him. "I'm done, Ma. She made her choice," Noah said.

"Noah, you have changed for that girl. She got you to get out of the streets. You went legit. She complements you; she always has. Way before you ever had any romantic feelings for Bleu, she was your soul mate. Even if Bleu stays with the father of her child, I don't think you want to give up the bond that you two share. She's your best friend, Noah. Some loves aren't meant for this lifetime, but your friendship with her"—Ms. Monica shook her head—"it's irreplaceable. She is going to need you, and if you want to be a part of her life you have to respect her relationship with her son's father. You may not be able to love her the way you want to, but you can still love her and her son. Bleu needs you. I've watched you love that girl back to life these past six months, Noah. You breathed for her when it was too hard for her to breathe for herself. You helped her get her footing in life again. You don't want to miss out on the next chapter of her life, and I'm willing to bet more than anything that she wants you there. But make it easy on her. Be a man. Shake her boyfriend's hand and be there for her like you always have been. Don't make her have to choose between her kid's father and you," Ms. Monica schooled him.

"How did you get so smart?" Noah asked as he leaned in and kissed his mother on the cheek.

"Lot of years on this earth, boy. I done learned a thang or two," she said with a wink. "Now what did she have?"

"A boy," Noah said.

"Go on back up there with her and remember what I said," Ms. Monica stated. "I'll clean up here."

Bleu lay in the hospital bed; the back of her head rested on Iman's chest as he sat with his feet propped up on the bed. They both barely fit, but they made it work as they watched a black-and-white movie on TV. He stroked her hair and then kissed her temple. Bleu felt all of his love and appreciation pouring into her each time he touched her.

"I love you so much," she whispered.

"I love you too," Iman replied.

Bleu sat up slowly, being careful with her movements so that she didn't hurt her incision. "No, Iman. I love you too much." He sat up in confusion. "The way that I love you is so consuming, so obsessive. It's overwhelming and it doesn't make sense at all."

"I don't understand, ma. Is that a bad thing?" he asked with a chuckle as he grabbed her hand and rubbed the top of it softly with his thumb.

"I come from a place of addiction. My mom was an addict; my daddy was an addict. I'm an addict. It's in my blood. The disease runs in my family, and even though I'm done with the drugs, I still get high off you. I can't let you go, even if I know that you're no good for me. You're my trigger, Iman. Every time I'm around you, the feelings I feel for you are too much. It's overwhelming. It's too intense. You're like a fire that warms me, but if it gets out of control it burns, and I can't control the way I feel about you. It makes me want to smoke dope. It's not healthy for me."

"So what you saying, ma?" Iman asked, visibly wounded by her confessions.

Bleu looked him in the eyes, her tears accumulating as she found the nerve to whisper, "I need you to walk away from me. I need you to let me go," as her tears fell and her lip trembled.

Iman shook his head as he drew his bottom lip into his mouth. "I can't do that, ma. I want to marry you. I want to pump you full of babies. I can't leave you alone," Iman refused.

"That's how I know you're not the man for me," Bleu admitted. "Noah is my best friend. Actually, he's more than that and I don't know what that means or if it's wrong to love both of you at the same time, but I do. With you it's all about you, but with him it's always about me. He will do anything for me, even if it means he sacrifices something himself. There is nothing he won't do for me, including letting me be with you if it's what he thinks I really want. His love is unselfish and I'm first. He puts me above himself and I am so in love with him because of that. He helped me get clean, Iman. He stood by me. He urged me to go back to school. He made me believe that I could. He made me believe again . . . in myself, and I just want to love him for forever for that. But you're like a flame and I'm the moth that's flying toward you. I need you to walk away. We can be parents to our son, but please let me go," she pleaded. She was bawling at this point, her tears rolling freely down her face, and it was breaking her heart.

Iman knew that he had fucked up when he had let her come back to Flint alone. She had found her way without him and it hurt him deeply. He was grateful for Noah, for saving her, but jealous because he hadn't been the one to do it. He was Bleu's weakness. He didn't make her better. Noah gave her strength. It was a hard pill to swallow.

"Sh-h," Iman whispered as he wiped her tears and pulled her back down to lie on his chest again.

"Are you mad?" She sobbed.

"No, ma, never. I could never be mad at you," he said, but he was heartbroken. She had just broken him and he knew that he only had himself to blame.

He listened to Bleu cry herself to sleep, enjoying the feeling of her in his arms. He knew that he would never hold her like this again. When he was sure she was asleep, he stood. He bent down and kissed her forehead one more time. "I love you enough to set you free."

As he walked out, Noah was headed toward the room. The two men stood toe to toe. Each was destroyed by the presence of the other. Iman held out his hand and Noah shook it firmly in respect. It was a ten-second interaction, but it symbolized so much. They both loved Bleu enough to respect each other. No lines had been crossed. Their only beef had been they had loved the same girl at the same time.

Iman walked off and Noah headed into Bleu's room. When

he saw that she was sound asleep he made his way to the NICU and peered in on her son. It was crazy how Noah's heart swelled at the sight of him. You would have thought Noah was staring at his own son.

Noah stood there for hours, until a nurse rolled Bleu up to the window beside him.

"I thought you left," she said.

"I did, but my mama made me realize that even if I can't be here for you like I want to be, there is no other place I'd rather be," Noah admitted. "You're my day one, B. I'd rather have you as a friend than nothing at all."

Bleu struggled to her feet and stepped into Noah's space.

"I asked him to leave, Noah. I chose you," Bleu whispered.

Noah smiled as he bit his lip and shook his head from side to side in disbelief. Even with all of her flaws, Bleu was his dream girl.

"I love you," she said. "I want you."

When he kissed her, he felt it in his soul and promised himself that he would love her the way a man was supposed to love a woman. With integrity, with honor, with faithfulness and loyalty. He wasn't ready to get married, but he had already found his queen. One day he would change her last name, but today he would just appreciate her for everything she had been to him and everything she had yet to become.

Bleu was so grateful to God. She was being discharged today, and even though her son wasn't healthy enough to leave with her, he was getting stronger every single day. Her doctor walked in and handed her paperwork to sign.

"Are you going to name your baby boy before you leave today?" the doctor asked.

"I'm going to name him Saviour Iman Montclair," she said. "He saved my life. Without him I would have no reason to get clean."

"It's a beautiful name for a beautiful boy," the doctor said. "Good luck, Bleu."

Bleu smiled as Noah pushed the wheelchair up to the bed. Bleu sighed. "I can walk. It's been a week. It hurts, but I'm not crippled." She laughed.

"You let him take care of you," the doctor said. "Besides, it's hospital policy. You can walk as much as you want when you get home. Although I think then you will be wishing you had a wheelchair."

Bleu laughed as she sat down. Noah leaned down and kissed her lips before heading toward the exit. Bleu lifted her head to the sky as soon as they were outside, and the sight of the clear blue sky reminded her of her mother. Bleu wondered if Sienna could see her now, if she would be proud.

Boom!

The sound of the gunshot was surreal as Bleu looked down at the blood splatter that covered her body. It took her a second to realize that it wasn't hers. She turned around and saw Noah laid out on the ground, gasping for air.

"No!!!" she screamed. She didn't care that she was bursting all her staples open as she scrambled toward him. "No!!! Somebody help me!!!"

He was choking as blood gushed out of his mouth. Bleu lifted his head into her lap as he stared into her eyes. He reached for her head, blood dripping everywhere and staining her hair as he fisted it.

"No, don't leave me," she sobbed. "No! You wake up!" she shouted as she shook him, but she could see the life leaving him. She could feel his grip loosening as his hand slid out of her hair. His lips moved as he tried to say something. She already knew what he was trying to get out, but the blood never allowed the words to be free.

"I love you; oh God, I love you!" she cried.

His eyes were panicked and in them she saw a fear that broke her heart. "Sh-h . . . it's okay. It's okay." She knew that it was hopeless. Their time was coming to a tragic end. Hospital staff surrounded her, but he was already gone by the time they got there. "Don't be afraid. Heaven is waiting," she said. "Oh God!" she sobbed. The doctors and nurses who crowded around knew that it was too late and the scene before them brought tears to their eyes. They witnessed death every day but had never seen grief like this before. Bleu had lost her soul mate and when he drew his last breath a little piece of her had gone into the sky with him. So much for a beautiful day.

Naomi caressed the side of Demarcus's face as they sped out of the parking lot of the hospital. The same nigga she was supposed to kill months ago was the one she had used to kill the man she used to love. There was no remorse in her heart. Noah had played her and there was a price to pay for that. Noah had chosen Bleu over her; he had embarrassed her and disregarded her. He had tossed her aside as if she hadn't helped him climb to the top. Resentment had built in Naomi for months, and when she linked up with Demarcus they had a common enemy. Noah had never seen it coming and revenge had been sweet.

"He got exactly what he deserved," she whispered to herself, smirking in satisfaction. That's why men had to be careful whom they crowned a queen, because a queen scorned would slit the king's throat without thinking twice.

Final Chapter

Four Years Later

Bleu took a deep breath as the graduation song played in the large arena. She couldn't believe that she had made it this far. Tears filled her eyes as she thought of everything that it took to get to this moment. Now she was standing in line, waiting to receive her Bachelor of Science in Social Work. It was unreal. It felt like a dream, and she wrung her fingers together nervously while waiting for her turn on the stage.

"Bleu Montclair—"

Bleu looked behind her and her eyes fell on Saviour, Ms. Monica, Eddie, Marta, and Iman. She smiled and blew them a kiss as she walked gracefully across the stage to receive her degree.

She sat through the rest of the ceremony on cloud nine and when it was over she rushed to hug her baby.

He was four years old and sharp as a whip. She picked him up. "Did you see Mommy?" she asked in excitement.

"Uh-huh. You wore a funny hat," he said, causing a big grin to spread across her face.

"I did all of this for you!" Bleu exclaimed as she kissed his cheek. "Give me a big hug."

His little arms around her neck felt so good. He had been through so much. Two surgeries in the first two years of his life and countless hours of therapy. All of his milestones had been delayed for the first two years of his life, but he was strong and with time, patience, and God's will he caught up just fine. He was a healthy and happy little boy Bleu was so grateful for. He had truly changed her life.

"I'm so proud of you, Bleu," Ms. Monica said.

"Thank you. Thank you so much. I love you," Bleu said.

"Oh, baby girl, I love you too," Ms. Monica replied, hugging her tightly. "Come on to Grandma," Ms. Monica said as she held out her hands for Saviour.

Iman stepped up to Bleu last and held out a large bouquet of peach roses for her. "Thank you," she said.

"You did good, ma," he affectionately said. "I'm proud of you. As a woman, a mother, you're amazing. You've always been amazing."

They had never gotten back together, although if Bleu allowed him to he would marry her without thinking twice. He already spent half of his time in Michigan visiting Saviour but would gladly move if it meant that Bleu would give their family a chance. She always turned Iman down, however. They were good co-parents to Saviour and great friends, but

Bleu would never allow herself to open the door that she had shut with him all those years ago.

"Can I take you to lunch? To celebrate?" he asked.

"Um, rain check?" she asked. "I kind of have somewhere I need to be."

"Yeah, sure," Iman said.

Bleu kissed his cheek and gave his hand a squeeze before she hurried off. She turned on her heels. "Don't keep Saviour out too late. He has pre-school in the morning."

"You're the boss, ma," Iman said, giving her a wink as he watched her disappear in the crowd.

Bleu pulled up to the graveyard and kicked off her shoes as she walked over to Noah's grave. "You see me?" she asked as she looked at his headstone, her eyes filling with tears. "I did it. You always said I could." She lay down right on top of his grave and let her fingers glide through the grass. She came there every week to just talk to the love of her life. "I miss you so much. I wish you were here with me. I'm so lucky to have been loved by you, Noah. You saved my life. You pulled me off the streets and you believed in me. You are and will always be my priority. You are first in my heart. Always and forever. Rest peacefully, my love." She wiped her eyes and kissed his name before taking off her cap and hanging it from the corner of his headstone. "I'll see you on the other side. I know you're watching and I know you're waiting. I'll live for both of us, until we meet again."

Bleu felt a breeze on her face and she knew that it was Noah. Bleu could feel him smiling down on her. She closed her eyes and enjoyed his essence until the breeze passed. God had sent so many people into her life. Iman had been for a season, but Noah had been sent for a reason and when he had taught her the lesson that God had intended God had called him home. She understood that everything had happened as it was supposed to and she was no longer embarrassed by her journey. It was her story, it was her test, and now she had the ultimate testimony. Bleu turned proudly with her head held high and walked out of the cemetery, knowing that she was a lucky girl because she had been loved by the best.